I0659602

GORILLAZ IN THE BAY 4

De'Kari

**Lock Down Publications and Ca$h
Presents**
Gorillaz in the Bay 4
A Novel by De'Kari

Lock Down Publications
P.O. Box 870494
Mesquite, Tx 75187

Visit our website @
www.lockdownpublications.com

Copyright 2019 by De'Kari
Gorillaz in the Bay 4

All rights reserved. No part of this book may be reproduced in any form or by electronic or mechanical means, including information storage and retrieval systems without permission in writing from the publisher, except by a reviewer who may quote brief passages in review.
First Edition November 2019
Printed in the United States of America

This is a work of fiction. Names, characters, places, and incidents either are products of the author's imagination or are used fictitiously. Any similarity to actual events or locales or persons, living or dead, is entirely coincidental.

Lock Down Publications
Like our page on Facebook: Lock Down Publications @
www.facebook.com/lockdownpublications.ldp
Cover design and layout by: **Dynasty Cover Me**
Book interior design by: **Shawn Walker**
Edited by: **Tam Jernigan**

Stay Connected with Us!

Text **LOCKDOWN** to 22828 to stay up-to-date with new releases, sneak peaks, contests and more…

Thank you.

Dedication

This book is dedicated to the Loving Memory of Tyrell Demetrius Hayes AKA Lil Rell, my nephew and a true Neva Die Dragon. The highest-ranking Angels are called the Seraphim. Their bright splendor gives light to the Throne of Glory, God's throne. The Seraphim are Dragons with heads of a crocodile and sapphire eyes. Their bodies are covered with eyes (scales). They have six wings which are symbolic to the number of days in Creation.

Lil Rell you are "Our" Immortalized Dragon, our Eternal Angel.

Moja, Upendo, Mwezi
Minakupenda
One Aim, One Struggle, One Goal

Neva Die
Revenge Is Promised!

Author's Note

The following are the words of my Big Brother and Commander in Chief, Dok Holliday, written to his first born Prince and now Eternal son.

2015: Lord forgive me for my sin; past, present and future. May my glory and praise of your love & blessings reach your recognition...

These are my humbly, chosen words in prayer & hope, of them to be accepted by our Heavenly Father & sent threw his beloved son & received by my beloved son, Tyrell D. Hayes... There has neva been a moment during my children's existence, that I have not acknowledged them as the greatest part of my existence. The love between parent & child is absolutely unconditional. It starts even before a child's birth. It is the only love your heart will ever know that exist without your permission or say-so. It's a love not built through bond, or earned from "trial and error", nor formed by familiarity... It's pure, effortless, endless. No mistakes, mishaps, miscalculated judgements, misfortune nor flaw, could ever even so much as dent the corner of this love. Not even a parent & child standing on the worst of terms could ever truly deny the fact of loving their child – loving their parent... Through children's growth they teach us (parents) who we truly are, because they are the mirror image of all of our elements. Ones we expose as well as conceal.

Our good, our bad, our strengths and weaknesses, gifts and greatness. And as they become adults, they then teach us whom they have become, who they are and it is the most amazing and humbling work of God one could ever encounter. If ever there is a question of how great God's love is, there definitely is an answer in parenthood. What more loving of a gift, than the gift of life?

My son, My young Prince, continued to amaze me throughout his years in the world. And now even in his too soon departure to behold the beautiful impact he made while here. The great imprint he left is absolutely phenomenal. And I know I speak true for all who knew him when I say "To know Rell was to love Rell & To be

loved by him is certainly a Blessing. So as we .... Naturally ....
Mourn and heal and he is returned to the essence from which he
came. Let us begin to passionately celebrate the gift of his life and
may his Heavenly wings keep him as Fly as he was on this Earth.

An Angel in this life, now an Angel for eternal life!

This Love, Our Love, will NEVA DIE!

.... With all my heart & soul

.... I love you Son!

Pops

NEVA DIE
276

Thanks

Thanks to Our Eternal Creator, Giver of Life, Light and Energy. Thank you, Father.

Thanks to Ca$h for giving me a platform to Immortalize Our Struggle and Our Fallen Comrades.

Thanks to my Queen & Team De'Kari for encouraging me to put pen to paper by their enthusiasm in typing my stories.

Thank you to all my Fans and Readers for lending an ear to Our Story and reading Our Struggle.

Thank You & God Bless You

Author De'Kari

De'Kari

CHAPTER I
Berkeley Marina, CA

After shooting Clarkola in the back of the head, Voorheeze hung his head low.

"If I lie to you, I will lie on you. If I lie on you, I will tell on you. If I threaten you, I will turn on you. If I turn on you, I will kill you."

They were raised by and lived by this mantra. They neva lied to nor threatened each other. No matter what. That was the rule! Clark knew the rule and he broke it when he threatened French Tip. She was their baby sister. They were supposed to protect her.

Voorheeze wondered what the hell Clark was thinking. He had to know that Voorheeze would eventually hear about and eliminate a threat to his little sister.

Voorheeze went into Clark's pocket and pulled out a bag of Berry Fusion Dutchess. "You ain't gonna need this rogue," he stated before throwing the faceless body of his older brother off of the pier like a sack of potatoes.

"He brought it on himself, Booger, the moment he threatened you. I wouldn't let God get away with that," he spoke as he rolled a blunt of the potent weed he pulled out of the bag.

They sat in silence thinking of their older brother for a few minutes. French Tip finally broke the silence.

"Brother, I know that now might not seem like the right time to bring this up." She hesitated trying to decide how to proceed.

Voorheeze hit the rolled blunt. He took a long drag on it, blew the smoke out and looked at his sister.

"So, bring it up. What's up?"

She couldn't figure out a subtle way to breach the subject so she just asked. "Well, what's up with you and Vieira?"

What you mean what's up?" The question completely caught him off guard.

"Shit, she's white!" French Tip spoke flat out. "Since when did you start fucking with white women?"

Voorheeze had neva been with a white woman. He'd always said he didn't know why so many brothers fucked with white women. His favorite line was "I'd neva get caught with a snow bunny."

He took a deep breath in contemplation. How could he break this down to his sister? She knew him better than anybody. He said fuck it and just kept it real!

"Okay, first, Booger, you gotta understand something. When we lost T'Rida, I lost a part of me. Blood was my brother. He came into my life at a time when I literally didn't have anybody. You know as much as I do that Clark was neva a big brother to me. I was waiting for the day that I would be recognized as his lil brother. The problem is, that day came but it was T'Rida that was my big brother. Neva Die was my family."

"When 'Rida died it felt like I was all alone again. So, I started back snorting the coke and trying to drown my pain in the alcohol. That shit only fucked with my head more. Had me realizing how bad I wanted Lisa but couldn't have her. I was constantly thinking about the abuse and shit from our childhood. Before long, I was hearing and seeing shit that wasn't there. Creating people and relationships that weren't real."

French Tip thought of all the empty photo frames and the photo of Lisa that said "Danika". She kept her thoughts to herself and listened.

".... I felt like a nigga stranded on a deserted island. Anyway, by the time I'd run into Vieira, a nigga was so lonely I just needed companionship. At the time I didn't give a fuck or think about that fact that she was white."

"Shit Vieira was real. And somewhere in my twisted mind, she was Lisa. Booger, I was all fucked up."

French Tip was so caught up in what she was hearing that she hadn't even hit the blunt, he'd passed it to her. It just burned in her fingertips.

"I take it that's why you didn't know about her being a cop." Considering what he just told her, she knew damn well that he wasn't on his safety and security.

"I ain't even gonna lie to you, sis. I was just fucking her. I didn't care about nothing else. But based on what's going on, it's a good thing that she has connections." He reached for the blunt that his sister was wasting.

He took a hit and let the Tropical Berry flavor marinate in his mouth and lungs. The flavor instantly reminding him of Fruit Loops.

After exhaling the smoke, he spoke sternly. "We're going to need her."

There was no sense in her inquiring about what his last comment meant. She knew her brother in and out, and knew that at any given moment he would be mulling over eight or nine different plans.

After finishing up the blunt. They got up and walked to their vehicles. Voorheeze followed her before heading to Hayward Hills.

**** **N. D.** ****

S.A.C. Andreatta had the latest edition high-resolution all-weather night vision digital goggles up to her eyes. At her leisure she could switch from night vision to thermo imaging for better details of what was going on, on the other side of the lens.

She sat low behind the tinted windows of an all-Black Dodge Charger with blacked out rims. Even the housing and covers of the headlights and tail lights were blacked out. These were the newest vehicles in the FEDS arsenal to fight crime in the urban communities.

The vehicles themselves were fitted with night vision sensors all around it. Its windshield was equipped with the latest in LED technology in the glass. Which allowed the driver to go from looking out a normal windshield to seeing compute images. With the ability to drive 210 mph. These cars were virtually ghost vehicles.

Agent Finnegan sat next to her in the driver's seat listening with high frequency head seats connected to a Mega Audible Voice Microphone. Agents Garcia and Daly were on the other side of the Marina on foot wearing stealth camouflage. Tracking the targets.

What started out as a regular multi-unit surveillance mission turned out to be the biggest breakthrough thus far in the case. The breakthrough that Andreatta was waiting for.

No one had any knowledge whatsoever that La'Mont Simpson had awaken from his coma. The other night when he walked out on stage at the Satin Doll Fashion Show,. S.A.C. Andreatta almost shitted on herself. Although she was not anticipating seeing La'Mont, she jumped into action just as fast as she would've if she had known.

She, along with her team had been surveilling La'Mont ever since that fateful night when he walked out on the stage. They were there for the meeting at the War Room and now in Berkeley at the Marina.

"I thought Blacks were tropical folk?" Agent Finnegan couldn't believe it was one something in the morning and the three siblings were still out on the pier.

"They are." Andreatta responded without moving the binoculars.

"Well it looks like they didn't get that memo." He replied, referring to the three siblings.

Just as he spoke S.A.C Andreatta could make out figures coming back her way. They were parked in the furthest corner of the parking lot in deeper shadows to ensure they wouldn't be seen.

As the images got closer, she noticed there were only two. She figured the third stayed behind for a while. Now she could see it was only La'Mont and the sister.

"Where's the oldest brother?" Finnegan asked out loud.

"Maybe they had a disagreement. Maybe he wasn't ready to go. Who knows?" She didn't care La'Mont was the target not the brother.

"Maybe he killed him." She joked.

"Garcia." She spoke into her comm's.

"Yeah, Boss."

"If they leave, we will stay with La'Mont. In case we've been made and this is a play I want you and Daly to stay here with the other brother and see what he does. Meet back up with us if it's nothing." She instructed.

"Alright Boss."

When they drove off, Finnegan waited a while and then pulled off with them.

They waited forty-five minutes without any movement. Finally, Garcia decided to stumble out to the pier, feigning drunkenness. The pier was completely empty. The only thing on it besides the birds and sea water were a few droplets of blood. He quickly gathered a sample and headed back wondering if the boss could be right. Did they kill their older brother? If so, why?"

**** N. D. ****
Oakland, CA

"Peace be still brethren. His response was understandable, in fact it was expected. Somewhere along the way Voorheeze lost his revolutionary principle and teachings. His ideology is once again focused on capitalism and self-gain.

"We however must continue to stay focused and remember our objectives and immediate aim. We will not return ignorance with ignorance. We will not start a war with our own because they are being misled. Now we will still carry out the sanctions of the Central Committee. His brothers will see the face of the dragon." Dok understood the anger within everyone's hearts in the office. Someone still had to remain level headed.

"I understand what you're saying and all, but he's gotta pay for that disrespectful ass shit." Gunz was furious. Voorheeze took shit to another level when he'd pulled them bangers out.

"That thinking is our old mentality. The thoughts of a reactionary is to stick without consideration. As visionary revolutionaries we must at all times analyze the body of facts as a whole. Our entire course must be fully mapped out before we begin our journey. You must elevate your mind and yourself, Gunz. A thinking man is a dangerous man!" Only a fool rushes into battle blindly. Dok learned this lesson the hard way years ago.

15

Although Gunz was already a boss, he took to the knowledge and teachings that Dok shared. His drive to better himself through enlightenment was the reason Gunz sided with Dok over Voorheeze.

"Come on, take a ride with me." Dok told Gunz as he grabbed his keys and stood up.

Scooter and Rell remained at the Koffee Shop while Dok and Gunz jumped in Dok's suped-up Chevy Camaro. Gunz didn't know where he was going and didn't care. He had his banger on his waist and his mentor on the side of him.

Dok used the time while driving to talk to Jeanette. He missed his wife something fierce but as long as Clark was alive she wasn't safe.

Twenty-Five minutes later they were cruising down Mission Blvd in Hayward. When Dok hung up Gunz could sense the mood change.

"You straight, brah?" He asked Dok.

"Nah, Bredren. I've gone too long without my rib. It's like all of me is shutting down little by little, mind, body and soul. We need to finish this shit soon so I can get my baby back." Dok was referring to the beef with Clark.

Ironically, Gunz knew exactly what he meant. He hadn't checked in on Nastasia in almost a month due to the beef. He missed his baby like fuck. He'd really wanted to take Clark out at the fashion show. Fuck all the FEDS. He'd listened to reason instead of his emotions.

Dok made a left on Garin Ave and drove up the hill. A short ways later he pulled over and pointed out a house to Gunz.

"What's that? Who lives there?" Gunz was curious, the large house was simple yet nice.

"A little over a year and a half ago a real estate agent named Steven Jackson had this house on the market. That is until he sold it to his big cousin." Dok paused and looked at Gunz. He smiled and added," His cousin as Voorheeze."

The smile must've been contagious because one instantly appeared on Gunz' face.

16

"If he was an issue we could've been touched him. Ever since the spot in Union City was compromised. This is his only house. He thinks no one knows about it.

A few minutes later Dok pulled off. The full ramifications of what he'd just learned began weighing on Gunz' mind.

****** N. D. ******
Somewhere in the Bay Area

"Back in elementary, I thrived off misery/ left me alone I grew up amongst a dying breed/ inside my mind I couldn't find a place to rest /until I got that thug life tatted on my chest / tell me can you feel me…

Beep

Beep

Incoming call from 510-825-212." He didn't need to hear the last digits to realize who it was. "Answer call." La'Mont called out. He was driving down highway 680 toward Dublin with no destination in mind. Later on he was meeting up with Vieira, but right now he was just driving lost in thought. He'd awaken from the coma in the middle of hell.

"La'Mont, what the fuck y'all got going on out there in Cali? And why in the hell didn't you call me and tell me about this little problem you had? Do I need to get on the next mothafucking plane and come out there? La'Mont, boy you better answer me. Don't make me act a fool!" The deadly venom that spewed out from the Bose speakers sent electric energy though his body.

La'Mont was silently chuckling to himself as she went on ranting and raving. "What's up cuz? It's good to hear your voice, too.''

Nigga, don't what's up cuz me? Boy you better answer my questions ,before I fuck you up." Cookie spit back to him.

Anita Cook aka Cookie was Voorheeze's favorite older cousin. She was the epitome of a Boss Bitch and a True Gangsta. Voorheeze respected her gangsta to the utmost and she loved his dirty draws.

"Okay, first of all I didn't call you because there was no need to have you all out in Vegas stressing over nothing. We've had a few misunderstandings that had to be ironed out but nothing to lose sleep over...

Cookie cut him off mid-sentence. "Misunderstandings, my ass. Little boy, I had to see on the news that you just woke up from an almost yearlong coma after almost losing your life twice. And how come no-one called me and told me about your brother? La'Mont don't make me call Peter.''

"Be easy wit all them names on the phone cuz. Look cousin, we've had a lot going on for a minute, but I'm getting everything back where it needs to be right now. I promise you once everything is right and I can dip off. I'm on the first thing smoking out to see you. Besides I miss my little cousin Ebony anyway. How is she doing?'' He figured he'd best change the subject and the momentum of the phone call.

"Lord Jesus, don't get me started on your cousin. I don't know if she gone make me have to kill her or if she gone fuck around and give me a heart attack." Cookie loved Ebony like she was her own daughter. Which is why she fussed over her so much.

"You know if you kill my cousin, I'mma have to come and see you about something. He joked.

"Shyyyyt, mothafucka, don't threaten me with a good time." He knew that would lighten the mood and get her to fall back.

Besides Mama B, Cookie was the only woman to ever make him feel nervous. The Black Widow may have been an assassin, but Cookie's gun play was beyond legendary. Her body count was rumored to be so high, mothafuckas from her era was actually happy when she took her dangerous-ass out to Nevada. She stayed pulling niggaz' hoe card.

"You know I don't want no problems wit you."

"Boy, I ain't worried about you. I know you better bring your ass out here like you said." He could hear it in her voice she was about to start crying.

"I am. I love you, cuz." He told her.

"I love you too, cuz."

18

It was Cookie who disconnected the call. Family or not, she wasn't going to let him hear her cry. She was too gangsta for that.

Tupac's "Shed So Many Tears" came back on. He hated the fact that he lied to his favorite cousin, but he loved her way too much to allow her to come back to Cali and get caught up in the shit that he had going on. She was a Gangsta though, so she would understand.

With that in mind, he decided to head over to meet up with Vieira.

****** N. D. ******
Sacramento

Angry and irate are two words that couldn't compare to the way Governor Nicholas Costa was feeling right at that moment. His anger and humiliation was beyond that. He was outright, fucking furious!

He'd just gotten off the phone having a lengthy, heated debate and argument with Jim Smith, a politician that was well-known for his "Make America Great" campaigns. The video of Deputy Purtle's murder had drawn so much attention that the Smith himself had to see it.

The public outcry for justice among the white community was immediate. A few groups even took to the streets holding marches and rallies carry signs that read. "White Lives Matter."

Tension was building on both sides of the racial divide.

The conversation started innocently enough with Smith offering any type of assistance Gov. Costa might need. Somehow in the middle of the conversation, if took on undertones of Costa not being able to control the situation.

Smith flat out verbally questioned if Costa was indeed competent enough to run a state, since he couldn't find one single culprit. That set of a string of comments that lead to outright cursing, disrespecting and threatening before Governor Costa had the balls to hang up on Smith.

"Nicholas, what was all of that, dear?" His loving wife asked him as she came walking into his study.

They were all alone, except for a few staff at the Governor's Mansion. She had heard the argument clearly but knew her husband would need to verbally vent.

"Would you believe that asshole Smith had the nerve to call me and question whether or not I was competent to do my job?" He was dumb founded.

"No?" She feigned surprise.

"Yes!"

"Which Smith, darling?" she asked.

"Jim Smith." When she looked at him questioningly. He continued.

"Jim Smith the politician from Texas, that fucking know-it-all!" She could tell that he was still heated.

"No, he didn't. What would make him do such a thing?" She already knew. It was only evident.

"There's this fucking wacko out here killing all these cops. Shit, I sent in the FEDS. You'd think they would get their head out of their asses and do their jobs." He was actually yelling as he slammed his fist down on the desk.

"Now, now, baby, calm down. You remember what the doctors have told you." She needed to keep him calm.

Before he ran for Governor, both he and his wife were Deputy Sheriffs in San Mateo County. Back then, Deputy Costa was in charge of 3-East which was Ad-Seg housing. Deputy Khaury was a classification Deputy. Both were good at their post and fought like hell to keep their love affair a secret. Their love for each other was so strong that it was hard keeping it secret. Especially on Costa's end. He couldn't keep his hands off of her. Every time she passed by the sight of her extremely phat, juicy ass would send him over board.

He was a weight lifting fanatic and she was the perfect Persian Persuasion. When he won the Govern ship they both resigned as Deputies. Got married and moved into the Governor's Mansion. Up until now he had a stellar run. This terrorist was fucking everything up.

He placed his hand on top of her hand that was resting on his shoulders. Then he grabbed her hand and guided her around the chair to stand in front of him.

Her long jet-black hair cascading down past her shoulders. Her plump juicy breast sitting nice and perky caused his dick to jump inside of his slacks.

He wrapped his arms around her waist bringing her closer, standing in between his legs. The soft sheer fabric did nothing to hide her steadily hardening and growing nipples that poked out under the gown.

"I remember exactly what the doctors said. I had to take it easy, but making love was good cardiovascular exercise." He huskily told her before opening her night gown and placing one of her aching breasts into his mouth.

Years of taking supplements and driving too hard on the weight pile gave him a weak heart, but that shit wasn't going to slow Governor Costa down. Fuck that shit!

They made passionate love right there in the study oblivious to the maid behind them staring from the doorway.

**** **N. D.** ****

Oakland, CA
9:47 p.m.

Big Roc was not only tired, but he was also on edge. All day his senses had been fucking with him like there was danger lurking around the next corner or something. No matter what, he couldn't shake the feeling. It was like a bad omen was lingering.

He started to mention it to Rell, but he figured he was tripping. Plus, he wasn't about to look like a pussy in front of the young killer. As they rode around Oakland picking up money, Roc kept his eyes open and his hand on his Glock 40mm.

Alert and ready!

Pulling over, they both jumped out. Rell walked inside of the apartment complex to see Big Moe while Rock stood on point with his .40 mm in his hand. The extended thirty dick was hanging out of the .40mm and looked menacing in the moon light.

All day the two of them had been riding around. Big Moe's was their last pick up. In the back of the jet-black Escalade was twenty-four duffle bags. Big Moe's would make twenty-five.

Big Moe was notorious in West Oakland for his pistol playing days. Big Roc had little to no worry that someone would try and jack them. Even so he stayed on point. The eerie feeling had him teetering on the edge.

A few moments later Rell came into view with a duffle bag thrown over his shoulder and a FN Herstal in his hand.

"Everything smooth, Big Homie?" Rell asked Roc as he walked up to him.

"Everything's good, young'n. Let's get the fuck outta here and grab something to eat." Big Roc walked around to the driver's side as Rell jumped in the passenger seat.

Neither of them saw the black Mustang GT with tinted windows lurking across the street back a ways.

Big Roc was always hungry. The amount of food that he waffled down was unbelievable.

"Fuck yeah, let's swing by Quarter Pounder and snatch up a few burgers 'fore we hit the freeway." Rell offered up.

"I like the way you think young'n," Big Roc was thinking the exact same thing as he turned onto San Pablo Ave.

A few minutes later they were turning into the parking lot of 1/4lb Burger on San Pablo Ave. There was only a couple of people at the 1/4lb Burger, which was usually packed.

" The nigga who stole yo shit just happens to be up here while we up at this bitch." Big Roc joked as he pulled up next to a dark drop top 1966 Lincoln continental.

Rell had the same exact car. All the way down to the spotless white wall tires on it. The only difference was the paint, Rell's Lincoln had a money green body with a peanut butter top. The Lincoln next to the Escalade was dark burgundy with a black top.

"If that was my shit the nigga driving it would be in Heaven already. I got you on the food Big Homie, you just watch all this money. What you want?" Rell let it be known before climbing out of the truck tucking his banger on his waist.

"Right on, young'n. Get me two number ones wit extra cheese and onions. And grab me an extra-large Dr. Pepper."

"Aight, I got you." With that he closed the door and walked over to the window to place their orders.

Big Roc was lost in deep thought. That fucked up feeling that he'd felt all day was fucking with his mind. He had been in the streets too long, damn near thirty years, for him to ignore the felling. His instincts had always kept him alive. He'd learned ages ago to follow his instincts. As many bodies that Roc had, he had to always be on his toes.

The black GT pulling into the parking lot drew his attention. When he'd pulled up the spot on 34th Ave. a black 2016 Mustang GT with tinted windows was parked a ways back on the street, he now recalled.

Roc cocked the .40mm and had it resting softly on top of his lap. The hairs on the back of his neck stood up. He checked his mirrors making sure no one was coming. The GT could be a distraction. He double checked all the mirrors.

On any given Sunday Roc would've stepped to the GT to see what was what. Hell, they could blaze it out if that was the case. Dok and Gunz had entrusted them with the responsibility of rounding up nearly a million dollars. Bad as he wanted to, he couldn't play no desperado cowboy shit.

Right as he was getting ready to say, *"Fuck It'* and let the .40mm hang out the window, Rell came walking up. Rell noticed the .40mm in Rock's hand and the look on his face and instantly became alert.

"What's hood, Big Brah?" Rell asked in a voice full of concern as he climbed in.

"I don't know that black Mustang over there was over by Moe's spot when we pulled up. Now the mothafucka pulls in and ain't nobody getting out that bitch. It's like it's waiting on something." Roc told him without taking his eyes off of the car.

"Where at?" Rell leaned over to get a better look." Aw, Big Brah that ain't shit. That's lil Zoe's shit."

He sat back straight in his seat. Big Roc looked at Rell to see if he was serious, then he looked back at the Mustang, wishing he could see through the tinted windows. The hairs on his neck wasn't just standing up. They were tingling now too.

"Lil Zoe? Who the hell is Lil Zoe?" Roc continued to look while trynna rack his mind for a face to go with the name.

He was so focused on the car when he looked at Rell that it hadn't registered yet that he didn't have any food with him.

Just then it hit him like a wrecking ball.

"Lil Zoe, you mean Big Zoe's son?"

When Roc turned around to get confirmation he was staring down the barrel of Rell's FN.

"The one and the same big homie. Let me get that." Rell told him as he reached over and grabbed the .40mm off of Big Roc's lap.

On cue the doors to the Mustang opened and out climbed Lil Zoe. He was the splitting image of his father whom Big Roe killed almost ten years ago, when they were taking over Oakland.

Zoe was the block lieutenant who ran 85th. He just happened to be on the block taking care of something when they came and Big Roc killed him.

Lil Zoe had been listening to the entire conversation via Blue Tooth. While he was sitting in his Mustang, Rell called him and left the phone on so Lil Zoe could hear what was going on. He walked up to the Escalade on the driver's side.

"What's up, old head?" Lil Zoe asked with a menacing look in his eyes.

"Young'n, it is what it is. I knew what it was when I participated. But if you think I'mma bout to sit here and cry like a little bi…"

BOOM! BOOM! BOOM!

The bullets from the 50 Cal made his head explode. Suddenly it was raining skull, blood, and brain matter all over the interior of the truck. For good measure, Lil Zoe leaned inside of the open window and fired off five more shots.

24

The thunderous sound disturbed the peaceful night.

Rell was busy loading the duffle bags out of the back of the Escalade and into the trunk to assist Lincoln. After killing Big Roc, Lil Zoe made his way to the back of the truck to assist Rell with the bags.

Gun shots in West Oakland wasn't an abnormal occurrence. So, there wasn't an immediate threat of police responding to the shots. Still they made haste to get the job done and get the fuck outta there!

A few months ago, Rell had dropped his Lincoln off at Raw Finish to get the new paint job just for tonight. As Rell pulled off the Young Fellons "Definition" blasted thru the speakers. Rell rapped along with Stone.

"You don't want the drama I sit on yo block rowdy/but you don't want the drama I bring/I bring beef to the White House death to yo front door/ you niggaz talk about it. Blah! You ain't neva seen war/ You ain't neva seen more Goons than the Ghoulies/or a murder scene shit you only seen in the movies/ niggaz wanna shoot me, what's wrong with they murking/ I slide thru they block and leave that whole bitch jerking/ My young niggaz lurking...

A good nigga was taken from the world the day them faggots stole Stone." Rell spoke to no one in particular as he thought of his mothafucking homeboy, driving down San Pablo Ave.

De'Kari

CHAPTER II
East Palo Alto

Voorheeze exited the elevator with a lot on his mind, a heavy heart and the world on his broad shoulders. He had a lot of shit to do and a lot of tough decisions to make. He was getting one out of the way now. Slowly, he walked down the hall to room 0428.

He waited for the door to open after he had knocked. A few moments later the door opened, with her standing there looking like a million-dollar baby doll.

Vieira rushed into his arms and held on tight. He had to admit that it felt good. She felt warm and soft, her scent tantalizing. It felt natural. After a long passionate kiss, he was able to get her to break free long enough to walk inside the suite.

"Oh my God, I am so glad to see you up walking about." She finally told him as she put her arms around him again.

Unable to hold her emotions back any longer, Vieira broke down and let all of her pain out. Voorheeze neva realized that he had developed real feelings for her until he felt her pain in his heart.

The feeling was foreign to him, because the only woman who ever held any piece of his mind or heat was Lisa. Before the coma he couldn't even use her name it was too painful. Sure, he'd fucked around with his share of woman even had a couple of relationships. Still Lisa always held his heart.

"Shh" he wiped away her tears and helped her sit down on the sofa.

"W-Why?...Why La'Mont, huh. Just tell me that. Why can't we be together?" She gripped him tightly.

"Vieira, babe look how you sound. Us be together? I'mma convict playing this shit the best way I can." He pulled his gun off of his waist and placed it on his lap. "I live by this, Fa'sho Fa'sho, and I'll die by it. I ain't scared of death and I ain't scared of introducing a mothafucka to him either. You the police, Vieira! Not just the police but you the mothafucking chief. The big dawg. How that sound, us being together? Where they do that at?" He didn't mean to raise his voice but she had to have lost her mothafucking mind.

"I don't care! I don't fucking care! I know that you are a drug dealer, I don't care! I'll quit my job if I have to I'll…" Vieira was far beyond hysterical. Her big, heavy breasts heaved up and down.

Voorheeze did the only sensible thing. He grabbed her by the shoulders and gave her the most passionate kiss that she had ever had in her life. As he kissed her he wrapped one arm around her shoulders and let his other hand run through her dirty blonde hair. That kiss did the trick. When he was done she was too out of breath to scream. Hell, she couldn't even talk.

"Listen" he began.

She shook her head no. She needed to get if off of her chest so she began.

"You listen, La'Mont, I didn't plan for it this way. When we met I didn't have any expectations, but I didn't expect to fall in love with you either. The sex was magnificent but when I felt that if was becoming more I had to do a background check on you to protect me.

"I knew who you were the first time you got shot at Anne's Funeral. I didn't care because by then I was already falling in love with you. These months I've spent by your side while you were in the coma only made my love grow deeper. La'Mont I would be lying if I didn't know who that Lisa woman was." She rolled her eyes and leaned backwards.

"Lord knows while you were in the coma you talked about her enough. So, I know your true feelings for that woman, b I still want you.

"I know you plan on looking for your friend to help him. The file that the FEDS have on you guys tells me how strong your bond is. You're going to need me." She was looking him dead in his eyes. Voorheeze just looked at her, stunned. He wasn't expecting any of what he'd heard. He needed a minute to run everything through his receptors.

She grabbed him gently by the chin and stared deeper into his eyes. "La'Mont, I love you. I'll do anything for you just please don't shut me out. I swear on my soul you can trust me."

Another kiss followed that statement. Her left hand reached down and picked up the gun. Then she placed it next to him.

Vieira broke the kiss and reached for his zipper. After unfastening his pants, she pulled out his semi-erect dick. Stroking it twice she licked her lips as she saw some pre-cum roll down the head that was steadily growing. First she licked it up. Then she put her lips right on the tip of his dick and sucked for more pre-cum.

He hadn't done shit since coming out of the coma. It had been almost a year since he had a woman's mouth on his shit. The anticipation was thru the fucking roof. Vieira sucked and slurped with all of her might. She needed La'Mont to know just how much she needed him now and in her life.

Her mouth felt too good. He had to stop her before he bust in her mouth. He needed to feel the softness of her insides. He raised her up and they both stood to their feet. While staring into each other's eyes lustfully they undressed. It was Voorheeze who broke the staring match. He had to take in her luscious milky mounds. Vieira's white porcelain skin was flawless. She was the only white woman he had ever been with, and she was addicting.

They kissed hungrily, fondling and caressing each other's body. He took one of her massive breast into his mouth and suckled the nipple. She gasp inwardly. His hot mouth electrifying her entire body beginning at her hardened nipple. The tingling sensations spread everywhere. Voorheeze right hand trailed a line of heat down her body as it made its way to her pulsating clitoris.

The moment his calloused fingers touched her clit, he bit down gently on her nipple. She came so powerfully that he had to literally hold her up with his free arm. He continued to suck on her nipple while he slipped two fingers deep inside her pussy which was literally dripping juices down his hand.

Finally, Voorheeze released the breast and kissed his way down her body until he was sitting flat on the ground. She anxiously waited for his next move.

As he sat down, he guided her over to stand directly in front of him. With a hand on each one of her voluptuous white ass cheeks, he guided her forward until her legs were standing on either side of his shoulders. Her pussy directly in front of her face.

Voorheeze didn't waste a moment. He dove right in, face first. Vieira's legs were already weak. The second his mouth closed around her pussy lips, her legs buckled. She actually had to hold on to the back of his head to keep from falling.

At first he sucked on her clitoris. He relinquished the hold he had on her clit and slid his tongue as deep as it would go into her. Then he expertly allowed his tongue to dance with her clit. Vieira couldn't take it.

"Oh…. Baby…." Her head was tilted backwards, eyes closed. She was engrossed in the best feeling in the world. "Baby I'm going to cum!"

The moment he heard that he squeezed her big ass cheeks as hard as he could. At the same time he held her clit in between his teeth and let his tongue go to work. Back and forth he rubbed it across her clit.

"Oh My Gawwwd! Yes! Yes! Yes, Baby! I'm Cuming!" She screamed. At the top of her lungs.

He sucked and licked every last drop of her cum off of her. She stepped back. He stood up. Both of their hearts were racing.

Chief Vieira was a cougar, but she was built like a stallion. She took hold of his rock-hard dick, gently squeezing it. Her pussy flooded again from the memories of how it felt, buried deep inside of her.

She put a hand on his chest and pushed him down on the sofa. As she straddled him, she took a deep breath, placed the head of his penis at the opening of her vagina and slowly slid down.

His massive size was stretching her inner walls to their limit.

"Ooooh Fuck, Daddy!" She bit down on her bottom lip as she said.

Voorheeze allowed his hands to glide across her 46-inch ass. He wasn't going to rush the moment. He just sat there rubbing her ass while she sat and waited for her pussy to adjust to his size. Vieira slowly eased up, when she did rivers of her juices flowed down his shaft and unto his balls.

Steadily she increased speed until she was fully bouncing up and down on his lamp so hard that the slapping sounds could be heard out in the hallway. Alternating from one to the other he hungrily devoured her breasts. When he smacked her on her ass, she really went crazy.

"Uff....ooh...again baby. Do that to me again. Spank me, baby." She managed to get the words out in between grunts and moans.

Voorheeze was trying to hold back but he could feel his balls swelling. A year was too long to go without pussy and Vieira was riding the dick like the stallion she was.

"T-take this god damn dick. That's right bitch, ride this mothafucka!" He called out as he matched her thrust for thrust.

Sweat covered both of their bodies. She arched her back.

"Oh, my Gawd! It's all most there." She alternated between bouncing on his dick and grinding down on it.

"Oooh....Ooooh...Oooh yeah... Fuck me. Fuck me. Fuccccck!" Her orgasm was so powerful at the point of climax that her breath caught in her lungs and her heart skipped a beat.

The contractions of her inner walls gripped and released him so spasmaticly that his balls blew and he erupted sending a years' worth of seamen as deep into her has he could.

When she was finally able to breathe again, it was in deep heavy breathe like she had just finished a mile-long sprint. The perspiration covering her pink skin caused her hair to stick all over in places. Their loving making was so intense that her entire body was a pinkish red which was a testament to how hot she was.

When she got up and walked towards the bedroom her ass cheeks were so red that they looked like she'd just been whooped with a belt, as they bounced up and down with each step.

She returned with a hot wash cloth and cleaned him up. She'd already cleaned herself in the bathroom.

"Look" He tried to think of the right words to say. Then said fuck it and just kept it real.

"While I lay there in that coma I was able to hear every word that you said to me. And that shit means a lot. You checking in on a nigga like that! You mean something special to me Vieira. I'm not gonna sit here and front like you don't.

"But my heart, no my soul belongs to one woman. Always have and always will. If I tried fucking with you on any level other than how we've been fucking with it. I would only be taking from you. Plus, the road I'm headed down. A nigga ain't gone say too much cause you them people. But, ain't no coming back from where I'm going!

"That's my big brother and he needs me. I'm not about to leave my brah out there alone like that. Especially when I'm the one that got him into this shit." He was looking into her eyes but his thoughts were back to that day he met Batman at the steak house. The day he pulled his brother into his personal shit.

Vieira reached with both arms and took his head into her hands. In the sweetest most sincere voice, she could muster she said.

"La'Mont, I don't care! I'm here! Tell me what to do."

He looked at her long and hard. Finally, he saw her for the very first time. He saw her conviction, her love and her sincerity.

**** **N. D.** ****
Two Hours Later

"Listen…You asking me if I/ know what real love feels like/ If I ever let anyone inside/ It could be serious…serious/ Cause I was the one giving all I had/ I kept my promises all intact/ For better or worst I honored that/ I could show you all about love!

Baby I can love you, love you, with my hands tied!"

It was Toni Braxton's song coming out of the super Bose speakers. But, it was Lisa's voice he heard and she was singing the song just for his ears, singing it to him.

This moment was a long time coming. Back, when he was a child she used to babysit him. She was a teenager and he was a child. Still he told everyone that one day she would be his wife. As he got older the streets swallowed him and she had gotten married.

As he was driving down Pulgas Avenue he approached the stop sign on the corner of Cypress and the school crossing guard waved at him. He waved back. The Lamborghini drew a lot of attention. He continued down to the end of Pulgas and then pulled into the parking lot of her company.

He got out of the Lambo and made his way across the parking lot.

He opened the door and walked over to the receptionist. The people in the office waiting to be helped smirked and whispered. He couldn't hear what they were saying but he knew it was about him.

"Yes. May I help you?" The slightly over-weight young girl asked with the warmest smile.

"I'm here to see Lisa." He responded with authority.

"Do you have an appointment, sir?" She wasn't being rude. She was just following procedure.

"No. But if you tell her I'm here, I'm sure she'll see me."

"And your name is?" The entire lobby got quiet.

"La'Mont Simpson."

"One moment, please." She picked up the phone, dialed some numbers, said a few words and hung up."

"Right this way please."

She led him down the long-carpeted hallway. The walls were decorated with the company logo of a Butterfly.

It was a nonprofit she'd started some years ago. Its main focus was assisting lost and abandoned children in urban communities. Due to Lisa's hard-work, dedication and warm heart., he company flourished and quickly became the largest non-profit organization in the Bay Area.

When he reached her door, the receptionist turned away. Voorheeze's nerves were all over the place. Right now, he wished he had a cigarette. Then a smile appeared on his face. He could kill any nigga without batting an eye and here he was shaking like a motor bike. Gathering his resolve, Voorheeze took a deep breath and knocked.

"Come in." Her voice was smoky like the late Billie Holiday. Voorheeze opened the door and stepped in.

For a moment they both just stared at each other with the biggest smiles on their faces. She stood up and walked around her desk. Neither of them had any way of knowing that the other was being attacked by the swarm of butterfly's in their stomachs.

"Well, hello stranger." Lisa greeted as she rounded the desk and gave him a hug.

"Finally." He returned the embrace.

"Excuse me?" She asked as she broke the embrace not sure if she'd heard him correctly or not.

"I'm just really glad I made the choice to finally come see you." He looked and sounded like a teenager going thru puberty.

"Um, I guess so." Her giggle made him follow her gaze.

When he looked down he realized his shit was standing at full attention. Voorheeze wasn't embarrassed at all. He had been in love with Lisa all his life. He had jacked-off countless nights while fantasizing about her.

"Excuse me" he did respect her still.

"It's okay. But, I'm afraid that everyone's seen your speech at your sister show. Believe me, these walls have ears, so if you don't mind, I think we should go somewhere and have this conversation."

"Mind? I wouldn't mind at all. You lead and trust me, I'll follow. The way he looked at her body when he said that made her temperature rise.

"Uh, I think you should go first."

He smirked cause he knew why she'd said it. Lisa stood 5'11 and she had milk chocolate skin. This woman possessed the smoothest, creamiest skin he ever seen on one of the most beautiful faces God ever created. Her black hair was flat ironed and hung three inches below her shoulders. She was exquisite.

As beautiful as she was, her face wasn't fucking with her body. Her 38 DD'S sat perfectly on her chest, complimenting a frame that carried a size 50-inch ass and hips. Lisa was every bit a "Brick House".

Voorheeze walked back the way he'd come, through the hallway filled with plaques and awards. After telling her secretary who gave her the "You go girl look" that she was heading out to lunch, Lisa met Voorheeze on the parking lot.

"I know you don't expect me to ride around in that little bitty thing." She gave him a look that said "Nigga, you're crazy."

"I'm a safe driver, Lisa. You ain't got nothing to worry about." She knew she didn't have to worry about anything because they were taking her car.

"Come on Boo, we're driving my car."

He stared at her for a minute. She looked so sexy. He told himself he should've stepped to her a long time ago.

"Is my sh... my car gonna be safe here?" He had to catch himself with his language. Just her presence made a nigga wanna be better.

"Sure. Come on." She told him as she led him towards her car. Voorheeze didn't pay any attention to where she was taking him. His eyes were stuck on her outrageous ass. The models in the Cheeks, Thick and Straight Stuntin Magazines ain't have shit on her! Not a damn thing.

He was so focused on her ass that he neva paid attention to the vehicle she was walking to. After she stopped he looked up and damn near shitted on himself.

They were standing in front of a brand new 4-door charcoal gray Honda Accord. Honda's were for woman and Asians. Not niggaz of his statue.

"What you got a problem with my car?" She asked him seeing the hesitation on his face.

"Yeah. It ain't moving let's go get that food." He laughed as he opened up the door for her to get in.

Once she was situated he walked around to the other side and got in. As soon as she started the car up, he pushed the button sending the automatic seat as far back as it would go.

She looked over at him and shook her head.

"You ought to be ashamed of yourself. I have a nice car." She told him.

"Lovely." Was his only response laughing at him she pulled out of the parking lot.

De'Kari

CHAPTER III
Cupertino, CA

The Outback Steakhouse was dimly lit and almost empty at this time of day. That was cool with Voorheeze. He didn't need any distractions. The waitress brought his Tokyo Tee and a Lemon Drop for Lisa. He ordered it for her knowing that it was her favorite. She declined at first but he was able to convince her to have just one.

"Tell me, where are we supposed to start after your speech the other night?", she finally asked after feeling uncomfortable from the way he was just staring at her and smiling.

"Oh yeah, about that. Look, I apologize for putting you on the spot like that. It's just laying up in that coma like that, not knowing if you gonna make it or not sort of puts things in perspective for you." He took a drink trying to formulate everything the right way.

"I hope so, because your body can't keep taking these beatings that you're dishing out to it."

"I'm not talking about that."

She looked him in the eyes. "Then, what are you talking about?"

"I'm talking bout life itself. Lisa, I've loved you as far back as I can remember. I tried my best to stay away from you because of my life, but I can't. You were married so I had no choice but to keep it G and respect that. You ain't married no more. I know this is sudden. But, I promise you I'll give you everything you could possibly have ever wanted. Whether its material things or your emotional needs, I got you. All you got to do is give me a chance. Just one. I've wanted this for way too long to mess it up. All I need is one chance Lisa just once" The sincerity she heard in his words moved her heart.

She'd had a couple of bad relationships, her experiences of ups and downs. She wanted what every woman wanted... to be loved. As she looked at the handsome, elegant man in front of her, she couldn't help but to see the little boy she used to baby sit when she was only fourteen.

"Wow! Uh…So I haven't seen you in nearly ten years and you expect a girl to stop everything she's doing and play a part in your little fantasy." His facial expression at the sound of the words "little fantasy" told her she may have chosen the wrong words.

"Not necessarily a fantasy per-se but it is virtually a dream that you believe that you can quit your lifestyle and be everything I need you to be. How do you even know we are right for each other?"

"Because I've had too much wrong in my life to be around it and not notice it." If you were wrong for me my sensors would've gone off a long time ago. I know it in my soul, we aren't right for each other we are perfect for each other.

Just then, as if right there was a perfect place to pause, their meals arrived. They ate in silence for the first ten minutes. She was thinking of everything that he'd told her and fighting with herself for allowing her heart to imagine the possibilities.

He was wondering if he'd said things the right way. Or if he'd said too much. Neva in his life had he been so nervous. Even just eating, his heart was going a million miles an hour.

"Look, I'm not asking for a lifelong commitment right now. I've still got some things I got to take care of. Plus, excellence is achieved not chose. I just want you to know that I'm old school "Checking for you" and I want you to at least be open to giving me a chance once I get all my ducks in a row." He knew all he needed was a chance. The rest he'd take care of.

"Well at the very least yes I will think it over."

The rest of their time was spent doing some catching up and just talking about life. While they ate she told him all about her plans of opening up another non-profit in Stockton, CA and the group homes that she wanted to open up. He was so moved by how big her heart was and her need to help people.

The more and more she talked, the more he knew that she was the one for him. He swore to himself that he was going to handle his business with Batman and the Mobb. So, he could hurry up and get back and take care of things with her.

When they pulled back into the parking lot of her job her receptionist came running out of the office.

"Lisa we have a huge problem!" She shouted out of breath as she ran up to them.

"What's wrong, Beverly?"

"Them." Beverly pointed to a line of men walking back and forth from a box truck to the front office. Voorheeze smiled and looked at Lisa."

"Just think about it."

"You didn't?" She looked at him shocked.

"Just think about it, Butterfly!" Then he strolled back to the Lambo. Of course, he was responsible for the box truck full of romance baskets and flowers. Carnations and Tulips. He gave the owner of the Boutique specific instructions for the two-hundred and fifty baskets. They all were to read.

"Just think about it!"

Vieira was asleep when Voorheeze walked back into the suite. He ordered room service then set up his Apple Chrome Notebook and then jumped into the shower. The hot water cascading over his muscles always helped him think clearer.

When he got out of the shower grabbed a Terri cloth towel and wrapped it around his waist. He checked on Vieira, she was still out like a light so he went back to the notebook.

Opening up Fire Fox he went to the tool bar and clicked on the icon for privacy mode. Now that his steps were untraceable he opened up Facebook. Typing the appropriate username and password his page opened up: Raider Nation 276. He typed 49er Empire Will Neva Die in the search box. He clicked on the message link and sent the following: *Football Season is coming around so I am back in town once again. Our active list is complete and injury reserved list is empty. We are no doubt ready to play, Guaranteed it's going down. What do you say we hook up for a scrimmage or pre-season game if your man enough! Anytime! Any place! Anywhere!*

He checked over the message and then clicked, send. A moment later a knock came from the door. He put a robe on top of the towel and grabbed his banger and slipped it in the pocket of the robe. Once he walked over to the door he checked the peep hole.

Seeing room service, he opened the door with his hand inside of the pocket gripping the banger. The little Mexican woman rolled the cart in and offered to unload it. Voorheeze declined and handed her a $50 tip. If she would've smiled any harder a whole book would be able to fit inside of it.

When he closed the door behind her and turned around Vieira was standing there wearing one of his t-shirts and clearly nothing else on under it.

"Smells good. What did you order?" She asked while stretching. The t-shirt rising just high enough to give a sneak peek at her curly pubic hair.

"Why don't you have a seat and let me show you." He pulled a chair out at the table as he spoke.

Vieira sat down and waited with a smile on her face while he fixed her plate. The food smelled so good she couldn't stop her mouth from watering

He sat the plate down in front of her and poured her a glass of orange juice. She licked her lips at the food. The plate consisted of two omelets, bacon, sausage and county potatoes. He also sat down a bowl of fresh fruit.

"This looks delicious. You're not eating?" she saw that he sat down without a plate.

"Naw, I had a bite while I was out."

"Did you see her?" She didn't mean to ask that question. It just slipped out.

"Yeah. Eat your food before it gets cold." He knew where she wanted to go. Now was not the time to go there.

"Well, you could at least tell me if you're leaving me." Vieira's heart was so heavy it was weighing down her entire chest.

The tears were fighting to fall. She fought twice as hard not to let them.

He reached over and took her hand in his. Yeah, he cared for this woman. Voorheeze didn't know where or when he'd started to develop emotions towards her, but he had them.

"I'm here, ain't I? Now eat your food before it gets cold."

A smile lit up her face. Vieira picked up her fork and dug into the omelet. To her surprise, it was a fresh lobster and spinach omelet with provolone and American sharp cheese.

When she bit into the cheesy omelet, she closed her eyes in bliss. It was the best omelet she had ever eaten. It was so moist and juicy that some of the creamy cheese spilled out of her mouth and down her chin.

While Vieira ate Voorheeze talked. Without telling her anything that she could use against him if she decided to cross him, he let her know what was what. Batman was his "brother from another". He wasn't just going to sit by while his brother needed him.

She needed to understand that he lived outside of the rules of the law and wasn't going to conform to those rules. She also needed to accept that he had feelings for her, but his heart belonged to Lisa. They could spend whatever time they had enjoying each other. But, when Lisa called he would come. That's just how it was.

He'd finished talking just as she was placing the last forkful into her mouth. The entire time he'd talked she listened. Vieira had neva met a young man like him before. He was smart, strong, confident and in control. All while still remaining humble and sweet.

She wiped her mouth and looked up into his eyes." So, tell me what do you want me to do? What do you need from me?"

****** N. D. ******
Dublin, CA

Gunz sat next to her bed holding her soft hand in his as the tears rolled down his cheeks. He couldn't believe that he had allowed her to become a victim of the life he lived. If anything, he should be the one laying in the hospital bed, not Nastasia.

It had been months since the tragic day Tut tried to kill her in their home. Months that caused Gunz to questions his entire life. All the things he'd done and all the things he now wanted. If he could re-write that one tragic day, rewind the hands of time just once. He'd gladly give up everything he had to prevent her from having that experience.

"What are you thinking about Leonard?" With her hand she wiped the rest of his tears away.

"You know what I'm thinking about already. I'm thinking of how I failed you. I'm actually wondering if marriage is right for us. A husband is supposed to be able to provide for his but also protect his. I couldn't protect you. I didn't keep you safe." He was too ashamed to look to look at her.

Hearing him say those words were like bullets flying into her chest all over again!

Of course, marriage was correct for them. They were the perfect couple. Why didn't he see that?

"Leonard, accidents happened all the time, all over the world. Okay, so some of your enemies came into our house. Babe, it could've easily been some intruder, some rapist or some other sick son of bitch.

"Random acts of violence occur every day all over the world. Leonard, it's called life. I thank God that I made it through and I thank God that you are still here with me! Now when I get out of this hospital tomorrow we are going to Las Vegas to get married and since you feel so guilty right now my honeymoon better be some place I can't spell or pronounce." Her words were having a wonderful effect on him, the effect she wanted. When she said the last line they both burst out laughing.

"Oh, so now you blackmailing a nigga, huh?"

"Call it whatever you like, but it better be more exotic then Bora Bora." She told him as she playfully punched him in the shoulder.

He also was just happy that she'd miraculously recovered fully. Especially, since one of the bullets that entered her chest came just a few centimeters away from her main artery.

Tomorrow they would be leaving. Going home to the new house he had bought in San Ramon. No-one beside the real estate agent knew about the house. But tonight, he had something to do.

He looked at his expensive Audemar watch. It was time to head out and take care of this shit. After tonight everything will be settled. Tomorrow he and Nastasia could began a new life. He neva thought he would ever know anything other than the game and he damn sure neva imagined he would leave it. Now he had a whole ass future to look forward to a future with this exquisite woman.

He stood up and gave her a kiss.

"I'll be here first thing in the morning miss somewhere I can't spell or pronounce.

She laughed at the man of her dreams.

"It better be somewhere like Instakavanauh Hot Springs." She said the most foreign shit she could make up.

"Well you just pronounced that so we can't go there. See how you mess everything up." I know how to read and spell "ass" Gunz couldn't help himself.

Being around her was so natural. It's like his whole reason for being was being around her. That's how strong his feelings were.

"Ok, Babe. I'll see you in the morning," she told him as she began to lay back down.

Giving her one last look, he blew her a kiss then turned to leave. Nastasia felt warm and fuzzy all over until he opened the door and crossed the threshold. The coldest chill she'd ever felt in her life washed down her spine, taking the smile she'd had on her face clear off.

"Leonard!" The panic made her scream his name at the top of her lungs.

Gunz came busting back in the room with is 44 Desert Eagle in his hand. Ready to act the fuck up!

"What's wrong?" He looked at a frightened Nastasia.

Before she could answer, he stormed the room looking inside of every nook and crevice. Searching for any kind of threat . Not finding anything, he walked back over to the bed.

Her scream drew the attention of spectators so he tucked the banger back on his waist. The look on her face was as if Nastasia had just seen the Devil.

"Babe. What's wrong?" He asked her as he gently stroked her face.

Nastasia could see written all over his face how much he loved her. The level of concern on his face was adorable. She knew he had business that he needed to handle so they could put it all behind them and finally be alone with his old lifestyle.

She couldn't hinder that. She couldn't fill his head with all kinds of madness.

But the feeling she felt was so scary. Nastasia didn't know exactly what it was. All she knew was it was bad. She wanted to tell Leonard to stay with her tonight. Climb right in bed and stay with her. But she didn't want to be one of those manic trauma survivors she wasn't a victim! She neva had been and neva would be a victim.

"Nothing babe. I'm okay, I just had a moment." She was referring to the flashbacks related to PTSD that the doctors told them about.

He sat down and took her into his arms. He gave her a tighter squeeze and a kiss on her forehead. "Babe, are you sure you're okay?"

"I'm sure babe." She kissed him on the cheeks.

"Really babe gone and take care of your business and come back to me as soon as you can."

He was hesitant. "You're sure?"

"Sure. I'm sure babe I'll be okay."

Gunz held her in his arms for another ten minutes before he finally got up and left.

**** N. D. ****

Dok had a cousin out of San Jose named Tree Top. Tree Top had been buying weight from Clark for a few years now. Top had been copping ever since Voorheeze opened that line and made the introductions.

Tonight, it was set up for Clark to meet Tree Top at a restaurant that Tree Top owned in San Jose called, "The Wellfare House." It was a soul food spot that'd been jumping since it opened.

As a favor to Dok and the family, Tree Top was closing the restaurant down for one day so that the meet could take place.

Dok had another plan for Clark and his fucking crew. He and Gunz along with some shooters would be waiting for Clark when he showed up. The plan sounded perfect to Gunz, especially considering they were going to be in the restaurant before Clark and his team.

Gunz was crossing the San Mateo Bridge when he decided to take 101 S to San Jose because traffic on 880 south was a mothafucka right now. He was just about to go around a slow ass Camaro when his phone rang. It was Dok.

"I'm crossing the Mateo Bridge, so I might lose you." Gunz told Dok as he answered the phone.

"Peace, God. Everything okay?" Dok asked.

"Everything's Gucci, big bra."

"That's good. I'm looking over the menu as we speak." Dok was letting Gunz know that he was at the restaurant already.

"Aaight. Depending on traffic I should be there between twenty and thirty-five minutes."

"I'll see you then, brotha."

"Aight." Gunz hung up the cellphone and sped past the slow ass Cameo.

He couldn't understand why motherfucker's bought fast cars and drove the mothafuckas as slow as dog shit.

He looked over at the driver of the Camaro as he passed. He started laughing so hard when he saw the little old black lady flip him off that he swerved. She looked like one of those little, old church ladies.

Still laughing ,he reached for the blunt he had rolled in the parking lot of the hospital, before he left. The taste of the Blueberry Widow hit his taste buds as soon as he lit the blunt and took a full pull off of it.

He started thinking about Nastasia and the life that they would soon live. Leaving the game would be easy. His little cousin had South Philly on lock and Gunz had over ten million put up. Although he neva had thought he would see a day like this, the game had treated him good. Gunz couldn't believe he was about to be a married man.

Right on cue DMX cut off and Tupac's "Me and My Girlfriend" came up on the playlist. Gunz turned the volume up full blast.

"All I need in this life of sin. Just me and my Girlfriend/Down to ride to the bloody end/ Just me and my Girlfriend.

As the first verse started Gunz began rapping right along with Tupac. Song after song Gunz rapped along with them as they played. Twenty-Six minutes later he pulled into the parking, feeling extremely good. The only car in the lot was Dok's Hell Cat.

He checked his Desert Eagle to make sure it was right before getting out of the car. The sun had gone down a couple of hours ago and the Bay Area breeze was blowing nice.

When he entered the restaurant, he paused to all allow his eyes to adjust to the dimly lit room. The smell of food was heavy in the air. It smelled fucking wonderful. Gunz stomach growled and he licked his lips.

When his eyes adjusted he saw Dok seated in the back. He made his way to the table while thinking about the unmistakable smell of fried pork chops.

The restaurant itself was in a medium size building. The design and décor resembled that of a Chinese restaurant more than a soul food joint. With the rice paper lamps and Chinese candles on the tables.

Gunz figured fuck the design, the food smelled on point like a mothafucka!

To his surprise as he walked up Dok was on the ass end of a plate of neck bones and gravy with black eyed peas on top of white rice, some jalapeno cheese cornbread, yams and collard greens with salt pork in it.

"Peace young God." Dok greeted Gunz as he reached the table.

"What's going on big brah?" Gunz took a seat across from Dok. "What's up with the food? This a dinner date or something?"

"Naw brah. He called saying he was running a little late. I didn't see no harm tasting this world famous corn bread while I waited for him to show up." Dok took another huge bit of the corn bread he'd dipped in gravy after he spoke.

After chewing enough of the cornbread to speak, Dok slid a menu across the table towards Gunz.

"Chef still in the kitchen." He told him. Then he went back to his plate.

Gunz picked up the menu and opened it He didn't see or hear the waiter who walked up behind him. Everything on the menu sounded delicious to Gunz. He was about to just tell the chef to bring whatever. Until he turned the first page.

Taped to the center of the second and third page was a newspaper article. He glanced up at Dok who was busy eating, then looked back at the article and begin reading it:

Oakland Tribune
August 07, 2002

Once again tragedy has struck in the streets of Oakland. Violence erupted today in the form of automatic gun fire in broad daylight in the streets of East Oakland, California. That took the lives of 29 people while stray bullets injured 11 more.

Witnesses (who wanted to remain anonymous) reported it was a scene out of a gangster movie in urban streets. Reportedly and estimated five or six shooters who got away in two or three vehicle opened fire on a group of individuals loitering on the side of the liquor store. Some speculate that the victims were indeed members of gang called The Black Guerilla Family and were selling drugs in the area. Our sources say that the shooting was indeed a statement letting the Figures of the Under World know that a new gang was taking over the block of 85th St. Among the dead was the notoriously known Big Zoe also knows as Gun Play. Who was a suspected lieutenant in the organization with influence rumored to spread all the way into North Richmond...

Gunz didn't continue reading the article. Instead he dropped the menu on the table.

"What the fuck is...."

His sentence was cut off by the bite of the garrote as the waiter threw it over his head, squeezing it as tight as he could. A sharp pain pierced through his right hand!

Gunz looked down at his right hand, only to see a big ass knife sticking all the way through it. His eyes looked up until they met Dok's eyes. What he saw staring back at him was pain and regret.

He knew fighting was futile ,but he had to try. There was not one ounce of bitch inside of Gunz' body! With his left hand he reached to his waist. The Desert Eagle was turned backwards because he was right handed.

Desperately, Gunz tried to pull it out. Droplets of blood ran down parts of his neck from where the garrote cut into his skin.

The waiter pulled it even tighter, with all of his might, he let out a grunt as he pulled.

A tear escaped from Gunz' left eye. It rolled slowly down his face.

BOOM!

The sound of the big 44 interrupted the night's peace. The muzzle flashed momentarily blinding everyone. The smell of gun powder replaced the aroma of the soul food.

They were so close to one another that Dok could see smoke coming out of the bullet hole in Gunz' shoulder. Dok lowered the big .44 Magnum.

"Believe me when I tell you, brotha, that this breaks my heart. But ,it's out of my hands, Young God. You guys knew that 85rth was a B.G.F. Block. So, you had to know that there would be repercussions. Not only that, but you killed a Joker. No-one authorized or sanctioned the hit.

"The move itself ruffled a lot of feathers and made a big stink. It also drew so much attention to 85th that the Dinosaurs decided that revenge should lay dormant. Well, they've decided the attention has faded. The face of the Dragon has come for you." A lone tear actually fell from Dok's eye as he spoke.

He had truly grown to like and respect Gunz. He had become like a little brother to Dok. Yet and still, the order was given. Even a General follows orders.

The bullet to the shoulder hit directly into a nerve severing his ability to move his arm at all. The white lights began going off in his head as his lungs screamed and cried out. Burning from lack of oxygen.

Thoughts of Nastasia swam through his mind. Maybe God knew that he was too tainted for her. His spawn would be too much on the soul of someone as sweet as her. So, this was the answer.

A glorious tragedy. First, he'd nearly lost her, only for her to actually lose him.

Fuck That!

A warrior dies on his feet! '*Uuurrggghh!*"

With all of his might Gunz pulled his hand with the knife still stuck in it out of the table, he lunged at Dok with the blade first.

BOOM! BOOM! BOOM!

This time there was no smoking bullet hole. The big .44 slugs burst Gunz head wide open!

"God damn, man!" Little Zoe yelled out as he released the garrote and jumping backwards.

Looking down he began knocking the pieces of skull fragments off of his Gucci shirt.

"Peace, Bredren. You can buy more clothes." Dok told him.

"Man, I don't give a fuck about this skirt. Bitch ass nigga made you smoke 'em, robbing me of my revenge." Lil Zoe was thinking of the night he was told that his daddy was neva coming home, while he was slowly waiting for Gunz to die.

Lil Zoe quickly rose through the ranks while making a name for himself in both East and West Oakland. Before he could rightfully take what was his, he needed to avenge his father. At first he wanted everyone involved. The elders talked him into understanding that only those who gave the order were responsible. The rest were just soldiers taking orders.

Big Tree Top came around the corner with a Draco 7.62 in his hands,. When he heard the first shot, he figured that was the shot to kill Gunz. So, when the other three rang out he decided, fuck that! He was going to investigate

"Peace, be still, big one." Dok called out at Tree Top coming out of the kitchen." Everything's copasetic. We're just finishing up dinner and had ungrateful guest. I'll call the cleaners and get it all taken care of."

"Don't sweat it, cuz. I've got an incinerator out back, we can throw all this shit in there and be done with it." Tree Top might've been cooking soul food, but he was still a street nigga!

The three of them spent the next two hours removing any trace of Gunz from the restaurant. By the time they were finished with the scrubbing, sanitizing, and reupholstering all three were dirt tired. The growl of Little Zoe's stomach was testimony to how much work they'd just done.

Big Tree Top really didn't need a reason to eat with his 6'6 270lb frame. He was always hungry. He'd mentioned there were some St. Louis style ribs, baked beans, macaroni and cheese and some peach cobbler in the kitchen. He was actually getting ready to fix him a plate before he heard the shooting earlier.

They made themselves plates and ate like they'd just pulled up from a long day of work.

When they were finished eating and tying up business Lil Zoe and Dok both took off going their separate ways, leaving Big Tree Top to lock up his establishment.

CHAPTER IV
Hospital in Dublin
10:17 a.m.

Nastasia couldn't stop looking at the clock. The nurse had been in there three times. The doctor had popped in twice, yet she refused to say a word to anyone. The stuffed teddy bear in her arms was soaking wet from the pools of tears she'd cried over the past hour and seventeen minutes.

At 9:00 a.m. Nastasia received her discharge from the hospital. Leonard was the most punctual man she had ever met in her life. She could feel it in her heart but she denied the feeling. The longer she sat there waiting for him, the more she thought about last night and the cold chill she'd gotten the moment he crossed the threshold. The river of tears came on their own.

Finally, Nastasia gathered her things along with the energy she needed to get up. She smelled the teddy bear one last time. Leonard had given it to her the first time he came to see her. It still had his smell on it.

She made her way slowly down the halls not talking to or even looking at anyone. There was a trash can at the end of one of the halls. She threw everything she was carrying away except her bear.

"Excuse me, Mam are you okay?" A concerned nurse who witnessed her throw everything away asked her.

Nastasia didn't even acknowledge her she just kept walking. She was in her own world.

It was one of them days you wished would just hurry up and end, nothing went right. Everything that could go wrong did. She decided to have a drink and let the alcohol sooth the anger out of her muscles.

"Excuse me miss, would you mind if I attempted to keep you company for a while?"

She looked up from the magazine she was reading. Standing before her smiling down at her was one of the finest young brothas she had seen. Though he was being proper, his whole being screamed Thug.

She thought, for the first time today something good was going to go her way.

Fate proved to be a playa hata when his phone rang just as she was gesturing for him to have a seat.

He'd sat down and had a brief conversation. Afterwards, he sprang from the seat. All sophistication was gone, only the Thug she saw under the surface remained.

"I hope whatever it is, it isn't so serious that I'm not going to be given the opportunity of finding out your name." Disappointment was heavy in Nastasia's voice.

After the day she'd been having she was ready to run off anywhere with his fine ass. She knew he was special!

He didn't respond. He picked up his drink and finished it in one gulp.

"I'm so sorry, beautiful. I wish we had the time to get to know each other more. I honestly think that it could've been a treat for both of us. but I have a family emergency. Luv, my name is Leonard, Leonard Johnson." His voice made her panties wet. It was deep and strong like Barry White.

"It's very nice to meet you Leonard. I understand emergencies, lord knows I do, it's okay." She'd had three emergencies in two different states in one day.

She reach into her purse pulled out a business card and handed it to him. As he walked away she prayed he would be safe, whatever he was going to do. She also prayed that he would use the card.

The morning air was warm and welcoming against her skin. The warmth enveloped her in a state of nostalgia. Nastasia involuntarily squeezed the teddy bear tighter in her arms. When she took a deep breath all she could smell was Leonard and a smile quickly spread across her face and then…

**** N. D. ****

The nurse who had asked Nastasia if she was okay hurried to catch up to her. Nurse Jackie was dead tired. She was finishing up a double shift. When the young lady ignored her show of concern, Nurse Jackie initially let it go and went back to her paperwork.

Nurse Jackie's motherly instincts kicked in. Instinctively she knew something was wrong. She took off in a sprint after Nastasia who'd already walked out of the main doors. Nurse Jackie was fifty-one years old but she was in good shape. She closed the distance relatively fast. However, she still wasn't fast enough.

Seeing her sprinting and calling-out in desperation to the young lady a few orderlies and paramedic's joined Nurse Jackie starting yelling at the top of her lungs.

Before anyone could get to her or snap her out of the state that she was in Nastasia stepped off the curb and into the street. The screaming intensified! Nurse Jackie willed her legs to move beyond their normal capacity. "Oh God, please Nooo!" She screamed.

BAM!

Everyone stopped dead in their tracks. The nurse Stared in horrid shock at Nastasia's body was being catapulted into the air. Nastasia neva saw the ambulance as it came barreling down the street. It was carrying a twelve year old gunshot victim. The little girl needed a blood transfusion A.S.A.P and possibly a couple of organs.

When her body finally hit the ground, people were shocked to see that she held a Teddy tightly snuggled in her arms. Nurse Jackie rushed over to her. By the death grip that she had on the bear and the peaceful smile that was on her face, Nurse Jackie knew that whatever had been troubling the young lady before? It was not troubling her any longer.

Nastasia's life was not the only one that ended due to the accident. The life of her unborn 3 ½ month old unborn baby ended as well. She had been waiting to surprise Gunz with the news that he was going to be a daddy.

A surprise that would never come to light.

**** N. D. ****
Fremont

Riders of Bay Area Rapid Transit also known as Bart, had complained about the rancid smell in the parking lot located at the eastern back side of the Bart compound. However, Bart officials paid no mind to the complaints. The Bart station was located not too far from Lake Elizabeth, the mating ground for goose. The smell of thousands of geese being in the area mating and shitting, was the cause for so many complaints.

Just by chance officer Winston Justice pulled over at the back of the Bart station. He had drank two Monster Energy drinks and two twenty-ounce Lipton Ice Teas with his lunch. His damn bladder felt like it was literally about to burst wide open, holding it wasn't an option. The nearest restroom was over one hundred fifty yards away, so he parked in the first empty spot he saw. As he threw his cruiser in park he jumped out without shutting the ignition off. His door slammed into the truck parked next to him.

The most God awful smell assaulted his nose. There was no time to worry about the fucking smell. He was fumbling with his zipper when all of a sudden.

"Holy Fuck!" Officer Justice shouted out!

If his weird behavior didn't draw any attention to himself, the loud shout most definitely did.

Bystanders looked at the cop who was staring into the truck like he saw a ghost. Officer Justice was so busy reaching and fumbling for the radio on his shoulders he didn't realize in his fright he forgot all about needing to piss. He was too busy worrying about the image he was looking at. The body was slumped all the way over. From what he could tell the male victim who was seated in the driver's seat had been shot twice in the back of the head. Either he was already leaning over when he got shot, or he ended up slumping all the way over after getting shot.

Either way it went, the body was all the way face down in the passenger seat. No-one saw the body laying down on the seat decaying.

Officer Justice radioed it in to his dispatch. He couldn't take his eyes off of the sight. The right side of the victims head was blown off. It looked like a watermelon had exploded. Maggots had begun crawling in and out of the head wound, while flies buzzed around inside of the truck.

When he finally snapped out of his trance, he moved to cordon off the area. That is when Officer Justice felt the cool dampness. In his shock at finding the body he didn't realize that he had forgotten to take a piss. Officer Justice had pissed his fucking pants.

Looking down at his pants was the worst thing he could've done. The onlookers followed his gaze to see what else he discovered. Snickers and laughter quickly broke out as they realized Officer Justice had pissed on himself.

Embarrassed, he went about taping the area off all the while wondering if he had made the right career choice. This indeed was one hell of a first day!

**** N. D. ****
A little while later

Hedgecock nearly crashed into an Infinity G35 that was pulling out of the parking lot as he sped into the same parking lot. It was Hedgecock's day off. He was at his favorite men's club. Blowing off some steam when he got the call. Immediately he made it his business to get there as soon as fucking possible.

As he sped into the Bart Station's parking lot. It looked like a car dealership for Government vehicles. Law enforcement personnel was all over the place. It didn't take long for word to circulate through the law enforcement channels that Lieutenant Randy Urena's body had been found decomposing inside of his truck, with what appeared to be two fatal gunshot wounds to the back of his head.

The tires screeched as Hedgecock came to a sudden stop. He and the lieutenant weren't that close, but still Lt. Urena was his superior officer. His death was a slap in the face to the entire department.

He got down from his monster truck and headed for the briefing area. His skin tight black leather pants drew attention from almost everyone. Sure, he wished he would've gone home first and changed. It just would've taken him another forty-five minutes to go across the Dumbarton Bridge and forty-five more to get back. He didn't have the luxury of time.

He spotted the FBI Special Agent and her team and made his way toward them. As he got closer, the smell was fucking atrocious. It meant the body had been rotting for some time. Instead of walking up to where the others were, Hedgecock chose to go see the body. He might've been a rookie, but being in the Bay Area he'd already seen his fair share of dead bodies.

Nothing could prepare him for the smell of a dead body that had been decaying in a vehicle under the sun for two weeks, with all of the windows rolled all the way up. The smell literally began choking him.

Once he was sure he could tolerate it, he walked closer. Still coughing, Hedgecock made sure not to step in or anything that could possibly be evidence. What he saw pissed him off!

The doors were now open, which attributed to the smell. It also left the corpse vulnerable to more files and other insects. *A man dedicated his life for the good of the people and this was the thanks he got*, is what he was thinking as he stared at the dead Lieutenant.

Careful again not to disturb anything, he turned away from the truck's cab and headed toward the area where Andreatta and her team were. He made it to the group just as Agent Finnegan came running back to the group.

"Hey boss, we got video." Agent Finnegan was nearly out of breath due to running from the Bart station's office to where they all were.

"I've been trying to get you on your cell but this damn things not getting any reception." He told her, holding up his cell phone.

Special Agent in Charge, Andreatta was in the middle of lecturing her team on what was expected from them on this case. Upon hearing the news of the video, she stopped what she was saying in mid-sentence. She turned around giving her attention to Agent Finnegan.

"Is it good footage?" she asked in a stern voice.

"I wanted you to know right away. I didn't look at it." Still struggling to catch his breath, Agent Finnegan's face reddened from embarrassment. He knew he should've looked at the video footage.

"Well, let's got see the video." She spun around walking in the direction Agent Finnegan just come from.

Hedgecock didn't see the need in saying a word. He just invited himself and tagged along with them.

A few minutes later, all five of them were crammed inside of the stations command center. It was a measly broom closet made into an office. Hedgecock noted that the office didn't smell too much nicer then the area by the truck.

Inside of the tiny office was a rinky-dink wooden desk that look like it came out of the principal's office at the local middle school. There was also a small, beat up, file cabinet. Finally, there were the only two things of worth in the office, a DVD player and a 32" Samsung flat screen TV that doubled as a camera monitor.

"This is Officer Justice. He is the lone officer on duty whom discovered the body of the Lieutenant. Officer Justice this is my S.A.C., Andreatta." Agent Finnegan made the introductions, still feeling a little warmth from his earlier embarrassment.

"S.A.C?" Officer Justice question with a puzzled look on his face, hoping he didn't have to stand up.

"It means Special Agent in charge. It's just a silly title, now let's see this video." Straight and to the point S.A.C. Andreatta was beginning to take all the deaths revolving around the shit going on in the streets of the Bay personally.

"Okay, so this was the night of Wednesday before last at 9:08 p.m. The camera system that we have is relatively new. They were just installed four months ago, so the footage is wonderful. How-ever, the light pole on the targeted area was broken out by some neighborhood kids earlier that same day." Officer Justice explained to them as he got the DVD player ready.

All the Agents exchanged looks with each other at the mention of the light. All of them thinking the same thing; *Neighborhood kids didn't knock the light out. It was preparation for later that night.*

The footage came to life on the screen. Just as Officer Justice said, the resolution was high quality. However, with the light being out it was too dark to get a clear visual. Lt. Urena's truck was already parked. Though they couldn't see inside of the truck, they assumed the Lieutenant was sitting in the truck waiting on someone. The time stamp on the screen was 9:01 p.m. They all waited in anticipation.

At 9:06 p.m. an all-black SUV with tinted windows pulled into the parking space to the right of Urena's truck. An elbow sticking out of the window was the only indication that someone was inside of the S.U.V. It was presumed that the driver of the SUV was talking through the open window to the occupant of the truck. Presumable Lt. Urena.

At 9:07 p.m. a figure was seen climbing out of the back passenger side of the SUV. The figure was covered in all black from its hooded sweatshirt to its black rubber sole boots.

Whoever the figure was, he or she quickly creeped around the back of both vehicles up to the driver's side window. The figure raised its right arm extending thru the open window and fired two shots into the truck.

Oddly enough the figure then opened the driver's door reached inside of the truck. Then placed whatever he or she just retrieved from the truck inside of the hooded sweat shirt. He or she turned the truck on for a moment then turned it back off. Afterwards the figure walks back to the S.U.V. climbs in and it drives away.

The coroner is the only one who can pronounce time of death. However, to S.A.C. Andreatta it was evident that he died at 9:08 that night.

"Okay guys, talk to me. What did we just see?" Andreatta asked her team.

Hedgecock instinctively spoke up.

"We just witnessed some scumbag murder a fine officer in cold blood."

All four of the Agents looked at him like he was crazy.

With a look of disdain on her face S.A.C. Andreatta turned to face him.

58

She looked him up and down. "Did you happen to forget your brain at the costume store when you were out shopping?"

The Crimson Tide aren't as red as Officer Hedgecock turned after the comment. He held his tongue and composure and just glared at her.

"Clearly, he reached in the truck and removed something that either was valuable or perhaps he didn't want found. But, why turn on the truck?" Agent Daly spoke up quickly to defuse the situation.

"Maybe there was something in the disc drive and he took it out." Finnegan tried his hand at it.

"Naw, the moon light would have reflected off of the CD." Garcia knew what he took.

"There was no phone found on the body. I'm betting the shooter took it because their number would've been in Urena's phone when the meeting was set up. I would've done the same thing." He looked over at the S.A.C. to see how she felt about it.

"I agree with you, Garcia." It was the only thing that made sense.

"Okay but why turn on the truck?" Daly called out.

S.A.C. Andreatta smiled at him like one of her children. "Easy, he was rolling up the windows. We see from the footage that both of the windows were down on the truck. He was talking through the passenger window. Clearly, we see the shooter stick his arm thru the driver's side window. Yet, when Officer Justice arrived at the scene." She turned and motioned towards the rookie sitting behind the desk.

"Both of the windows were rolled up. That was actually pretty smart. With the windows being up, the decomposed gases would stay trapped in the truck longer, hence the smell would be trapped. Which is why it took so long to discover the body."

"Hey, don't look at me I just started two days ago." Officer Justice spit out in defense when she looked his way.

If someone would've investigated the complaints from the Bart riders, it's possible the body would've been found earlier.

"Yeah ,Rookie, you might personally be in the clear, but right now, you are the representative for this station. So, you get the shit." *Life wasn't fair but she didn't make the rules* Andreatta thought.

"My guess is they're cleaning house...

"What a minute, hold up! Cleaning house?. Who's cleaning house?" Hedgecock interrupted her. He was clueless.

"If you spent more time doing police work and less time at your male strip club, excuse me, gentlemen's clubs, you would know what is going on." S.A.C Andreatta scolded him.

He was livid! How did she know about the clubs? More importantly who was she to think she could fucking talk to him that way? He wanted to bash her fucking head in. Who the fuck did she think she was? She was just like his fucking wife. She needed to be punched around a little to know her fucking place.

Fucking cunt wasn't worth his job. Fuck her and her prissy federal ass. Hedgecock pushed his way past her and Daly and stormed out of the office.

Fuck them and their investigation he would stick to his own!

On the ride back to the police station Hedgecock couldn't help but steam over the conversation with S.A.C. Andreatta. He wished they were alone he would've back handed the shit out of her.

As he listened to Hank Williams her comment about the gentlemen's club came to mind. Again, he wondered how she knew about it. Knowing the Feds, he figured they were probably following him. Hedgecock told himself that he would have to be careful. As he was telling himself this, he checked his rearview to see if anyone was tailing him now.

Just as he was getting off of the 880 Freeway at Dixon Landing, his cell phone started ringing. Officer Hedgecock didn't feel like being bothered, but when he glanced at the phone and saw the 209 area code, he immediately snatched the phone up. His mother lived out in Stockton. She was old and lonely, so he always was available to hear her complain about one thing or another.

This time it happened to be his mother's neighbor on the phone. His mother had fallen and broken her wrist. She was at San Joaquin Valley Medical.

After receiving all of the necessary information, Hedgecock made an illegal U-turn at the corner of Dixon Landing and Milpitas Blvd. and headed towards Stockton.

**** **N. D.** ****

De'Kari

CHAPTER V
Berkeley, CA

As he rolled over and climbed out of bed Dok wondered if he was making the right choice by giving this interview today. He would neva admit it to anyone, but he was nervous as fuck. To mask his nervousness, he created every excuse in the world why doing it wasn't right. In the end though, the Central Committee thought it was best for the direction they were heading in. Or at least the direction they wanted people to think they were heading in.

He couldn't make his mind up on whether he should wear something fancy or dress casual. In the end, won casual . He stepped out of the house in a pair of crisp grey Cavalli Jeans with a grey and black Cavil shirt, a black and grey Gucci belt with all black Gucci sneakers. A simple diamond chain and silver Oyster Perpetual Blue Face Rolex kept him A-1.

The drive from Berkley into the city took nearly an hour due to traffic. Twenty minutes later he was pulling up to the building. After being checked in and clearing security, Dok was escorted to Carla Daniels office.

"Mr. Hayes, good morning. It's nice to see you." Her smile was warm and inviting.

"Good morning, sistah." His discomfort was as clear as day.

"It will be a good morning once we get you to lighten up. Do you drink coffee? Come on, let's go." She didn't even wait for a response, instead she grabbed him by the arm and ushered him down the hallway.

A few minutes later they were inside an employee lounge. Dok was thrown completely off by the décor of the studio. He was expecting a big warehouse with screens and sound boards, stages and back drops.

Instead they were in a corporate office building.

"Okay, so look. Let me run this down to you. I'm only gone run it down once, so catch it when I throw it." Her entire demeanor, sentence structure and even her voice was different.

"This is the only room in dis whole mothafucka that's sound proof and has digital sound avoidance. That means what we say in here and here only, can't be heard. Anywhere else in this building a fart can be picked up ten floors away."

Dok was looking at her like she was crazy. The sophisticated, educated sistah was gone. Standing before him was a real hood rat.

"I was born on 23rd Street. I was raised in the Murda Dubbs until I was ten and then I moved with my mom, Gwen in the Lower Bottoms. So, I'm Deep East Oakland but I'm Town Official. My father's name is Dumela. This interview is not the white folks trynna embarrass you. This is a legitimate chance for the people voice to be heard. So, Dok you need to relax and do you." She was telling him all this while making two cups of coffee.

She handed him a cup just as she finished speaking. Smiling and shaking his head, he accepted the steaming hot cup of coffee. They continued talking and drinking their cups of coffee until it was time for Dok to go to stage preparations.

During the time they talked he learned a lot about Carla Daniels, whose name was formerly Margo James. Her father Dumela was a real militant comrade who died in a vicious gun fight with federal Agents. This took place after a daring escape attempt by Askari, a member of the Central Nerve of the Supreme Committee.

Dumela was a legend in the organization for his acts of bravery. Everyone within the organization knew who he was or knew of him. No-one, however, knew he had a daughter, except members of his immediate family and members of the Central Committee.

It never ceased to amaze Dok just how far the committee could reach.

Preparation didn't take long because Dok wasn't with all that make up shit. He didn't give a fuck how enhanced it would make him look on T.V. Just empty props and screens.

Ms. Daniels explained to him how the blue and green screens worked, the sound mics and a few other things. Then someone mic'd him up and it was show time.

"Okay, remember just keep this nice and easy. I'm just and old friend from back in the neighborhood that you're having a conversation with." Ms. Daniels told him as she re-adjusted her own microphone.

Dok simply nodded his head in agreement and the interview began.

"Good evening ladies and gentlemen and welcome. Today we are speaking with Brother Hayes. He is one of the founding members of Neva Die Ministries, as well as one of its most active organizers

"Now Neva Die Ministries is not only a spiritual mentorship. It is also the parent organization of the Nu Africa Village, Mecca House and I'm sure we're all familiar with Elysian Fields Community Centers.

"So, Mr. Hayes, let me first start by asking you, where does the drive and motivation to help so many helpless children came from?" Carla Daniels asked as she sat across from Dok with her legs crossed with some paper in her hands.

"Well, Miss Daniels, I myself am one of these helpless children. I grew up in South Berkeley, where I quickly became a victim of the streets because I didn't have anyone who cared. Unfortunately, that is the title song of most of the lives born in our urban communities.

"Thankfully, a group of brothas and myself decided to pull ourselves away from the streets. But, not before the sins of our youth caught up with us and forced us to pay heavy prices. We neva had any options but the ones we were given. We're just showing these little brothas and sistah's that now they do have an option. Their parents maybe on drugs or in jail or prison., but there is someone who cares." Dok looked good as he spoke. He was comfortable and relaxed, like he was right where he belonged.

"You say you were forced to pay the price for the sins of your youth. Would you care to elaborate on that?"

"Miss Daniels, I won't go into detail, but as I said I used to be in the streets. I was involved in a lot of illegal stuff. One of those things led to me spending twenty years of my life inside of the California Penal System."

Batman looked up from what he was doing and glanced over at the television. It was a little after ten and he was catching the Fox 2 Nightly News with Carla Daniels.

" So this nigga is just gone throw it all out on the table, huh?" He was talking to the T.V.

He reached for his Samuel Adams and took a long swig before turning his attention back to what he was doing. He hated typing with a passion and was glad that he was finally done.

He read over what he had just typed making certain everything was right before sending it.

Welcome back to the Grind Iron. You're absolutely right.

"It's going down!" After all you've been thru you must be crazy trying to scrimmage against me. Gone and sit this season out. You can cheer as I win the Pro Bowl! "LMAO" But if you just want to lose that badly you know where to find me. I don't do no hiding. I'm always in plain sight.

After checking everything he pressed send and the message was sent to Raider Nation 276. He was tempted to go on Rochelle's page and see how his baby was doing. but he knew that wasn't a good idea.

He missed looking in her eyes, staring at her beautiful smile and eating all of her delicious food. He'd lost thirty pounds since he let home. Since he didn't have her food, he just didn't have an appetite. Right now, he would kill himself for a plate of her chicken alfredo, four cheese noodles. With the egg noodles.

Instead he picked up the burrito that he got from the Mexican restaurant, which had become his 'go to' for a food source.

He turned his attention back to the interview:

"Tell us more about Nu African Village and Mecca House. How do they play apart in the Neva Die Ministry." Carla Daniels was well seasoned at interviewing people. She knew how to guide an interview the direction it needed to go.

"Well they are actually the corner-stones of the Neva Die Community. The Community is our end game so to speak. It is a self-sustained, fully functional community for our children. We're talking a complex with a ten block radius.

"The Community will have everything that a child would possibly need for nurturing and growth. Mecca House or "My Enlightened Children of African descent" are the foster homes the children will start in. As they grow and mature , they will leave Mecca House and go to Nu Africa which is the "Next Urban African American Fruits Restored in Christ like Awareness". These will be college dorms like group homes.

"Also, in the community will be K-12 schooling, community centers and after school activities. As I said, it would be an enclosed environment within our society." As Dok finished speaking he was actually smiling.

Batman didn't realize he was smiling until he glanced at the mirror. At least some good was coming from all of this. He remembered all the way back to 2000 before the birth of Neva Die when his brotha Voorheeze told him about "The Koffee Shop" That was the original name he'd wanted to use to help children. The Koffee Shop was the community.

Then, the wars started and Neva Die was born. It came about not as the answer to the Urban light as it was designed, but as the answer to the ruckus niggaz kicked up. Quickly thoughts of the Summer of Blood entered Batman's mind. He shut them out just as quick.

He grabbed the remote and turned the T.V. off. Fuck being positive. His mind had to stay in hell so he could continue with his carnage. Batman hadn't even scratched the surface.

**** **N. D.** ****
Meanwhile

Voorheeze lay in the huge California King bed watching the T.V. At first he was just channel surfing until he saw his brotha on T.V, Dok was giving an interview with some sistah on the Channel 2 News Special. He turned the volume up and listened.

"Too many times we as a people tend to spend too much time dwelling on the problem instead of the cause of the problem. It is essential to know and understand the cause of a problem in order for us to combat the issue or problem accordingly. However, and I strongly stress this, it is just as important, if not more important, to spend the necessary time on creating a solution."

"Sometimes we get so caught up with focusing on the negative, we forget that there's a positive to be had. We use so much time and energy dealing with the problem that we rush and don't give our all to the solution. Therefore, making it destined to fail and then we wonder why." As Dok was talking, Voorheeze thought about the night the two of them stayed up drinking coffee talking about the same issues.

"He seems very insightful. I like what he just said. That's so true about people spending more time griping about the problem than finding a feasible solution." Vieira stood there in all her beauty, soaking wet ,with a body towel in her hands, drying off.

Voorheeze neva even heard her get out of the shower. Her skin had turned a pinkish, reddish hue from the hot water. His dick started to rise at the thought of seeing that big red ass bouncing up and down on his dick as she rode him backwards. It was one of her latest specialties.

"He's a very intelligent brotha. The subject about the youth in the hood just happens to be one of his most passionate subjects" He told her as he took his focus off of her pussy and remained focused on the interview.

He neva would've thought in a million years that he would've seen Dok Holliday giving an interview on national television. Shit truly was changing.

Bloop! *Bloop*!

The notification on his phone went off. He reached for the phone just as Vieira reached for his dick. She saw the hunger in his eyes when he looked at her. It didn't escape her.

Voorheeze clicked on the notification and brought the Facebook Messenger up. Vieira's mouth was so hot and wet, it was hard for him to concentrate on the message. He didn't know how, but he read the message.

"Sit this one out and cheer as he wins the Pro Bowl." Did he forget Voorheeze started this shit. Batman must have been out of his mind thinking that Voorheeze would sit this one out.

Vieira took her mouth off of him for a minute, "Can a girl get some attention?" After telling him this she went back to sucking the life out of his dick.

Her slurping sounds drove him crazy. Since he knew that this was going to be their last night together, he stopped focusing on Batman and the havoc they were going to wreak.

He dropped the phone and reached down to pulled her on top of him. When she stopped at his midsection he encouraged her to keep climbing until her pussy was directly on top of his mouth. For the next ten minutes he ate her pussy like he invented pussy eating. Then, he gave her that good, Mandingo dick .It had her literally trying to crawl up the walls.

The next morning, he left her at the Embassy Suites and drove to Newark. He left a little after five in the morning, so it was still cold and pretty dark outside.

He thought about last night's sexcapades with Vieira. He would've neva thought he'd end up with a white chick, an O.G. at that. But boy, that pussy was volcano.

It didn't take him long to reach the townhouses. He thought how crazy Batman had to be to come right back to the town houses they had raided, but he had to smile at the irony. They would neva expect to find him there. Batman always hid right in plain sight.

He circled the block twice scanning everything. Once he was sure he wasn't followed and no-one was watching the townhouses. He pulled up to back garages.

The funny thing about having an I.T. guy was everything could be altered. Niggaz stayed putting stash spots in cars and shit. Batman always did the unthinkable.

He figured a nigga neva knew when he needed access to one of the houses they used. Instead of carrying all those garage door openers, all of the garages were rigged.

Voorheeze turned the radio to AM 6.50 then he pulled out his iPhone and dialed 444-9xxx. He placed his I-Phone next to the radio and pressed send. A little static was heard and then the garage door opened up. He drove in and pressed end on the call and the garage door closed .

He got out of the car and walked through the man door that lead to the backyard. Walking across the backyard he couldn't shake the feeling that he was being watched. He ignored the feeling and kept walking towards the sliding door,

Preforming a similar process with the cell phone unlocked the digital key pad on the sliding door. Instead of punching in Rachel's phone number, he dialed 10201986 and the glass door unlocked.

The townhouse was quiet, too quiet. Voorheeze had expected to be greeted by the barrel of a gun instead of an empty house. Feeling like something wasn't right, he pulled one of his dragons out of the holster and made his way thru the house.

He checked both upstairs and downstairs but didn't find Batman. He knew Batman had been there, but he wasn't there any longer. Instead of leaving, he decided to wait awhile and see what happened.

The windows were blocked, so no light got out. A surveillance station was set up and from what he could see was operational. The air smelled of burnt smoke like there had been a fire there before.

Voorheeze walked over to the surveillance station and looked at the monitors. He was careful not to touch anything. Knowing Batman, any and everything could be body trapped.

**** N. D. ****
One hour earlier

Hedgecock was tired, hungry, irritated and grumpy. After driving all the way to Stockton to check on his mother. She didn't want to stay at home by herself all alone. It turned out that she had cracked her hip along with breaking her wrist.

He didn't want to argue with her or disappoint her, but he didn't have room in his house for another body. It was cramped enough with his wife and the kids. Having his mother move into as already tense situation with all of her nagging and complaining was the last thing he needed.

Getting her a room at the Embassy Suites in Milpitas was the perfect solution. He'd been up fifty-six straight hours by the time he walked out of the main doors. Hedgecock felt like he would drop at any minute. The frigid cold air didn't even bother him as he staggered across the parking lot in his leather pants. He had actually walked past it before his mind registered what he just walked past.

All the fatigue evaporated from his body immediately. Hedgecock became fully awake as adrenaline raced through his body and a smile crossed his face, He hurried over to his truck. He had no clue how long the car had been there. Nor did he know how long it was going to be. What he did know was when it moved, he would move.

Hedgecock didn't know how long he sat in the parking lot fighting sleep watching the car. But just when Hedgecock thought he couldn't last another second, he came strolling out.

Hedgecock was so happy he literally squealed like a pig in his truck. When he saw the Lamborghini, he knew it belonged to Simpson, but he didn't want to get his hopes up. Listening to the Dixie Chicks, Hedgecock followed the Lamborghini down highway 880 from Milpitas to Newark. he sang along with the music wondering where Simpson was going.

When he exited onto Thornton Ave Officer Hedgecock didn't know why he would be heading there, but he knew where Simpson was heading. Confirmation came when he made the left next to Chubby Burgers.

By now the sun was beginning to come up. His instincts told Hedgecock that Simpson would circle the block doing a security sweep. So Hedgecock pulled over in front of the apartment complex at 71103 Magnolia and waited.

Sure, enough the Lamborghini circled the block a few times before pulling into the driveway behind the town houses. Hedgecock wanted to get a better look so he repositioned his truck directly across the street from the complex.

He didn't know what it was, but his instincts always told him that Simpson was not only a scum bag, but he was at the center of it all. For a brief second Hedgecock reached for his phone to call it in but quickly realized Simpson hadn't done anything wrong.

Since the murder charges against him had been dropped a few months back, there was nothing to get Simpson on.

If it hadn't of been for the sun coming up, Hedgecock would not have seen the figure sticking to the shadows as he walked down the street. Hedgecock couldn't make any of his features out due to the skull cap pulled down low on his head. The long, thick pea coat had its collar turned up blocking the lower half of the figures face.

From its size and built Hedgecock could tell it was a male. He thought to himself, *could it be? How idiotic?* Silently he thanked the gods if indeed that was Jenkins walking up Magnolia St.

Fuck back up and those fucking FEDS! Them and that stuck up cunt that was running the show. Hedgecock was going at this on his own. If he captured Levell Jenkins and La'Mont Simpson it would sky rocket his career.

As stealthily as he could, Hedgecock climbed out of the cab of his big truck. He put his cellphone in his tight ass pocket after the third try. He had to get a better look so he slowly crept behind the figure he suspected to be Jenkins.

**** N. D. ****

A light breeze blew by pricking the hairs on the back of Batman neck. A natural predator, he could feel the elements and climate telling him that he was now the prey. He slowed as he waited for his opportunity to make his move.

There was enough daylight out now for Hedgecock to see the dark brown skin covered with salt and pepper baby hair on the figures neck. His heartbeat raced as he wrestled with himself about what he was going to do, if this was Jenkins he had the drop on him. If it wasn't then there would only be a little embarrassment. *What to do? What to do?* He debated. It was now or neva!

"FREEZE! Milpitas P.D. Levell Jenkins put your hands above your head and slowly lay on the ground!" Hedgecock was scared as shit. This man was responsible for the deaths of dozens of cops.

"I'm sorry officer, but you got the wrong man!" Batman called out over his shoulder as he raised his arms.

"I said put your fucking hands up! Lay down on the motherfucking ground!" He didn't realize his normally steady hands were shaking. Batman smiled sinisterly to himself. He could hear the fear in the mothafuckas voice. Not only that, but he could smell the stink of fear gushing out of his pores.

"My arms are up, pig! What you gone do kill me, pig? Are you gone shoot you a coon?" He taunted the cop as he slowly turned around. If Batman was going to die, the cop was going to have to shoot him while facing him.

"Look, you sorry son of a bitch! I'm not playing with your black ass! All the mayhem you've caused I could kill you right now and get a medal. Lay the fuck on the ground!" Hedgecock was getting even more nervous even though he had the gun.

"Guess we got us a problem, pig. I'm not an animal, so I'm not bout to lay on the fucking ground like one." Just as Batman was saying this a big ass wasp flew by him landing on his nose.

Batman was scared of wasp; his reflexes were faster than his instincts. He swatted the wasp while ducking low. Forgetting all about the cop.

"Don't move! Freeze!

"*Boc! Boc!*

BOOM! BOOM! BOOM! BOOM! BOOM! BOOM!

De'Kari

CHAPTER VI

Voorheeze continued to watch the monitors all the while wondering where the fuck was Batman was. As he watched the screens a big monster truck pulled up and parked across from the complex.

The truck was clean as shit, but that's not why Voorheeze was interested in it. He could've sworn he saw the same truck in the parking lot of the Embassy when he left this morning. An uneasy feeling shot through his body.

Fuck booby traps and shit, a nigga needed a better visual. He took a quick scan of all the equipment, there were six monitors linked in to twelve cameras positioned all around the complex. After a quick study he was able to figure things out enough to work the joy stick attached to the keyboard enough to zoom in on the truck.

The fat white boy had police written all over him. Immediately Voorheeze looked at all of the other monitors. Looking for people sitting in other cars or construction worker and early morning joggers. Anything that would resemble more pigs in the area. Anything!

In one of the monitors he caught a glimpse at a figure weaving in and out of the shadows. Where there fuck was Batman! He kept wondering. All kinds of wild ass thoughts ran through his mind.

Mothafuckas had Jason Voorheeze fucked up if they thought shit was sweet around here! He was just going to have to show these faggot ass cops what that Dragon Gang was like!

Something about the figure caught his attention, He zoomed in on the figure. The sun was beginning to peek over the horizon bringing more light to the shadows. He knew that walk anywhere. That figure was his big brotha!

Movement brought his attention to the other screen. The white boy was sliding out of the truck like he was trynna creep. Voorheeze didn't need ESP to see what was going down. Batman was just turning up into the complex as Voorheeze was bolting through the back door. He burst through the garage door so fast he nearly tore the mothafucka off its hinges.

His rubber soled Timberlands didn't make a sound as he came around the corner of the front of the complex. For a big nigga, Voorheeze moved fast as fuck.

As he neared the front of the complex, he slowed down eyes on swivel. He couldn't let no other pigs get the jump on him. He didn't see nor sense any danger. He could hear the pig yelling orders. He bit down on his bottom lip to control the anger boiling within.

When he parked around the brick column into the courtyard. His brotha was wearing a beanie pulled down low with a dark pea coat on. He had his hands raised in the air talking to the pig.

"...A problem, pig. I'm not an animal so I'm not bout to lay on the fucking ground like one!"

Voorheeze had the pig in his sights, but if he squeezed and the pig had his finger on the trigger, reflexes would make him pull it. He was at odds with himself when all of a sudden....

Something made Batman flinch!

"Don't move! Freeze!"

BOC! BOC!

Voorheeze couldn't believe what he was witnessing the pig opened fire.

BOOM! BOOM! BOOM! BOOM! BOOM! BOOM!

He emptied the entire cylinder into the pig. Not giving a fuck where he hit him at. He just squeezed!

Batman spun around from the shot and hit the ground. The pig dropped right after Batman did. Voorheeze pulled his other Dragon with murderous vengeance on his mind, until common sense alerted his instincts. No doubt the loud as dragon woke up everybody in the complex.

He rushed over to his brotha. There was a lot of blood coming from his so he couldn't tell where he was hit. By now it was light outside as the clear, blue sky came to life.

He tried to pick his brotha up.

"Nigga, if you don't get your hands off of me! Yo ass always on some emotional shit! Nigga, look out!" Batman pushed Voorheeze out of his way as he climbed to his feet.

"Nigga, I didn't know where you was hit, but I know we gotta get the fuck outta here." As Voorheeze looked around, sure enough there were faces peeking out of curtains in windows.

As the two of them ran toward the garage Voorheeze was glad his brotha was alright. When he fell the beanie, cap was knocked off of his head. Two bald-headed killas rushed inside of the garage.

There was no time to grab anything out of the house. Seconds after they entered the garage, the Lamborghini came roaring up outta there.

Vrrrrrrrrrrrrrrrrrrrrrrr!

Before it shot out of the parking lot. Later witnesses would recall seeing a blur of red and black as a high powered foreign looking race car sped away.

10 Minutes Later

"What's up, Pop?" DJ answered. He'd just finished his morning workout.

"Son, I'm burning up. I need to cool down" He hated to bring heat to his son's house but DJ was the closest reliable person to him.

"Alright pop when."

"Five to ten minutes." Voorheeze answered his son.

"Aaight, do you need the doctor?" DJ was seeing how bad things were.

"A.S.A.P., Rocky!" He had no way of gauging Batman's injury.

Bullet wounds were funny like that. One minute shit was good and the next minute everything was going to hell.

He glanced over at Batman, who was looking like he didn't have a care in the world.

"You look good, old man." He smirked at his brotha.

"Fuck you, Robin! I know you wanna check me." Batman was holding strong and sounding tough, but his chest burned like a mothafucka.

"Naw, brah. I can't get on you bout dis one." Voorheeze took a deep breath as he turned unto Tennyson Ave in Hayward.

"I think that mothafucka followed me here."

"Don't matter, I still should've felt his eyes on me. Thanks, by the way." Batman was bitter about nor feeling the cop watching him.

"Rogue, what I tell you about thanking me?" Voorheeze didn't like his people thanking him. He figured anything that he did had to be done, so, it was his job. You don't thank a nigga for doing his job.

"Tell me something though, what the fuck happened back there?"

"Rogue, a fucking wasp landed right on my mothafuck'n nose. I just reacted, I didn't even think about what I was doing." Batman shook his head as he thought about that shit.

Voorheeze sounded like a lion roaring as he burst out laughing. He knew Batman was scared of wasps. It all made sense now. Voorheeze had seen Batman do some pretty dumb shit over the years behind wasps. He couldn't say shit about his brothas phobia, hell, he was petrified of spiders. Two, stone cold killas were scared of little bitty insects. Where the fuck they do that at?

DJ lived in an apartment complex off of Lionell St. It wasn't the hood but it was close to it. It was mostly people on section 8 housing, low income and welfare. DJ was waiting down by the car port when they pulled in. He wasn't too worried about nosey ass neighbors. Hell, all types of shit went down in his complex. That's why he loved living there. It still felt like the hood.

Once they parked the two brothas climbed out of the Lamborghini. DJ greeted his pops first then his uncle, letting them know that Dok was on his way.

"Uncle Vell, you don't look too bad." DJ was glad it wasn't his pops who was injured but nevertheless Batman was still his uncle. He didn't want to see his uncle all fucked up either.

"Yeah, I'm good nephew." Batman responded as he started towards the sidewalk.

Two steps were all he took before he collapsed. They rushed to his aide and carried him inside of the first floor apartment. Inside the apartment Voorheeze took of the pea coat and his shirt. DJ went to his back room to retrieve a first aid kit.

His girl Isis came to offer her assistance, but DJ let her know they had everything taken care of. They located the wound which was located high above the right side of his chest, just below the collar bone. They cleaned the wound with some peroxide and applied gauze to the front and back sides.

Batman was still unconscious when Dok came through the door. Always the professional, Dok ignored both Voorheeze and DJ and went straight to work on Batman.

It turned out he collapsed from losing a great deal of blood. The first thing Dok did was hook an I.V. up to Batman. There's a new form of synthetic blood that was out that was non type specific. A few pints of this was given as well. Next he tended to the wound.

As Dok was finishing up with Batman, DJ came running out of the back room.

"Pop, I need yo keys, Safety and Security." The look in his sons eyes made Voorheeze want to ask what was up. However, the words "Safety and Security" made him reach into his pocket and retrieve his key and phone with no hesitation.

DJ was out the front door like Usain Bolt. Hearing the front door slam, Isis came running from the back room.

"Dwayne!" She yelled and screamed over and over as she tore out the door after him.

Dragon in his hand, Voorheeze raced right behind her! When his son asked for the keys he didn't think anything of it because DJ used "Safety and Security". Seeing the look on his girls face, now he was worried.

It took a minute to fully get her attention. By then a few neighbors were getting their nosey on .When he asked her where his son was going she just mean mugged him and stormed off.

Inside of the house, Dok barely acknowledged them coming back into the apartment. Isis walked over to the couch, picked up the remote and turned on the T.V.

Jessica Aguire was on for NBC 2 / Bay Area. She was in the middle of recapping this morning's breaking news. There was no need for Voorheeze to watch the segment. He already knew what they all were going to see. Instead, he pulled his cell phone out of his pocket and made a call.

"Hello?" Keak sounded like he had been awakened out of hibernation.

"Man, we got a problem."

"What's up?" Keak's favorite two words.

"I'm at you brothers spot. I need you."

"Come on, rogue, it's seven something in the fucking morning!"

"Safety and Security. I need you!" Voorheeze knew his son. He knew the nigga was not a morning person.

"Fuck! Bye!" When Keak hung up on him, Voorheeze also knew he was on his way, hands down, no questions asked.

For the first time, he took in the apartment, it looked like Simmy's apartment in Coming to America. Everything was plush and state of art.

Isis was on one of the couch crying. She had been trying DJ's number to no avail ever since they came back into the apartment. She just kept shaking her head and holding the phone while the tears rolled down her cheeks.

Voorheeze found his son's number and pressed send. He got the voicemail. He tried three more times and got same results.

"It's been a long time my friend." Dok said as he walked up to Voorheeze drawing his attention.

He had washed up and was looking sharp as a razor blade as always. Voorheeze had first met Dok back when they were still forming Neva Die. T'Rida was nearly killed in a shoot-out. Anne had saved his life in the shoot-out and Dok saved it literally at Jenn's house..

Dok had been the go-to man for the Mobb ever since then.

"Yeah, and every time we meet it's under the most fucked circumstances." Voorheeze shook the man's hand then asked.

"How is he?"

"He's alright. He just lost too much blood. That's why he fainted. The bullet went thru so there's no damage. He just needed rest and food." Dok had seen way worse pull through.

"Thanks Dok. I'mma have to hit you later. I didn't expect my son to pull a Houdini in my shit."

You've got your hands full on this one young gun slinger. Don't worry about the money. Hell, I've made so much over the years thanks to y'all. You just be careful young gun slinger cause them white folks ain't playing no more." He nodded his head indicating the T.V. screen.

Both Voorheeze and Batman's faces were on the screen with their government names under the pictures. A FBI hotline number was scrolled across the very bottom with a $100,000 reward.

The screen switched to footage of Voorheeze shooting Officer Hedgecock six times. One of the bullets crashing into the back of his skull forcing a spray of blood and brain matter out of his forehead. Cop killers were in big black letters at the top of the screen.

The next shot was the scene that sent DJ into action. It was a shot of them running into the garage and moments later the Lamborghini racing out of the garage and down the driveway. Friends, acquaintances or neighbors, if anybody saw the news and saw the Lambo outside they were fa'sho gone call it in for a hundred stacks.

Jessica Aguire was now reciting script about the mayhem Batman had been causing in Northern California. Even showing traffic cam footage of Batman in disguise driving away from the Dublin Police Department bombing.

"Gawd damn ,young gun slinger, y'all been some busy little niggaz." Dok looked at Voorheeze like he literally stepped out of a Friday the 13th movie.

Voorheeze's iPhone rang before he could respond. It was DJ.

"Where you at?"

"Look, Pop I love you. We ain't got time for a long drawn out conversation." Voorheeze could hear sirens in the background as his son spoke which made his heart beat faster.

"When I saw the news, there wasn't time for no talking so I acted. If anybody saw the Lambo sitting out there it was a wrap.

You know a mothafucka would've called in on y'all fast once they saw that reward. Unc needed help so I bought y'all some time."

"D., where you at?" Voorheeze felt like Déjà vu was kicking his ass. A decade ago it was T'Rida that he was talking to while the police were in the background.

"I'm crossing the San Mateo Bridge. I got this, Pop. Won't nothing happen to me. You need to take advantage of this distraction. My car is in the garage. Pop, y'all can use that and get up out of there, cause ain't no telling how much time y'all got." DJ switched gears and opened up on 'em. In the rear view he watched the distance between him and the cops behind him open up.

"DJ, look…"

"This time, Pop, you look. This is about "Safety and Security". Take my car and get my uncle outta there. I got this. You've taught me enough. I'll be alright." DJ cut Voorheeze off and to make things even worse, he hung up the phone before Voorheeze's could say a word.

Voorheeze pulled the phone away from his ear. He looked over at Isis who was still in the same position. It's as if she didn't even hear the conversation. Voorheeze was just beginning to wonder if she did, when she spoke.

"You would've only been wasting your time. I know Dwayne and once his mind is made up, it's made up. I know he loves you, because he's told me. So, I know he'll do whatever he can to help you. I just pray he makes it back to me." The tears cascaded down even heavier.

"Young gun slingers, it's time for me to get outta here. You take care of yourself, alright." Dok had love for Voorheeze and the Mobb but he wasn't about to go to prison for them.

"Yeah, Dok you right. Thanks again." As he patted Dok on the back Voorheeze briefly questioned if he could still trust the old man.

He quickly pushed that thought out of his head. After all these years Dok could've already snitched them out if he wanted to.

He walked Dok to the door and thanked him again before he walked out of the apartment.

The gangster in Voorheeze wrestled with the man as he turned around and looked at Isis. She was a slim, little cutie pie who would normally resemble a Victoria Secret model. However, at the moment in her vulnerable state, she looked like a frail little girl. The man and father in him wanted to comfort and consoled her. The gangster knew he needed to fucking skedaddle the fuck up out of there!

Voorheeze desperately wanted to get to his son, but he knew DJ's words were true. He'd raised him as best as he could and given him as many tools as he would need to navigate life. DJ wasn't a little boy no more. He was a grown ass man capable of making his own decisions and accepting whatever consequences.

Shocking him once again, Isis stood up and began talking.

"Now, it was nice meeting you. I really wish it was under better circumstances, but nevertheless it was nice. But, y'all got to get out of here. D was adamant about that. My baby is risking his life to make sure that you get away. I couldn't imagine if he was doing what he's doing and it was all for nothing." The moment the word 'nothing' left her little peach colored lips, someone knocked on the door.

Voorheeze yanked out the big 45 and turned to the door. He turned back to Isis and told her to yell "Who is it?" He wasn't about to play any games. If the wrong fucking words came thru that door, Voorheeze was going to air that bitch out.

"It's Keak, man, open the door. It's cold as fuck out here!!" Typical Keak, he's always gonna be there when you need him, but he's gone talk shit the entire time.

l With his banger still in his hand, Voorheeze opened the door. Keak looked at the 45 and said,

"Damn first you wake a nigga out his sleep. Then, you wanna shoot 'em for coming to help." He laughed as he stepped past Voorheeze into his brother's apartment. Seeing Batman laid out on the sofa bandaged up he asked,

"Damn what happened to Velly?"

"I forgot you don't watch the news. We ain't got time to talk. Help me get him into your brother's car. Afterward I want you to

83

stay and hold Isis down until we find out what happens to your brother.."

"What's wrong wit DJ?" Keak cut him off.

"Isis can fill you in. Right now I got to get your uncle out of here before we have a shoot-out with every fucking cop in the Bay. "Safety and Security". Let's move.

Isis gave him the key to her man's baby and clicked the garage open. Keak walked out of the apartment first, double clutching twin Glock 50's as he stepped out. Voorheeze was carrying Batman over his shoulder with his dragon ready in his left hand. Both men had their eyes on the swivel.

DJ"s car was a 2020 Nissan 350Z twin turbo. It was metallic grey with tinted windows. After getting Batman inside of the car, Voorheeze turned and had a brief conversation with Keak. He opened the driver's door then hesitated. Without warning he ran back into the apartment and gave Isis a hug and a kiss on the cheek.

"It was nice meeting you, too. I can see my boy picked a winner. I'm sorry that this is all we'll see of each other but tell my Lil Man I'm proud of him." He reached into his pocket and pulled out a Samsung Galaxy S9 and handed it to her. Give this to my son when he gets home."

She took the phone and watched him leave. The smile on her face couldn't compare to the one in her heart. As much as DJ'd told her about how much he respected his father and how much his opinion means to DJ, to have him say that to her, meant the world to Isis.

Her warm feelings evaporated as she sat down and looked at the screen. More Breaking News was showing. This time it was a high-speed pursuit involving the Lamborghini.

"Keak!" Isis shouted at the top of her lungs.

Watching his father drive away, Keak was thinking of the times they used to go fishing when he was a kid. Everything was innocent back then.

Those thoughts were interrupted by the sound of Isis screaming his name like she was being attacked. He had the Glocks in his hand ready to get it popping when he raced through the door. Isis was standing with her back to the front door facing the T.V. Isis was bouncing up and down, flailing her hands. Rushing to her side, that's when Keak saw the reason for her scream.

De'Kari

CHAPTER VII
101 Freeway

"Push it to the limit."

The speakers was knocking so loud DJ could feel his ear drums vibrating. The red and blue lights flashed in his rear view but he couldn't hear the sirens. The speedometer on the dash read 110 mph but he was toying with the police. His objective was to buy his Pops as much time as he could.

Rick Ross was talking bout pushing them thangs, but DJ was pushing his Need For Speed. The song was old as fuck but he knew why his Pops still knocked it. The shit slapped!

Feeling his phone vibrate he hit the mute button on the radio.

"Yo .What's Up!" The cell phone was on speaker so he had to yell a little.

"Yo D. It's me. Come thru nigga I got you." The caller spoke into the phone.

"Where you at?" DJ asked grateful to hear his brother's voice coming thru the phone.

"I'm at the spot. Aye, but you gotta lose that camera." Although that was easier said than done.

"Aaight. Bet! Give me one minute!" DJ called out before checking his rearview and coming up with an idea.

He began to drastically slow down. There were twenty-two different law enforcement vehicles stopped fifty feet behind him, nervously awaiting his next move. The only thing that could be heard were the rotors on the helicopter hovering above filming the entire scene.

DJ pulled a lighter out his pants pocket and grabbed the half of blunt that was in the ashtray. He lit the blunt, savoring the taste of the smoke as it rolled over his tongue and down into his lungs.

None of the cops attempted to make any move to get out of their cars. The news copter steadily hovered. Suddenly, the doors lifted into the air.

The tension surrounding this area was thicker than Chloe Kardashian in a G-string. A few patrol cars began opening their doors and then more joined them.

It was a little after 10:00 a.m. by now. Traffic on the other side of the freeway began slowing down as people became more interested in what was going on instead of getting to their destination.

"Driver! Stick your hands out the door and step out of the vehicle!" The voice carried through the bell horn.

DJ wasn't paying that shit no attention. He hit the blunt and fucked with the radio. In the rearview he could see the police walking around talking to each other. They really didn't know what to do.

DJ knew what he was gonna do, He pressed the play button on the radio. The sound of Push It To The Limit blared out the speakers at full volume.

He stepped down on the clutch and smashed down on the gas! The Foreign Beast came to life as the RPM'S raced to life. The back tires screamed and hollered as the rubber on them began smoking.

The cops quickly raced into action in preparation of what was coming. It didn't matter what they did though, the Dodge Chargers weren't fucking with the Lambo!

DJ took another pull on the blunt, threw the Lambo into first, then slapped the clutch just as the chorus came one. The Lambo took off like a dope fiend that snatched a nigga's bundle! There was hardly any wind blowing so the smoke hung in the air. Even though the police reacted as quickly as possible, it seemed like five seconds after his foot came off the clutch, he was already a quarter mile ahead of them.

**** N. D. ****

"Oh my God! Just when it looked like there was going to be some closure to this gruesome and tragic ordeal, the suspect has just taken off again on what appears to be a car chase at a very high rate of speed." Pam Moore of KRON-TV/KRON 4 was speaking from the news desk about the high speed chase.

"Ladies and gentlemen I am receiving word from the KRON 4 news chopper that the Lamborghini Veron is now going 190 mph. The driver is showing no regard for anything that suspected cop killer La'Mont Simpson was involved in with authorities on highway 101.

"Ladies and Gentlemen, I am receiving word as we speak from the KRON 4 News Chopper. Our calculation had the Lamborghini that the suspect is driving now traveling at speeds faster than 160 mph. The driver is showing a complete disregard for safety as he dangerously weaves in and out of the slight traffic that he encounters.

"OH MY GOD! WHOA! As you can see ladies and gentlemen the driver just missed smashing into the back of that work van that crossed into its lane. Ladies and gentlemen there is no telling how this chase will end. Our hearts here at KRON 4 go out to the family of the officer who lost his life today. And to the family of those officers who tragically were murdered before this." Pam Moor almost looked as if she was close to tears as she spoke.

"Right, you know Pam, it's just heart crushing when you think of all the lives that were affected by the hands of the two people. Good lives of good honest people."

"We all remember the bombing of the Police Station over in Dublin. The public outcry from that incident was unbelievable. And now to learn that all of these horrific acts were at the hands of the same person. That's just....Well it's just down right un-American." Tom Sinkovitz, co-anchor added.

This was scheduled to be his last coverage and what a coverage it was!

"The suspect has taken the ramp to Guadalupe Expwy. You know Tom, we've been discussing this chase as we follow it live, but we have yet to mention where the likelihood is we think he is headed. Also, do we have any idea whether it's just one of the suspects or both?" Pam Moore asked, looking a little more composed.

"Well Pam, we have no idea of how many people are in the car or even if it is the suspects. Holy Toledo!" Tom Sinkovitz actually threw his hands up and jumped up in his seat at the near collision the Lamborghini just escaped. "I'll tell you this much Pam, if he keeps doing like that this, chase is gonna end badly on this Freeway. Also…"

"Wait a minute, Tom." Pam cut in, "Are you seeing, what I am seeing? There is a line of motorist that have pulled over on the Freeway. Some are holding signs and oh! There is a banner! Chopper 4 can you zoom in on that so we can read what it says." She paused as she waited for the chopper to zoom in.

"Oh my God! Black Lives Matter! appears to be written on the banner. Tom, it seems like the motorists are actually in support of the suspects."

"Pam, that doesn't surprise me in the least. In today's society, people just want to feel like they are a part of something. They just want to belong even if it's to some ignorance." Tom Sinkovitz spoke with disdain.

"What? Wait a minute Tom, are you saying that the Black Lives Movement is ignorant? What do you mean Tom?" Pam Moore was completely shocked.

"No, I'm not saying the movement is ignorant at all. It's tragic what is happening to Black People across the U.S. What I'm saying is, when a movement or something of the like ,gets so much attention, it becomes hard to navigate its cause, and the fanatics will then abuse it for their own interest." Tom Sinkovitz rightfully defended his stance.

Before Pam Moore could comment KRON 4 came over the ear piece. It looked like the suspect was headed for the airport. Because of the federal "No-Fly Zones" over airports. The chopper would have to fall back.

The significance of this was that Law Enforcement personnel were over three miles behind them. The Lamborghini had out-run the Chargers from the gate. The Chopper was the only thing capable of staying with the vehicle. With the car now heading for the airport they would lose the trial.

**** N. D. ****
Meanwhile

"A-6!" Was the only thing that he needed to yell into the phone?

"Bet! I'm on my way!" The caller on the other end of the phone responded.

DJ bent a hard right, sped down one of the rows, and then made a left. Which brought him down long term parking terminal isle A. Within seconds he was parking in parking space 6.

He grabbed the bottle of Bacardi 151 as he raced out of his back room. Cracking the top, he opened the door, then began dowsing the expensive leather with the alcohol. He Made sure to douse the driver's seat and steering wheel after he stood up.

Next, he popped the trunk before throwing the key fob back into the car. He relit the other half of his blunt with his zippo lighter. With the sun beaming down on him, DJ tossed the zippo into the car. The Bacardi ignited instantaneously. Within seconds the interior was engulfed in flames.

With the half of blunt still hanging from his lips, he walked to the back of the trunk and retrieved two black duffle bags. DJ knew his Pops always had those two bags in the trunk and he'd be damned if he left them!

Right on time like a sunrise, a cherry red Mitsubishi Eclipse with Twin Chargers came speeding up the aisle. It came to a screeching halt right in front of DJ. The driver was obscured behind the tinted windows. That was okay, DJ knew who the driver was.

The trunk came open and he tossed the bags inside, then he jumped in the passenger seat.

"Man! Good looking out, brah!" He told his brother as the Eclipse sped out of there.

"Come on, brah, you know I got your back." Andrew told him as he navigated his way thru the airport.

A thick black column of smoke was now rising from the other side of the airport, into the sky.

"That shit was live though! The whole time that I was waiting for you I was watching the chase. You mothafuckas is starting to make some major noise. Organizations and gangs all across the U.S. are starting to feel and support the cause! They say this is the new Black Lives Matter Movement." An overly excited Andrew told his lifelong friend.

"No doubt." Was all DJ responded with.

His mind and focused was on his father and Isis. He pulled out his cell phone as Andrew sped down the freeway. The police were just pulling into the airport.

"Oh my God! Dwayne, baby please tell me are you okay?" Baby, you're not hurt or anything are you? Do you need me to do anything?" Isis was such a nervous wreck, she just rambled on. She wouldn't let him get a word in.

When she finally stopped to catch her breath, he told her,

"Babe, calm down. Everything's okay. I'm with Drew. I didn't want you worrying so I called. I got to get rid of this phone, so I don't want you to worry. Just to be on the safe side in case them people on me. But, I'll be there in a few hours." He told her. Then he took the last hit off the blunt roach.

"D. Please baby come home! I need you, daddy, please." The prospect of losing him only showed her just how much she loved him.

"I'll be there. I promise. I love you."

"I love you too, babe! Oh, I almost forgot ,your brother's here." She was so happy to hear from him, she'd forgotten about Keak.

"Let me talk to him."

"Okay. I love you, baby."

"I love you too."

"Aww. I love you too, Boo Boo!" Andrew joked in the background.

"What's up, Keak? They good?" DJ was referring to his father and uncle.

"Yeah ,it's all good. I can't believe yo ass had the fucking Z all this time and didn't say nothing." The two brothers were speed-junkies from cars to dirt bikes to motorcycles. They lived for speed.

"I was waiting to bring her out on the twin's birthday. I still had something to do to her. But oh, well." He was already thinking about what he was gonna replace her with.

"You need me to stay here with Isis?"

"Naw. It's good. Just tell her I'll be there for dinner."

"Aaight. Bet."

"One"

The moment DJ hung up the phone Drew got on him.

"Oh, greedy mothafucka didn't even pass me the blunt! And that smelt like some Wonder Woman!"

"My bad, brah. You know my mind was on Isis."

"I'm just fucking with you. Open the glove box." Drew told him.

When DJ opened the glove box there was a large Ziploc bag with what had to be about one hundred blunts in it.

"Nigga, fire up!" Drew told him as he pushed play on the stereo.

"It's 187 on da D.A. / Cause they ain't trynna give a young mothafucka no leadway / 187 on the whole courtroom mothafuck'em all / you better swing, batter swing /Yes, Yes, Y'all / cause once you get your third felony you 50 years you gotta bring / it's a deadly game of baseball/ so when they try to pull you over, shoot 'em in the face y'all."

Old school C-Bo blared out the speakers just as they were getting off on Willow Road. DJ would chill over at Drew's house in Menlo Park for a few hours before heading home.

De'Kari

CHAPTER VIII

"God damn it!" S.A.C. Andreatta yelled the moment the black smoke columns rose into the air.

She wasn't stupid. Neither was Agent Finnegan ,who was behind the wheel of the all black Dodge Charger speeding into the San Jose Airport. Both of whom had been on the job far too long to believe in coincidences. They both knew that the black smoke had something to do with Simpson.

Their car took the lead in the pursuit while it was still on highway 101. Her team had been taking control of the scene in Newark at the Town House Complex when the call came over the radio of a possible spotting of La'Mont Simpson's Lamborghini.

Agent Daly was left in charge of the crime scene while the rest of the team mobilized to join the pursuit. Cutting across the Dumbarton Bridge and speeding down University Ave, they were able to catch the chase just as the sports car came racing by.

"I want Highway Patrol and SJPD to lock down the roads. All access in and out of the airport is cut off. Tell TSA under direct clause of the Patriot Act, I want all flights grounded.

She was just spewing out orders but Agent Garcia knew she was talking to him. "Finnegan, when we stop I want you to get me as many agents as you can. And where the hell are the SSU people? I want this God forsaken airport combed and those sons of bitches found."

Following the smoke column Finnegan found the Lamborghini. Fully ablaze. Parked in a long-term parking space. One look at the vehicle confirmed this was self-induced arson! S.A.C. Andreatta was studying the charred remains. Something was wrong. She got out of the car oblivious to the smoke, the suns blistering heat or anything else. She was in full concentration mode and communication with her instincts.

Then it hit her! Why was the trunk open?

"Garcia get airport security on the phone now. Come get in the car." She yelled as she hurriedly turned around and jumped back into the car.

"Tell security I want camera footage of this area twenty minutes prior to the smoke column and I want it now! Finnegan head to TSA'S office."

"What's going on, Chief?" Agent Finnegan asked as he put the car in gear.

"They're not here!" She spoke with conviction.

"What?" Both Garcia and Finnegan asked at the same time.

"They either had an accomplice waiting for them or they met them here. But, someone helped them get away." Something was pulled out of the trunk.

No-one would risk pulling something out of a trunk and hauling it on foot if they were being pursued. They wouldn't pull it out unless they had a second vehicle to put it in.

Finnegan brought the Charger to another screeching halt. People scrambled frantically to get out of the way of the all black Chargers with flashing lights barreling down on them.

As they entered the airport it was Agent Garcia who took the lead.

"This way!" He shouted as he took off in the direction the person on the phone guided him.

They all raced through the airport screaming and hollering for people to get out of the way! Four TSA agents joined in the race. At the sight of them in their uniforms running with the three plain clothes maniacs, everyone got out of the way, fast.

Once they reached the TSA office there, was no time for introductions.

"S.A.C., Andreatta, FBI. What you got?" She held her badge up for inspection as she asked.

The head of TSA was a middle-aged, super thick, black woman with a beautiful, baby face and on enormous set of breasts. She'd been with TSA for ten years after quitting her job as a nurse at the San Mateo County Jail.

"Hi, I'm Stephanie, Agent in Charge of TSA." Her long black dreadlocks swayed as she stood to greet the agents.

"I had the surveillance cameras footage rewound to the time your agent specified on the phone." Her beautiful, black Hershey, skin shinned in the light.

"That's great, thank you. Do you have a remote control?" Andreatta asked.

"Here you go. The system is very easy to operate." Agent Stephanie told her as she handed over the remote to the video system.

It didn't take long for S.A.C. Andreatta to find what she was looking for. They all watched as she played the footage of the red Eclipse pulling up and picking up the driver off the Lamborghini and leaving the airport.

They were all shocked to see that not only was there one person in the Lamborghini, but that person wasn't even Simpson. She rewound the video, played it again, slowed it down and zoomed in on the driver that got out of the Lamborghini as well as the license plate of the Eclipse.

"I wanna know who the hell the owner of that car is! And who the hell is our mystery man is!" S.A.C. Andreatta called out, not speaking to no one in particular.

"I'm already on it, chief." Garcia responded back.

"And I want this video feed on every Bay Area news station in an hour."

"Right, Chief. I got it." Finnegan told her as he looked to Agent Stephanie.

"I can have a copy burned for you in a minute." Agent Stephanie told him before he could even speak. looking towards the S.A.C. Andreatta she asked.

"Is it's okay to clear my flights for scheduled departures?"

"Yes, thank you for your support." S.A.C. Andreatta told her before heading out of the office.

This time they walked through the airport like normal passengers. They didn't draw any attention as they exited the front doors. A few pedestrians looked as they climbed into the Chargers but most ignored them. People were more interested in getting out of the heat, than paying attention to the Mexican and two white people.

**** N. D. ****

No one had heard from or seen Clark in months. It was as if he'd just vanished. The Usalama Squad was out in full force searching for him. Both Dok and Mtambo felt it would be a waste of resources for the E.G.U. to assist in the man hunt. So, they were assigned new detail until he was located.

Figuring that Clark either relocated or got knocked down, Dok felt relaxed enough to bring his baby back home.

"Now what are you over there thinking about, old man?" Jeannetta teased her husband, as she came into the room, bringing him a plate of food.

Picking up one of the pastrami sandwiches he fired back.

"I was just thinking of how jealous you must be of this marble statue physique since you're feeding me all this bread. Trynna get me fat." He took a huge bite out of the mouthwatering sandwich to keep from laughing.

Jeanette had just sat down, but she jumped right back up and modeled for him.

"Oh, believe me, baby, I don't have nothing to be jealous about ,not with all of this!"

He couldn't help admiring his wife, with her long silky hair, and high yellow complexion that was just barely kissed by the sun. She was gorgeous and her "Get the fuck outta here" body just made her the perfect specimen in his eyes.

He lightly spanked her on her butt. "Woman, you better sit down before you start something. I done told you 'bout starting grass fires in the summertime."

"Mr. Hayes, are you threatening me with a good time?" She asked him and then bent all the way over in front of him. Shaking her plump ass right in his face, giggling and teasing him. When she spanked herself on her ass cheek, that did it. Dok wasn't about to play around with her.

His cell phone had other ideas though. No sooner did he stand up its little song began. Time with his wife superseded just about everything and everybody. When he saw his son's number on the screen that was one of the things it didn't supersede considering Rell was his security.

"Peace, God," Dok answered the phone while his angry wife shot him a look that would kill.

"We got four cars approaching. No I.D. on the personnel but the movement of the vehicles say that it's a trained detail. I've already alerted Mtambo. Eta. Of the nearest strike unit is five minutes." Rell spoke clear and precise as he ran down the situation.

Dok didn't waste time responding, instead he turned to his wife who he would neva let anything happen to.

"Now! Go to the panic room!"

A ton of fear gripped Jeanette's heart but she didn't utter a word or hesitate. She took off down the back hall to the panic room. Using the word "Now" at the beginning of a sentence was their safety and security word.

The panic room was built to Dok's personal specifications. It could literally withstand an attack from an army platoon. He knew his wife would be safe from any harm until ground force troops arrived.

His mind set in military mode, he hit a series of buttons on the coffee table and the top slid back revealing a weapons cache. As quick as a kid puts on a back pack, he threw on his Kevlar body suit. The new suits were state of the art, the newest thing in military defense. It fit snug like on under armor shirt. Designed like a button down dress shirt, it protected the entire upper body.

Mothafuckas had the nerve to come to his mothafuck'n castle! The fumes of anger and rage coming through his pores could ignite themselves. As he approached his front doors Dok could see the vehicles pulling up.

A black Tahoe was the lead vehicle followed by a Range Rover and two more Tahoe's. Dok didn't give a fuck about the details for the vehicles. The mothafuckas in them wouldn't live to drive them away!

When the vehicles stopped the doors to all of the Tahoe's came open and niggaz climbed out. Just then vehicles from both directions come screeching to a halt boxing the caravan in. The nig-gaz who had gotten out of the Tahoe's paid no attention to the screeching cars nor the young killas who jumped out of them strapped and ready for war.

The front door of the house opened and Dok stepped out onto the porch with twin Smith & Wesson .40 cals on his waist. Both weapons were equipped with fifty round hockey sticks. In his hands was a customized M16A3. It was the short rifle machine gun built especially for the Navy Seals. That mothafucka was ready to do some damage and so was Dok.

The screeching tires drew some attention from neighbors who absent mindedly looked out of drapes and blinds. When they saw the shit that was going down at the Hayes residence, they got the fuck out the way fast!

Dok was a hood nigga thru and thru. Naturally, he still lived in the hood and everybody knew who he was and what he was about. They loved him and were proud of the things he was doing.

One of the henchmen, a big, black, King Kong looking motha-fucka opened the back door of the Range Rover.

Dok lifted the rifle and took aim with his finger slightly resting on the trigger!

"Nigga, you a dead mothafucka!" Dok spoke under his breath, just waiting.

As the occupant stepped out of the truck Dok was dumb-founded. Rell and Scooter who were both holding AR-15's were shocked. The nigga was no bigger than 5 foot 4, 5 foot 5 he weighed, maybe 140 pounds soaking wet He was a light skinned, pretty mothafucka with an old school, 1970's Pimp Perm.

The little Supa Fly looking, mothafucka was actually dressed like he walked out of a Willie Dolomite movie. He looked at Dok and smiled. Dok slowly lowered the barrel of the machine gun. He didn't know why he was at his house or how he even knew where Dok lived, but Dok knew who the man was. He was a legend!

Dok walked down the walk way to greet him.

"Habari Gani, little brother." The man greeted Dok. Before they embraced.

'Habari Gani, Mwezi. You're a long way from home." Dok was really thinking.

"What the fuck are you doing here?"

"Forgive me for popping up unannounced, but we need to talk." The look in his deadly eyes told Dok it was important. It really had to be very important for him to make the long drive unannounced.

The little pimp look alike with the deadly eyes was none other than Floyd Perkins aka Suja. Suja was not only Ground Force Commander of Field Operations, but he was also Regional Commander of Overall Operations in the Valley with direct ties to both the Central Committee and the Supreme Council. He'd been selected for a position on the Central Committee three times and refused the appointment each time.

Like Voorheeze and Dok, he came into his rank and position at an early age. He was Ground Force Commander of Stockton, where he's from, by age nineteen. a failed assassination attempt on his life resulted in him receiving five life sentences for the murders of five of the men who tried to kill him. The sixth man lived and testified against him.

It took a little over twenty years to get all of the sentences over turned. After a lot of hard work, a real nigga came back to the streets. Now he ruled them majestically.

Dok called out orders to Rell and Scooter. Suja did the same to his men and the two generals walked into his house. Inside, Dok put the weapons away before going to the panic room and retrieving his wife. He explained to her what was going on and then excused himself and Suja to his study. Jeanette was just happy that he was okay. She knew the life of a revolutionaries wife but it didn't make things any easier.

The study was dark and comfortable. It was nothing fancy, just a couple couches made of dark Old English Leather with a dark Mahogany desk and a dark Mahogany bookshelf. Close inspection of the volumes on the bookshelf would reveal nearly fifty grand in books. This Included original volumes of Confucius, the original leather bound copy of "Recording the Oral History of the Bakabe,"

Journal of African History Vol. 1, No. 2 even the old Ibn Al-Khafif Murtadi, and The Egyptian History: Treating of the Pyramids London 1672, which was a gift from Voorheeze.

"Again, my apologies for intruding my brotha, but the matters of my heart are grave and dear." Suja explained after they were seated.

"Would you care for a drink?" When Suja declined Dok asked him.

"So, what tragedies brings me the pleasure of meeting such a great man?"

"Before I begin, let me assure you this is not a game nor is it a test. I've come to you on my own not as a member of any squad." His words caused Dok to go on alert.

It was known that the higher ranking personnel, specifically the Council would periodically test its Commanding personnel to test their loyalty. This was a viable tactic in weeding out those who had gone astray from the ideologies of the organization.

Dok sized the man up wondering about possible angles, while trying to detect the slightest hint of deception.

"I'm listening," It was better just to play it safe.

"I warn you, young brotha, though my words and intentions are not treasonous, I assure you they walk the line of insurgency so closely that I have gone through great lengths to ensure the utmost level of clandestine." Suja paused to see if he could get a read off of Dok. Dok's mind was full of a million questions but his face was stone. He'd learned the art of patience years ago.

"I won't procrastinate nor beat around the bush with you. We both know the stance that the Committee has taken in regard to the situation regarding Voorheeze and Batman. I've known Voorheeze a long time. Though he's my little brother, he's more like a son to me. Simply put, I can't just sit back and allow him to engage the enemy in a revolutionary battle and not offer him aid and assistance." Suja stopped talking and leaned back on the couch. A method used to engage one to talk.

"Why bring this to me? Your position and status in the organization is far greater than mine. Surely, you must know that what

102

you would require for what you are suggesting is far greater than the aid or authority that I possess." This was spoken neutrally so that Dok didn't reveal a feeling either way.

Or at least that's what he thought. But Suja had been doing this espionage and intelligence shit for too long. The fact that Dok was questioning his intentions instead of showing him the door told Suja that his assumption of the love the young General had for his brother is still strong, despite their little quarrel.

Suja uncrossed his legs and leaned forward placing his elbows on his knees.

"My brotha, your authority is all I need, your aid is all that I require." For the first time since they 'd met, those killer eyes showed a hint of warmth.

Suja ran everything down to Dok Holliday. The conversation between those two men would unknowingly change the nation!

De'Kari

CHAPTER IX
Windsor, CA

When Batman woke up his throat was dryer then the plains of the Serengeti. He tried to swallow and only ended up choking.

"Okay, old man. Fuck around and cough up a lung the way you're over there sounding." Voorheeze came to his aid with a glass of cold water in his hands. "Here, drink this big brah. "He handed him the glass.

Batman poured a mouthful into his parched mouth and let it sit for a while before swallowing it. He repeated that two more times, making sure his mouth was fully hydrated before killing off the glass. When the glass was empty, Voorheeze handed him a glass of Simply Orange, Orange Juice and another of V8 juice.

They'd been here and far worst before together so they both knew what to do. Batman had to hydrate, plus he ended vitamins and electrolytes. V8 would be too thick for him to swallow without lubricating his mouth and esophagus.

While Batman got some fluids in him. Voorheeze went to town on two huge bacon, egg, cheese and hash brown sandwiches he had just made.

"Nigga next time you wanna lose a bucket of blood make sure we ain't on the run. Had a nigga pulling over the side of the road trynna coax you ass into drinking on the Straw and shit." He told him with a mouthful of food.

"Nigga, fuck all that! Nigga, gimmie a bite of one of them sandwiches." The food smelled so good made a nigga wanna jump up and snatch the plate.

Voorheeze took another big-ass bite, closed his eyes and shook his head." Mmm." Teasing his brotha.

"Nigga, you know the rules, hydrate that ass up! When you done with the V8, I've got a phat ass plate for you and a big ass bottle of Gatorade, nigga. The blue kind, too." That was Batman's favorite kind.

They were laying-low at one of Voorheeze's time shares. Years ago, Lisa had put him up on World Mark by Wyndham. After hearing her talk about how fabulous it was, he had gotten one. The way World Mark was setup, you could virtually go to any of the nine hundred plus locations on a whim as long as you still had credits. When he signed up, he enrolled in the Diamond Elite Membership so his credits were always phat.

Batman may have been down, but he was far from a sucka. The moment he heard about the food he bounced up. He moved so quickly that he got dizzy for a minute. Once the dizziness subsided he went and got the plate and the Gatorade.

The room was laid out like a suite, with a living room dining room, full kitchen, two bedrooms one being a master and two bathrooms.

Batman was so focused on the two huge mouthwatering sandwiches he didn't even notice that the T.V. was on. Voorheeze's cooking skills were legendary to those who knew him. Batman neva could wait to get his hands on something his brotha cooked.

"What you watching?" Batman finally asked as food sprayed out of his mouth like an animal. Instead of wiping up the food particles he took another jaw stretching bite.

"Jim Smith is giving a speech at the University down in San Diego. Looks like you've pissed off a lot of white folk's, nigga." Voorheeze answered before taking another bite of his sandwich.

"What's he talking bout?" Batman's eyes was glued to his plate.

"Same ole' fuckery and bullshit. Make America great again, terrorist in our country are more of a reason to fund building his wall. Yatta yatta yatta! But, fuck all that! He's coming to Sacramento next month!"

Batman knew his brotha. He knew when he had something floating in his mind. So he had to cut in.

"What yo crazy ass over the thinking, nigga?"

"Rogue you been hella busy from what these mothafuckas are sayin'. Niggaz across dis country paying attention. Not just paying attention but rallying behind a mothafucka." He paused and wiped his mouth with his hands before sucking in his teeth before he continued. "I say while we got their attention, while we know they're looking, let's give they ass something to watch!"

This got Batman amped.

"Nigga, now you talking! That's my nigga!" He looked up and pointed in the air.

"Is that the Bat Symbol in the air?"

"You see it, nigga! Bat Symbol is in the air." Voorheeze called out.

They joked back and forth for a while. It had been a tiring two years. A high strung, tense race. Now it felt good to relax a bit. The only time they let their guards completely down was with each other.

Voorheeze was glad that his brotha was alright. He loved this nigga. Looking over at Batman, a vision of Clark appeared before his eyes.

They were kids living on Central Ave in Fremont. Mama B had grown tired of them arguing and fighting so she had bought them a pair of boxing gloves. The two of them were going at it in the front yard. Clark was beating the shit out of him the whole first two rounds.

All of their friends were out there watching Voorheeze was 11 or 12 which made Clark 13 or 14, Voorheeze was embarrassed from getting his ass kicked. Especially since his girlfriend ,Tasha, was watching. Just when he had but had given up, Clark rushed in for the kill, Voorheeze side stepped the punch and BAM! He caught Clark with a left hook right smack dead in the eye. Clark shit swelled up instantaneously. Shit looked like Rodney King after the police got in his ass. The weirdest part about it was Voorheeze be-came scared as fuck that his brother was gone really fuck him up.

But when he looked at Clark, he was shocked to see a look of admiration or pride in his older brother eyes. It was as if his brother was only pushing him until he learned to fight back. It was weird but it felt good to have his big brother's attention.

"...Voorheeze! Voorheeze!" Batman called out in alarm.

"Oh, huh? What's up, big brah?" Voorheeze snapped out of his trip down memory lane.

"Nigga, where'd chou go?" Batman was still looking concerned.

"Nothing, brah. Ghost and memories."

Thankfully, his iPhone started ringing. It was the perfect interruption to the awkward moment that was beginning to form.

Considering it was a brand-new phone, he knew who it was that was calling him. He had only reached out to one person, is son.

"What's up Pop?" DJ didn't even wait for him to answer before he spoke.

"Shit, you good?" Voorheeze asked full of concern.

"Yeah. I'm straight, Pop. Y'all good?"

"You know me. Long as you good, I'm good. But, check this out, tell your auntie I want everybody to go to sleep. There's a storm coming so everybody should sleep through it." In code he just told DJ that the family needed to go to ground cause he was planning something major.

"Aaight, I got you pop. Do you need me?"

"If I do I'll get at you. Oh, D, check me out." He almost forgot.

"What's up, Pop?"

"She's a keeper, son. I'm proud of you." He was referring to Isis.

"Thanks, Pops."

"Don't be a fool like me, son. Don't fuck it up." Voorheeze was talking about Lisa. He really had wanted to spend the rest of his life with her.

DJ knew what his father was hinting at.

"I won't, pops. I promise, she's the one. You just make sure you're at the wedding so you can witness me make the best move of my life. I promise, Pop."

He could hear the happiness and excitement in his son's voice so he knew that he was being genuine.

"I love you, son."

"I love you too, Pops." DJ hung up feeling good. He had wanted needed his pop's approval of Isis but he was gangsta. He couldn't ask for it. That would've made him look weak.

He was glad his pops approved of her. It meant she was truly the one.

"Everything aaight?" Batman asked once he hung up.

"Yeah, shit's cool." He replied.

"Good, nigga, then get up and go fix another one of them sandwiches." Batman told him.

"Oh, a nigga gets shot and now a mothafucka think he Tookie Williams or mothafuck'n Larry Hoover in dis bitch!"

"Nigga, you can fuck around and see King David in dis bitch if I don't get no sandwich." Batman joked.

"Yeah, okay ,your highness. Keep watching that news and see what else pop up."

"Nigga ,you ain't told me what you got planned yet."

"Good, nigga so pay attention to everything." He instructed as he headed in the kitchen to whip something else up. They both ate like bears 24/7 so he had to put something down.

One of the many perks about World Mark was the service. When he reserved the suite Voorheeze was able to give the concierge a list of things he needed. All of which would be paid for with the credit card on file and delivered to the suite put away nicely and ready for him when he arrived.

The smothered pork chops, rice and gravy, steamed vegetables and bottle of Simply Lemonade that he carried into the living room were on the list of groceries he had delivered. The World Mark account was under one of his many aliases, which meant they could relax long enough to enjoy the food.

"Nigga, it took yo ass long enough." Batman joked when he saw Voorheeze enter with the food." Shit, a nigga can't get no good service round dis mothafucka now-a-days."

"Keep talking nigga, yo ass will be eating Top Ramen like you was back in Solano," he shot back as he sat the tray down.

"Damn! Now niggaz getting all sensitive and shit. Nigga, shut up and give me my plate." Batman wasn't trynna hear any of that.

"Aaight, old man, keep playing! Nigga, I don't discriminate, lil nigga, old nigga, woman, retard, cripple, nigga Any Body Can Get It." Both of them burst out laughing. Batman laughed so hard his chest started hurting.

"Here, it's time for you to pop a couple of these anyway." Voorheeze handed him a bottle of Oxycodone's 30 mg.

"Nigga, what's these?"

"The reason yo ass ain't in pain."

He didn't need to hear nothing else! They ate and talked while the news continued to play low in the background. Batman filled Voorheeze in on everything he'd done since the shooting.

Voorheeze was shocked to hear just how busy his brotha had been. Batman's been knocking shit the fuck down since Voorheeze was hit. Subconsciously, Voorheeze rubbed his hand across his chest touching the gunshot wounds.

Hearing that Batman's inspiration behind his rampage was the plight of Blacks in America… set a new fire ablaze under Voorheeze ass. He had no idea the amount of his people who were being murdered in the so-called land of the free where so many, until Batman ran it down to him. He knew about Sandra Bland and Oscar Grant, Freddie Gray, and Michael Brown but that was only because those deaths were highly publicized. What Batman was telling him was outright racial genocide.

Fuck That Shit! At first he was only going to make a statement. He was going to kidnap Jim Smith. Now though, fuck making a statement! He was about to teach the racist mothafuckas a lesson. Jason Voorheeze was going to kill Jim Smith's racist ass!

CHAPTER X

Voorheeze woke up to the smell of Folgers. After taking a piss and washing his face he made his way to the kitchen.

"As loud as you were snoring, nigga, I just knew you'd sleep for another few hours." Batman told Voorheeze when he saw him in the kitchen.

The best part of waking up is Folgers in your cup." His imitation of the commercial jingle was his reply.

After pouring a cup of coffee for himself he headed to the dining table to join Batman, who was on the Apple laptop.

"What yo ass doing up this early anyway? Them Oxy's should have had you snoring like a cave man." He asked him as he sat down.

"Nigga, yo ass! First it was the snoring then..." He paused cause he knew it was a sensitive subject. He lowered his voice a couple of octaves.

"You were having one of those nightmares again."

Voorheeze had been having nightmares all of his life. Still, it was a sensitive subject because of what happened back then.

"My bad big, brah." That was all he could say. Batman knew the whole story, but the shit still made Voorheeze uncomfortable.

"Ain't shit, nigga! Whip up some breakfast and it's all good." Batman was trynna make light of the situation.

The nightmares were bad. He cried, yelled, screamed, fought and cursed. Back when they were first thuggin, Batman would run in the room when he heard all the noise only to find Voorheeze fighting the air. After the second time, he'd brought up the subject of the nightmares. Voorheeze told him that was a subject that was off limits. After a couple of years when their bond was closer, Voorheeze finally confided in him what the nightmares were all about.

As Voorheeze headed to the kitchen he called over his shoulder.

"After breakfast we gotta pack everything up and be ready to go. If yo chest bothering you then I'll knock it all out while you kick it."

"What's up?," Batman looked up from the laptop.

"Shit. We gone need some help for what I got in mind so I went on and took care of that. WE gone need a bigger spot. Plus, the penthouse is out of the way." He started laying thick slices of Hormel Bacon into a skillet as he talked.

"Okay, so who's the help? And what you got on you mind." This conversation was more interesting than the laptop, so Batman closed it.

"I called lil brah last night, his flight will be here in a couple hours…"

"Lil Brah, who? Nigga, we got a lot of brothers." Batman cut him off.

"I sent for Big Texas." Batman looked like he wanted to say something but Voorheeze didn't let him."

"As for what I got in mind…..Brah, I'mma kill Jim Smith, leader of one of the largest white supremacist groups known. He's been hiding behind his political position and using his authority to hurt people of color especially Blacks."

Batman didn't say a word. He was stunned and completely silent. He knew that his brotha was crazy, but he stared at him to see if he was really as crazy as he sounded. The look on his face left no room for error.

"No shit?" Was all he could say.

"Black Lives Don't Matter, if they only matter to us. I'mma bout to make sure they matter to the whole fucking world."

"Fuck you mean, I'mma?" He threw his hands up and made quotations when he said "I'mma".

Voorheeze stared his brotha in the eyes,

"Brah, think about Rachel. I can't ask you to do this with me."

"Nigga, is you crazy? Did you not hear the shit I told you last night? I blew up a police station! They know who the fuck I am. Ain't no turning back, I'm in!" He slammed his fist down on the laptop for emphasis.

In all actuality Batman didn't give a fuck. Voorheeze was the first nigga he started fucking with when he first moved to Cali from Mississippi. He was the only nigga Batman considered family that didn't have Jenkins blood in him. He would stand with and by his brotha till the mothafuck'n caskets dropped.

"Nigga, is breaking the laptop 'pose to make you tough?" Voorheeze joked as he stirred some Carnation evaporated milk into his famous cheese grits.

"I'll fuck around have that ass feeling like Al Green in dis bitch."

Instantly the tension left as they broke out in laughter. That's just how they were, genuine brothers.

"How's Tex getting here from the airport?' Batman asked realizing it wasn't too smart for them to be on the road right now.

Voorheeze looked at him with *that* look on his face.

"I took care of that already."

They continued to talk while Voorheeze finished cooking. Once the bacon, cheese eggs, hash browns, cheese grits and Pillsbury Grand's Buttermilk Biscuit layers was done, wasn't no talking, they got they're grub on.

3 Hours Later

The Penthouse Suite was as plush as one would expect with all of the commodities, but Voorheeze wasn't paying attention to that shit. He was trynna figure out just how he was going to do the impossible. Assassinate Jim Smith!

This dude was untouchable. He had a serious security squad around him at all times, Vin Diesel looking mothafuckas. Voorheeze was good at handling difficult situations so he knew he would figure this shit out.

He got up out of the recliner to answer the door. In his wife beater and sweatpants, he looked like the average Joe Blow citizen answering the door. At least that was true until you noticed the big ass canon in his hand, down by his side.

"Big Brah! What's up nigga?" Kwashay aka Big Texas rushed his big brotha and put him in a bear hug, completely ignoring the gun in his hand.

When Kwashay finally put him down and he caught his breath Voorheeze spoke. "Damn, lil brah, fuck you doing down there eating whole cows in Texas, nigga?"

"Aw, you know, big brah, everything's big in Texas!" Kwashay flexed on him as he said that.

Voorheeze looked at DJ and Keak who had walked in and took seats on the leather sofas.

"What took so long? Y'all run into problems or something?"

"Only problem we had was not passing a food joint his big ass didn't want to stop at. I swear, pop, I neva thought I would see somebody eat more then you." DJ responded as he was rolling up a blunt.

"Shit, little nigga, get yo weight up." Kwashay joked. He stood 6'2 and weighed 298lbs of pure Houston Texas muscle. That's how he got the name Big Texas.

Hearing all of the noise, Batman woke up and came into the living room. The first forty-five minutes they talked shit and laughed like niggaz do. Kwashay did most of the talking, telling them all stories about Texas and the wild shit he was doing. All the while the weed smoke dominated the air.

When it was time to get down to business, Voorheeze threw it on the table. Mapping out his plans for the destruction he was about to cause took another twenty something minutes. When he was done talking, Keak was the first to speak.

"Fuck you think this is an urban book or something? Nigga, how in the fuck we gone kill Jim Smith? First off, how we gonna get close enough to him? These racist, white mothafuckas ain't playing! Not to mention, earth to pops. A nigga ain't neva killed one of these racist leaders." Keak thought his had to be the dumbest shit he ever heard.

Voorheeze just smiled for a while. Keak didn't realize the magnitude of his own words.

"Exactly! Throughout history they done fucked us and fucked over us time and time again because they knew they can. Ain't nobody do shit about it. These mothafuckas think they're untouchable cause ain't nobody touching they ass. Now that they're dropping it's a mothafuck'n problem. Shit is unpatriotic. Fuck that! They need to know its consequences and repercussions for fucking wit us! Naw nigga, dis ain't no urban book, but we fa'sho bout to act like it is!" The passion in his words were so raw, so electrifying, pure fire.

"Big Brah got a point, in Texas they killing us like it's a sport and ain't nobody doing shit. That shit dey did to Jordan Baker in Houston a few years back was fucked up. Lil homie ain't even do shit, dey get' on him just cause he had a hoodie on. They shot the homie in cold blood. The same shit with the home girl Sandra or the homie Anthony Ross. Crackers killed homie over there in Dallas for pounding on the hood of a car. Something's gotta be done bout dis shit." Big Texas paused for a minute like a light just went off in his head.

"We always popping that gangsta shit, well let's do some gangsta shit!" Kwashay knew he didn't catch the first plane to Cali for some bullshit. He didn't know shit was this real, but he was bout that life nevertheless!

"Shit. Keak, anything is possible if a nigga put his mind to it." Batman explained to Keak before taking a sip on his Hennessey.

"Shit. Pop, you always told us to go hard or go home. Shit, I'mma go hard. What's up?" DJ wasn't about to miss out on this shit.

"Hold up, D. I've been thinking a lot bout that."

"I need you and your brothers help on a few things. That's why I called you, but when this shit go down y'all gone be as far away from this shit is possible...."

DJ cut in "Hold up, Pop."

"Ain't no hold up! Now me and yo uncle, it is what it is for us. But y'all still got a chance and a whole ass life ahead of you. And a beautiful woman whom I know loves you. Now the way y'all done held it down these last couple of years ain't nobody doubting yo gangsta. Somebody gotta hold the family together and protect the women. That's that!" He felt like shit having them this involved as it was. Voorheeze wasn't gonna throw his sons' lives away. They still had a chance and enough money to do whatever they wanted to do.

This time it was Keak that spoke up.

"Man, fuck that! Even though I think you mothafuckas is crazy, if we in, then we in. You ain't bout to measure our gangsta wit 'chou yardstick, man fuck that."

This was the shit he wanted to avoid. He wasn't trying to damage their egos he was only trying to protect his boyz. A pissing contest wouldn't get them nowhere and he knew it. Still his job was to protect them.

"Hey, Robin." He looked over at Batman once he called him.

"I know how you feeling right now. Hell, I understand I would feel the same way. But they've got a point. In for a penny in for a dollar. We family, nigga, right wrong or indifferent we ride!" Batman was just glad he wasn't in the position to make that decision.

"Let's take care of what we got to take care of and go from there.

"Everybody could see that Voorheeze was pissed off as he snatched up his I-Pod touch and ear buds and stormed out of the suite to go workout.

**** N. D. ****
East Palo Alto

"Nigga, I'm just saying why would that nigga smack his brother? It don't make sense, that nigga loves his brother, Rogue." Steven was finding the shit he was hearing hard to believe.

"Shit, nigga, I'm just saying. Mothafuckas are saying that nigga woke up out that coma on some other shit. The way I hear it, he ran up on own niggaz like "nigga do it moving." That niggaz mainey, rogue, and you know how that nigga be when he off that shit. Ain't no telling, but my guess is he knocked that nigga down." Linell said on the other line.

No one had seen Clark since the night he told Man Man and them that he was meeting up with his brother and sister. The streets were starting to talk. Word was that everybody was saying Voor-heeze probably killed Clark.

"Damn, Rogue, that'll be some cold shit. I wonder what that nigga Clark did. But look, I gotta holla at you later, Rogue. I'm pulling up to my appointment." Steve told Linell as he pulled into the gate.

"Aaight Rogue bet."

"One."

After parking his brand new big body Maserati, Steven gathered his briefcase, checked himself in the mirror then he got out of the car.

As he stood outside of the Maserati putting his suit jacket on he looked up to the sky and silently thanked God for all of his many blessings. The street life looked glamorous and inviting at times with the expensive cars, the sexy ass model type females, and stacks on top of stacks of money. He was glad that he'd chosen to stay on the legal path instead of succumbing to the temptation of fast money.

But he chose the hard road of school, sacrifice and work. All the while neva giving up. When his cousins were on top of the world, he was a book worm. He wanted to give up plenty of times and join the hustle. He didn't want to let his mom down though, so he stuck to the script.

Today he was the most successful real-estate tycoon in California. The transactions that Voorheeze made with all the houses before his coma plus the million he let him hold was a nice little nest egg for Steven to start his successful real-estate firm. His success has been tremendously wonderful.

"Good morning, I have a 10:30 a.m. appointment with Lisa my name is Steven Braxton." He told the young receptionist who was openly admiring him.

"Okay, Sir. One moment please." She told him after batting her eyes.

She picked up the phone and called Lisa. A minute later she came down the hallway with the warmest smile on her face and a natural glow about her.

"Hey, Steven. Right this way., honey." Lisa's entire essence was purity and warmth. Her smile was sunshine he could see why his cousin was in love with her.

He followed her into her office where she offered him something to drink which he respectfully declined.

"Well then what's this urgent matter of business that we have to discuss Steven?" Since their conversation the day before yesterday, she'd been eager to see just what business they had to discuss.

They weren't strangers. Lisa grew up with Steven's' mom and she watched him grow from a well-mannered little boy into a nice, and very successful, young gentleman.

"Okay. Well, for starters I am here on behalf of someone very close to me, who has the strongest of feelings for you. He picked his briefcase up.

She used that moment to spring her question on him. "And just who is this person that is close to you?"

Steven ignored her question though. He had his own agenda.

"May I?"

He was asking her if he could sit his briefcase on top of her desk. It was a nice spacious desk that wasn't too cluttered. But with enough stuff on it to let you know she was a busy woman. Once she gestured to him that it was okay. Steven sat the case down on top of the desk and opened it.

The briefcase was full of file folders which he began pulling out. She moved some things to give him room. He pulled out stack after stack. Lisa wanted to ask him what they were but since he'd ignored her first question, she wouldn't pose a second.

After the eighth file was pulled out of the briefcase and laid in front of her, he began speaking.

"I know you're curious, so let me share with you. Each one of these files I am placing on your desk contains all the information and deeds to properties around the Bay Area." He continued grabbing files and laying them in front of her.

"There are fifteen in total. Only two of the properties are not located in the Bay Area. One is a three-story, beach house in Aptos and the other is a three-story, mansion style, brick house in Missouri City Texas."

"Okay Steven, hold up! Wait a minute ,buddy. I know you doing you're thing now, but I'm not looking to buy no house and I'm sure I can't afford no beach house or brick mansion, buddy." Lisa pushed her hands out in front of her as she talked like she was pushing him away.

Steven smiled that signature smile of his.

"I'm not forcing you to buy anything. I'm not even asking you to buy anything. That would be illegal." He pulled out his thousand-dollar, gold incased, ink pen and opened the first file folder.

"I just need you to initial a few places and sign each one. All fifteen of them belong to you. Your signature officially makes these your properties."

The words "Dumb Founded" would not have described the puzzlingly shocked look on her face. She had no idea how long she sat staring at him like he was crazy. The laughter that erupted out of his mouth broke the shocked silence.

What do you mean that all fifteen of these properties belong to me? Wait you trying to get me on some scheme or something." She was thinking this fool had bumped his head and lost his mind.

"It's simple. The owner of all the properties have signed them over to you. The moment you initial and sign, each deed belongs to you. The homes are yours."

"Who's the owner?" she questioned.

In response he picked up a file opened it and handed it to her. It didn't take long for Lisa to see what she was looking for. The property that the folder in her hand belong to was at 31374 Santa Elena Way, Union City and the registered owner on file was listed as Lisa Prescott CEO and owner of PreStevens United. Estimated value of the 4-bedroom, 2 bath houses was $975,000 and it had been gifted to her.

When she was done she looked up at Steven.

"Are you serious?"

"Yup" Was all he said.

One by one she flipped thru each file only finding the same exact results with only one difference. Some of the deeds were under a foundation called PreStevens United. Apparently, Voorheeze had been so in love with Lisa that from the beginning of Neva Die reign he created the corporation and had all of his assets listed under the title of this corporation {This was done in hopes of one day having the life with Lisa and living happily ever after. However, if things ended badly for him all of his assets would already be in her name so the Feds couldn't find them and take it all. Nothing was ever put in his name}..

He reached into the briefcase and removed another file and handed it to her. She couldn't help herself as she screamed at the top of her lungs upon reading it.

PreStevens United was an international corporation valued at seventeen million dollars. It too now belonged to her. Both of her daughters Rachel and Renee ran into her office to make sure she was okay. Their responses were identical when she told them everything.

Sitting in his car, Steven thought about everything. It took almost an hour to finish things up with Lisa. Before leaving her office he retrieved an envelope and gave it to her. Instructing her that she was to read it at home tonight.

He pulled out a cellphone and sent a text message.

Everything Done
Catch 22

After sending the message he broke the phone and pulled out of the parking lot.

CHAPTER XI
Sunnyvale, CA

The day was long and drawn out. Aside from her meeting with Steven that left her breathless, the rest of the day was hectic. Lisa could hear her dogs, Brownie and Chico, barking as she put her keys in the door. Inside the apartment the barking became ear piercing as the two little dogs yapped as loud as they could.

Brownie was a light & dark brown miniature pincher. Chico was a vanilla and tan colored Maltese mix. Neither of them was bigger than a house-cat but thought they were more vicious then a red nose pit bull.

Lisa went about her normal routine, she opened the windows to let some air in, changed their doggy pad, put more food and water into their bowels, then sat down to catch her breath. She thought about the envelope that Steven had given her. The entire she was at work her mind went back and forth about what the letter might contain. So many thoughts went through her mind, she finally had to let the wondering go.

Finally, after grabbing a small bite to eat out of the refrigerator, Lisa made herself a nice, scolding hot bubble bath, turned on her playlist and climbed into the tub as Levert sang to her.

Nearly ten minutes went by with Lisa just relaxing with her eyes closed while listening to the songs play. While Ginuwine's "Differences" was playing and he was singing about his whole life changing she decided to reach for the envelope and see what was in it. She couldn't possibly imagine what more there could be. The beach house alone was worth eight point six million dollars. All fifteen properties were valued at twenty million dollars. Lisa couldn't believe someone in the streets ever came across that type of money, let alone giving it all away. She'd tried calling his phone after Steven left but the line was out of service.

What she had no-way of knowing was that T'Rida, Gunz and Voorheeze had been on top of the drug world in the Bay Area for close to twenty years. Money was the one problem they neva had after that night in West Oakland when they'd knocked Bamma's dick in the dirt. They had plenty other problems along the way.

Inside of the envelope she found a handwritten note. The Isley Brothers began telling a woman that she deserved better as Lisa read the note.

Butterfly,

Ever since way back on the 1300 block of Sevier we neva had anything or even dreamed of having anything. The one thing I always wanted I couldn't have, that was you, Lisa. I've worshiped the ground you walked on since I was a little child. But, then we both got married, you to him and me to the streets. So, I watched from the shadows and longed for you. I neva wanted to disrespect you so I wouldn't step to you until I was ready to leave the streets. That's what our lunch was about. Unfortunately, I placed myself in a predicament that I may get out of but I can neva come back from. Unfortunately, my lifelong dream of making you my wife and making love to you on a black, sandy, beach will neva happen. I can at least let you know that I've had my share of women, but I've neva loved anyone as I do you. I'm sorry that my choices robbed us both of that chance. All the properties, money and the corporation I leave to you because you are my everything, so I give you everything. The government would've seized everything that was in my name, now it's all in your name. It's a legal deal so no-one can ever take it. I'll love you until love doesn't love anymore. Take care.

La'Mont

Lisa hadn't even realized that she was crying. His words were so beautiful. No one had ever said anything so sweet to her. *Why Lord why?* She wondered. She had seen the news just like everyone else. She knew about the cop killed in Newark and the string of police murders he was supposedly linked to. She just couldn't believe it.

What La'Mont didn't know was she had always liked him, but she didn't want to come off like some bopper or gold digger. So, she just waited to see if he would ever step to her. The entire time telling herself that if it was meant to be it would happen. Another reason Lisa was hesitant was that she didn't know if La'Mont felt the same way and she didn't want to be embarrassed. Now she knew he did feel the same way but it was too late.

When she heard the front door open and slam shut, Lisa quickly hid the letter. To cover the tears she'd cried she took her hands and splashed water on her face .

"What the fuck you doing in here taking a fucking bath and my God damn food ain't on the fucking table!"

No one knew that Lisa was in a dysfunctional relationship for the past few years with an alcoholic and she was too embarrassed to say anything about it. He would get drunk after work each day. He would come home making demands and was constantly verbally abusive. She never knew what to expect. No more though, not after tonight. With the financial resources she had now, she could finally escape it all.

"Fucking, rich mothafuckas thinking they own the world! Some rich, asshole parked in front of the house blocking part of the driveway?" He yelled from the back room.

He would neva receive a response. Lisa decided she wouldn't waste another precious moment of her life with a fucking bum. She grabbed her two dogs and walked out, leaving the front door wide-open.

When he walked in the living room and found the door open he was furious. When he stepped through the front door all he saw was the Bentley that was posted in front of the house pulling off. There was no sign of Lisa. Just as he was turning to walk back into the house, he heard the squeaky voice of that dog of hers. To his surprise, Chewy was looking out of the back window of the Bentley barking at him.

**** N. D. ****
Los Altos Hills

S.A.C. Andreatta sat with her eyes closed, naked ,soaking in the Jacuzzi.. Her muscles were tight and stiff from this morning's workout and five mile run. The hot, bubbling Jacuzzi water helped sooth away the stiffness and pain. Every day she started off the same one hour workout and a run followed by a naked soak in her outdoor Jacuzzi in her back yard.

More than the pain from any workout, the stress from this case was beginning to get the best of her! She was more determined than ever to catch La'Mont Simpson.

She reached her arms high behind her head. Her 32B breast broke the surface of the water as she stretched. The sunlight dancing off of the water made her breast look like tiny snow-covered mountains. A smile came across her face as a gently gusts of wind blow. The contrasting temperatures from the waters heat to the cold wind was exhilaratingly refreshing.

All of a sudden her eyes flickered open and she bolted upright in the water like she had been electrocuted, nearly losing her footing. "That's it!"

With no regard for her own safety she bolted from the Jacuzzi, heading for her sliding glass doors. With her muscle toned, petite, alabaster body with just the right amount of curves, she looked more like a Victoria Secret Model than an FBI agent.

What she was thinking had to be outrageously crazy. It was the most insensible thing she could imagine. Yet it made perfect sense. For weeks the Agency had wondered why they hadn't heard a thing from either Simpson or Jenkins. Some agents believed they had gone underground from fear of the heat they were drawing. Andreatta didn't agree. It just didn't match anything that was in either of their files.

Above her head, in the distance a hawk called out. She slowed and put her arm out as she neared the door. Just then she got goose bumps before her eye caught light reflecting off of something in the distance. Instinctively she began to duck and crowd dawn but, it was too late!

The bullet crashed into her with so much force that is sent her crashing thru the glass sliding door!

She lay helplessly bleeding, naked on a pile of glass, wondering would this be the last day of her life.

****** N. D. ******

Kitana was watching her little, pale pink ass cheeks barely jiggling as S.A.C. Andreatta ran toward the door. Each cheek couldn't have been bigger than a ripe cantaloupe. Kitana was thinking how she would love to be cupping such fine ass cheeks while smothering her face between Andreatta's legs. Oh well fuck it! She was there to kill the hoe not suck on her pussy.

In her scope she followed Andreatta across the deck. Just before she reached the glass door, Kitana let out her breath, then held perfectly still. All thoughts were pushed out of her head, then she aimed and fired. The rifle made a sound similar to someone spitting. Kitana watched as she crashed violently through the glass. She waited a moment, looking for the slightest movement. Once Kitana was satisfied with her work, she took her eye off the scope and began breaking it down so she could get ghost.

****** N. D. ******

Both state police and Federal Law Enforcement Agents were everywhere. Spectators were trying their hardest to get a look while news reporters were trying to get a scoop. Nothing like this had every happened in the hills of Los Altos before.

Special Agent Finnegan nearly ran over a news reporter as his car came speeding up to the scene, tires, screeching and whining as he skidded to a reckless halt. Seeing the way he drove up, everyone got out of the way of the little blonde haired Agent as he jumped out of the car and ran up to the house.

The front of the house only had a little police tape keeping people back. The backyard had police tape everywhere. Finnegan briskly made his way through some officers who were in a huddle discussing possibilities and up the step leading to the deck.

Shattered glass was all over the place. There was blood splatter on some of the glass still attached to the frame. It was a clear indication of blood spray from a bullet.

Taking the side door, he entered the big house. There were probably thirty officers and Federal agents. inside the living room that Finnegan had to make his way through. When he finally made his way through to her, S.A.C. Andreatta was seated on an ottoman telling the Assistant Director everything while paramedics bandaged her up.

"The assassination attempt on S.A.C. Andreatta was unsuccessful. She was soaking in her Jacuzzi after working out when something regarding a case came to her. She was running inside to act on her thoughts, when the reflection of light caught her attention causing her to begin a tactical roll to avoid being shot. It is believed that this evasive move is what saved her life. The bullet that unmistakably was meant to end her life wound up entering the muscle area of her upper back and exiting cleanly out of her upper chest." While Carla Daniels was reporting an all-black Dodge, Charger came flying down the street nearly barreling into onlookers as it screeched to a haunt.

"It appears Special Agent Finnegan is now arriving on the scene." She stated as a blond haired, white man in plain clothes bolted from the car, headed for the house.

"Though there's nothing confirming this speculation, sources tell me that it is believed that Levell Jenkins and La'Mont Simpson are somehow behind the attempt. This is Carla Daniels reporting live from the Los Altos Hills for Fox 2 KTV U News.."

The screen shot went back to the news anchor. Voorheeze muted the screen. The segment was a pre-recorded segment from early that morning. This was his third time watching it and he still couldn't figure it out.

"I don't know why you're wracking yo brain on that shit, Robin. It ain't important. Somebody tried to hit that white bitch and missed. So what?" Batman looked up from his plate of food with his mouth full . This was his third time saying that.

"Oh, it's important Rouge. I just don't understand it."

"How's it important to us?" Batman questioned.

"First of all, because now they're looking for us in an area we ain't nowhere near. Secondly, we ain't bust a move in weeks. So, they were probably trynna figure out what we was up to and not knowing is making them nervous. Them thinking that this is us is throwing them completely off what were up to. But, most importantly this means we ain't in the game alone no more. Somebody else is playing on our side!" He told him with finality.

Voorheeze didn't know who just threw their hat in the ring, but he would have to keep an eye on the situation. It could be a good thing, but then again it could also be a very bad thing.

The news segment also gave him an idea . As he was thinking Kwashay, DJ and Keak came in. It had been two weeks since the three arrived at the Penthouse. A gruesome two weeks it has been. The days were full of studying, training and planning. The nights we filled with long hard workouts lead by Keak.

They were up against unbelievable odds, trained professionals and only God knew how many racist white fanatics who worshipped the ground this racist pig walked on.

Although they'd been laying low, Voorheeze felt like they'd been in one spot for too long. They were already packed and ready to go, now all they needed to do was spend time wiping down the suite. In the morning they were headed out to Angels Camp.

Now that they were in a new location it was time for some extensive training. Keak had taught Voorheeze how to ride the Harley Road Glide Motorcycle well enough for him to feel comfortable riding on the freeway. Now, he needed to teach him evasive maneuvering in a hostile environment. The thought terrified him but he wasn't letting nobody know especially his sons.

"Batman, check it out." Voorheeze called out while reading over what he just wrote.

"What's up?" DJ was just coming from the bathroom.

"My bad but we need to unpack all the electronics. We need a small digital station. Don't trip, I'll help with pulling the shit out and setting it up. What I need to know is can you bounce the signal continuously from state to state, while masking the Digital Foot Print?" Voorheeze had learned a lot about electronics reading Dan Browns Digital Fortress.

DJ thought about it for a second.

"Yeah. I can do it pop. That part's easy. However if you're talking about doing it now, I won't have enough time for an infinite skip. Eventually somebody could build a program that would allow them to predict the next skip and jump at the right time to land square on our back. They'll be able to retrieve the print then." All the money spent on education paid off. Electronics, gismos and gadget were his thing.

"What's the longest you could give us?"

"About two three days, tops."

"Let's get it done."

Both Keak and Kwashay came over to help. Thirty minutes later everything was unpacked, setup and ready to go. The food was cold, but what they were bout to do was real Gangsta shit! Fuck some food!

While working they all talked about what they were doing and all of the men were juiced. Mothafuckas would respect this shit.

CHAPTER XII
Long Beach

His muscles couldn't help but to flex involuntarily as he ironed his brand new wife beater. Old prison tattoos covered his body along with the battle scars that were memories of his life. The life of a Rolling 20's Long Beach Crips. Quake Loc was in his 50's now. A 5-star General for the hood. He had started at the bottom and climbed his way to the top of the Crip organization.

Along the way, he'd been shot three times, stabbed five, hit by a car and some more shit. He's done everything from being a look-out as a Tiny Locs to armed bank robbery and he had the prison numbers and war stories to back it all up. Though he's slightly crazy, Quake Loc is one of the last of the original gang bangers. He grew up gang banging in Long Beach in the 80's when shit was real and gang banging was just that Banging!

"Hell, naw cuz! These niggaz is on some other shit! Play that shit back, Cuz. Let me see it again," He told Baby S., one of the little homies.

Baby S. slid his finger backwards on the time bar rewinding the video that had gone viral last night. Everybody in the Beach was talking about it. When Baby S. heard about it, he came straight to the Big homie. He remembered the stories Quake Loc had told him about Voorheeze when they were in Jamestown State Penitentiary in California. After seeing Voorheeze blow that white pigs head off, Quake told all the homies how he and Voorheeze were so close he used to call the crazy little nigga his nephew. Voorheeze was a good lil nigga, but a bad politician. He didn't know shit about diplomacy. He reminded Quake of himself.

"For the past thirty years we've been slaughtering the shit out if each other. Blood, Cuz, Folks, Peastone, Vice Lords, Sex Money Murder, G-Unit, Nutt Case, T.B., The A-Team, Neva Die.... Shit I can go on and on. But, it's senseless and time is of the essence. While we've been killing each other, the world as left us behind.

Yes, a few of us got money, but the sacrifices it look to get it wasn't worth it."

"Everyone remembers or knows about Cointelpro and all the illegal shit the government did to the panthers from killing Fred Hampton to the bombings in L.A and the murder of those in the Symbionese Liberation Army. But what none of you are aware of is the Domestic Spying Program. The implantation of counter terrorism experts and counter-intelligence operatives into the hood and some of, if not all our gangs. Some niggaz right now are doubting this. Well think about niggaz like Alpo and Frank Lucas or organizations that fell because of rats. Think about Big Block, Sex Money Murda and The Jamaica Posse. It's a fucking epidemic! Most of these federal informants planted in the organization are the ones that start the beef and then fade into the background or disappear.

"I urge you, right now to look this up. A nigga named Jermaine Jones, who was once a cop back East, killed little Man-Man from the Taliban. He would later lose his trial and receive twenty-five years to life. He also became a key witness in the Sunny Day murders, along with a few other cases. Now I want you to do the math. He fought his case for six years in the county. Upon his sentencing he was given over ten thousand days credit for time served. That's more the thirty years credit. Jermaine Jones is not listed anywhere in the California or Federal Justice System. Jermaine Jones A.K.A Caviar disappeared for five months before surfacing on the SNY (special needs yard)."

"Check it out" In 2011 11,092 unarmed blacks were killed by the police 2012, 12,000 2014 3,600 2015 2,608 and this year alone 3,357 have been killed, all unarmed. All by the hands of racist white police. Black police ain't killing us! Mexican police ain't killing us! It's mothafuck'n peckerwoods!" It was Batman talking now. Neither he nor Voorheeze bothered coving their faces. The FEDS already knew who they were. Putting a face to the message would make it stronger.

"Until we do something about it they gone keep killing us. They might not be using a rope and a tree but they are still lynching us. How you mothafuckas running around talking bout you a gangsta when the police knocking homies down and you niggaz ain't doing shit? I know the pigs done killed some Crips. Nigga why y'all not riding? Tell me ain't no Bloods been knocked down by the police. What you do about it, Slime? Pigs ain't smacked no G.D's, Folks? Nigga, I'm from the Bay so I know the police have murdered a lot of Norteños. What the fuck y'all do bout it, holmes?"

Voorheeze began speaking. . Juiced up off of the adrenaline following through his body.

"They telling you y'all on the news that we crazy, two niggaz who went loony. Naw, nigga, they murdered our mothafuck'n brother so we doing something bout it. All your homeboys, comrades and homies that they killed and you scary mothafuckas didn't do nothing bout it. Or maybe they wasn't important enough for you to ride. My nigga, dis why we riding!" Voorheeze lifted his hand which held some type of device. He pressed a button and instantly the Sony Speaker came to life behind him via Bluetooth,.

"Okay these mothafuckas wanna take it there, then niggle's take it there!" It was T'Rida's voice on the recording. The sound of metal grinding on metal could be heard as he reloaded the Mack-90.

"This is your last chance come out with your hands in the air." A cop's voice came over a bull horn.

"Mothafucka, do I look like I give a fuck about your last warning...Nigga, it's Neva Die or Nothing," T'Rida yelled at the top of his lungs. The sound that followed was the roar of the Mack-90 as he told that bitch to do the talking for him.

Over the next few minutes they played the heroic last moments of T'Rida's life. This was the recording that Voorheeze played over and over at times when he felt he'd let his brotha down.

"You see, my nigga I don't talk that gangsta shit ,I live that gangsta shit! Now you niggaz can either talk that shit or live that shit! If you living it then let them mothafuckas know. Start waking their mothafucking game up, nigga! Cause to me, my nigga, "Black Lives Matter!"

The screen went black then a message appeared on the screen.

"IF A NIGGA KILLED YOUR FOLKS YOU WOULD KILL HIM! BUT WHEN THESE WHITE BOYZ MURDER YOUR NIGGAZ YOU AIN'T DO SHIT."

Under the message where five 7.62mm bullets and under the bullets were the words.

\"Body for Body. Are you Really Gangsta!

The message stayed on the screen for ten seconds, then the video shut off.

"Big Homie, that nigga done lost his mind, cuz?: Baby Half Pint called out after the video stopped.

"You niggaz heard the Big Homie say cuz was crazy nigga." Baby S. Told Baby Half Pint, who was getting ready to fuck wit the PS4.

Half Breed looked up from the blunt he was rolling. "I don't give a fuck what you niggaz say, cuz. Them niggaz there on some real life gangsta shit with a capital G. Fuck them faggot ass cops, nigga, dey bleed too." He lit the blunt, then passed to Quake Loc.

'Here, Big Homie." The he rolled one for himself.

Quake Loc hit the blunt that was laced with crack. He'd been smoking his blunts like this for years. He was a 5- Star G. He could do what the fuck he wanted to. While he smoked he sat in silence thinking about what the two niggaz said on the video.

Voorheeze was a good little nigga. He looked out for the Loc at a time when cuz wasn't doing so good. That didn't have nothing to do with his decision. Neither did all the 'rah-rah' that kept on going between the Locs. Thoughts of Baby Insane, O.G. Curly and the Homie Goldie Lock, all killed by Long Beach P.D filled his head. These thoughts forced him make his decision.

"Half Breed….I want you to round up five or six of the Tiny Locs. Tell them lil niggaz I said it's time to put that work in, cuz." Quake Loc took a hit off the sweet one and said. 'Nigga, dis Long Beach C.R.I.P."

"Aaight, Big Homie. That's what I'm talking bout" Half Breed responded.

"Carriiip carriip!" Everyone else called out.

**** **N. D.** ****

"God damn, cock sucking, sons of bitches!" S.A. Finnegan yelled out loud as he slammed the phone down on the receiver.

He was furious. He couldn't believe the words he was just told, *fucking motherfuckers thought they were invincible!* The mouse for his computer clinked and clicked violently as he forced it to do his bidding.

Daly came marching inside of the office with Garcia right behind him.

"What's going on Finn? Sounds like you're about to have an aneurism in here" It was Daly who asked the question. They both crowd his desk.

"Why don't the both of you come around here and take a look." He responded moving his chair out of the way. "Just got off the phone with Anderson over there in Counter Intelligence and Electronic Surveillance. He told me bout this video." He clicked on his mouse and adjusted the monitor.

"Here take a look."

Playing in front of them was the video clip that a quarter of the country had seen. It had only been on the net for two days and already it's at seventy-five million views and fifty million likes. This was unsettling to say the least. Each agent made his share of comments and remarks while the video played.

When it was done it was Daly who spoke up first.

This can't be authentic. Clearly someone has done a voice over. These guys wouldn't show their faces like that." Daly was ready to brush it off as a hoax.

"Tech guys say it's official. And why would they care about showing their faces. We've already had them splattered all over the T.V." Special Agent Finnegan was too pissed to respond to senseless, idiotic questions.

He reached for the phone. Sure, S.A.C Andreatta was out on mandatory short medical leave. Sure, he was in charge and sure he was ready to lead the team, but she needed to know and he needed her opinion.

133

****** N. D. ******
Los Altos Hills

Andreatta had already been expecting the call when it came through. Her shoulders and chest were sore as fuck from the bullet wound, but she could take it. Ironically she was shot in the same exact spot that Batman was shot in, only her bullet entered where his exited.

She was laying in her queen size Tempur-Pedic watching the Ellen DeGeneres show when she received the call from Electronic Surveillance informing her about the video.

"I guess we have to give them credit. They are a lot wiser than we thought." Was the way S.A.C. Andreatta answered the phone.

"Credit my ass! These self-righteous, low down, ghetto scum pieces of shit get no credit from me. They need to be taken out somewhere and hung from a fucking tree!" Shit Finnegan was fucking pissed.

"Calm down now, Finnegan." S.A.C. Andreatta knew very well where all of this was coming from.

Four years ago, S.A. Finnegan's brother was a gang task force Sergeant. He was killed in a shoot-out with gang members during a gang related drug bust.

"We will get these assholes, I promise. In order to do that though, we must keep a level head and look at everything analytically from a pro-active stand point." While she was talking to him she was watching the video on her MacBook Pro. "The message is not literal. They're trying to throw us off."

"What do you mean it's not literal? Throw us off of what?" S.A. Finnegan wasn't sure if the medication was clouding her head.

"The message was meant to ruffle our feathers and throw us into a frenzy. They want to throw us off of what they are truly planning. Exactly what that is I have no clue. But I'm sure this is why they released this video." She'd been working with this hypothesis all morning.

Her being shot had been the mitigating factor .Why would they shoot her instead of killing her? She couldn't figure it out at first but then it hit her. If the attention was focused on her it wouldn't be focused on what they were doing or going to do.

"Well, these mothafucking crazies are going to take it literally." He was referring to the people in the hood.

Andreatta was typing fast on the notebook while thinking about how she should respond to his comment. The truth was fucked up but it is what it is.

"Yes, they'll take it literally and there's going to be a fallout. But, that's not our problem nor is it going to be. That's what they want. They want us to focus on the fallout instead of the target. We won't be doing that. The state and local police will have to deal with that. We will focus on the case. Focus on catching these assholes!" She finished what she was typing as she was finishing up her comment.

She clicked send, sending the brief letter to the Assistant Director.

"There's is gonna be a shit storm" was all he could reply back.

"Unfortunately, Finny, that's exactly what it's going to be." She agreed.

They hung up the phone and S.A.C Andreatta thought about the letter she'd just sent her boss. If she was right this could very well put an end to this fiasco. If she was wrong that was her ass!

**** **N. D.** ****

As he sat in the car, he thought back to the conversation that he and French Tip had a couple of months ago at the Berkeley Marina.

Voorheeze hadn't lied to his sister when he told her what was going on with Vieira. He hadn't had any emotional attachments to her prior to the coma. But as he lay in the hospital bed day in and day out listening to Vieira pour her heart out to him, he realized how loyal she was. He felt something for her but wasn't sure what it was.

Loyalty meant everything to him. Most of his life he was either let down or betrayed. Which is why he wouldn't allow himself to become attached to Vieira. He was loyal to the cause.

There was no room for her no matter how loyal she was. No matter how committed she claimed to be. He was committed to the Mobb! Any and everybody else was just a means to an end. Until then, he'd continue to give her that good dick and finesse her. It was the only way.

Voorheeze fired up another Newport as his eyes continued to survey the scene. He'd been here for two hours watching and observing. Looking for anything that didn't fit. He saw her when she pulled in forty-five minutes ago and still he watched thru the binoculars.

Finally, he put the binoculars down and drove over to the motel. With his gloves on and dragons in both hands he exited the car and crept along the shadows across the parking lot. Making his way to the door, he stopped and listened. Everything was silent.

He raised his right hand, still clutching the gun and knocked on the door with his knuckles. Then he took two steps backward, off to the left side of the door. He still could hear footsteps approaching.

"Who is it?" He didn't respond when she called out.

She tried again with the same results. Voorheeze heard the doors unlock. When she opened the door, he charged and bolted through the door like old school Jerome Bettis of the Pittsburg Steelers, "The Bus".

She's wearing a sexy cotton candy pink see thru teddy with matching brah and G-String but Voorheeze didn't pay that shit no attention. Both arms raised and ready, he stormed through the little room checking everything.

She watched him, too scared to move, with a look of shock on her pretty little pale face. She was so terrified she could hear her heart racing in her ears. She'd neva seen this part of him.

After scanning the area and seeing nothing out of the ordinary, he closed the door. Satisfied that no one was in the room, he tucked one of his guns in the holster.

He turned to face her. She still doesn't know what to do, so she just stands there with her heart racing and legs trembling.

"Come here, lil mama." He stretched out his arms and she walked slowly into them.

'Don't be afraid babe, but a nigga gotta stay on point at all times."

She was literally shaking in his arms. In the tiniest voice imaginable she tells him.

"La'Mont I've told you that I am in love with you. My life could neva be if you aren't in it, baby. I will neva betray you, disobey you or dishonor you. I told you I would quit my job right now if you tell me." Slowly the tears begin to roll down Chief Vieira's face as she silently thanks God that his intentions with the guns were not towards her while she pours out her heart.

"Babe, I hear you. But, you gotta understand these mothafuckas want my dick in the dirt. So, I gotta stay on point at all times. Trust will get a nigga killed out here." He wiped her tears away as he talked to her.

"You don't have to be on point when you're with me, baby, I promise you I got you," She couldn't understand why he couldn't see what he meant to her or what she would do for him. Why didn't he understand that his wish was her command?

"Aaight, little mama, it's good. Where's the stuff at?" He asked as he broke their embrace and walked toward the bed.

"It's in the closet, baby, let me get it." A smile was on Vieira face as she walked toward the closet. She was happy, knowing that she'd please him.

Voorheeze laid the Dragon on the nightstand within arm's reach. His senses were still alert. If Vieira was setting him up he won't hesitate to blow her fucking head off!

Seeing the way her ass is swallowing that fucking G-string his dick was hard as rock. Fuck pleasure, though he knew he had to take care of business. He nearly loses the battle with lust though when she bends over to retrieve the duffle bag out of the closet. Both her asshole and her phat, juicy pussy winked at him.

When Vieira walked back and dropped the duffle bag on the bed she saw the print of his dick standing up. She licked her lips but got her mind off of it. She wanted him to see that she was down with him. So, she unzipped the bag and took the contents out and laid them neatly on the bed.

He picked them up and studied them thoroughly. Satisfied he set them down and asked her.

"If for any reason these are found, would they lead back to you?"

"Not at all, baby." She knew he was content.

"Put them back in the bag and toss it back in the closet." As she began putting the stuff up he told her,

"Thank you, little mama, you really came through."

Vieira loved it when he called her 'Little Mama", it turned her on so much. As she walked to the closet pussy juices dripped down her leg.

It'd been weeks since Vieira had that big, black dick inside of her and she can't wait a second longer. When she turned around from closing the closet door he was already undressed. His long, thick, black dick stood fully erect, waiting to take her body where she needed to be taken.

Vieira took a deep breath as her pussy vibrated in anticipation of the thrashing she knew she was going to get. She walked slowly across the room and into his arms. He kissed her lips tenderly while his hand glided across all of her curves. Just his touch, alone make her nearly cum all over herself. Her body temperature rose, as her breathing became deep and heavy.

Breaking their kiss, he planted soft kisses all around her neck, to her shoulder blades, down her back all the way to her ankles. When he got to her big ass, his dick started jumping like it was having a seizure as he bit down gently on her flesh. He kissed his way down one leg and kissed his way up the other. His muscular arms swallowed her as he wrapped his arms around her and bit and suck on her neck.

"Ssss, ooh, baby." She could feel that rock hard dick poking against her ass cheeks.

138

While Vieira continued to grind her ass up against his dick Voorheeze untied the front of the Teddy allowing her big breasts to spill out into his hands. Her nipples instantly went from soft and suckable to ice hard. Another moan escaped her mouth when he squeezed both nipples with his finger.

For doing a good job with getting the shit he needed he was going to give her that good long dope dick, since he was playing wit his nose earlier in the car.

She turned her head to the side. When she did he bit her neck. Both of them could feel the pre-cum coming out his dick and coating her ass cheeks.

"Baby, I want you to punish me. Fuck me like I've disobeyed you. This pussy needs to know it's yours." As she told him what she wanted, her hand was already teasing her pussy. Voorheeze was covering his fingers in her warm honey.

"Is that what you want?" He ask her as his hand climbs her body looking for her neck.

"Yes.."

"You sure, babe?" He whispers seductively into her ears.

"Yes, babe I'm sure." It was more of a plea than a confirmation.

As the words left her lips, he forcefully wrapped his hand around her throat, she looked terrified and turned on at the same time. He stares intensely into her eyes. It felt like he was staring into her soul. Searching for her dark secrets. Her lips parted slightly. Only to be devoured hungrily by his mouth.

His mouth felt like a hot furnace trying to suck her soul out of her body through her mouth she moans loudly into his mouth. The kiss was deep and hard. Vieira closed her eyes savoring the feeling. His hard-muscular body was thrust into her pinning her body against the wall.

He bit down on her lip when he finally came up for air. The bite wasn't too hard but hard enough to draw blood. She loved the force! She needed to be ravished.

Before she knew what happened, he bent down and scooped her up in one swift move her foot knocked the lamp that was on the nightstand over in the process. One arm wrapped around her waist while his other hand was filled with her ass cheeks. Instinctively she wrapped her thick legs around his waist, not realizing that this move lined her pussy up perfectly in front of his dick. It jumped again.

He didn't waste any time. He thrust up and forward! Driving every bit of his 10 inches as deep inside of her as he could.

The shriek that escaped her mouth from the pain was silenced the moment his mouth covered hers again. The heat inside of her hat, soaking pussy made him almost lose control. Savagely he kissed her sore, bleeding lips, savoring the passion right along with the coppery taste.

His hips were thrusting furiously in and out of her as he thrashed her pussy. The white light of pain she first felt the moment he penetrated her was replaced with a pleasures pain as his big dick opened her up deliciously stretching her walls. His heavy nut sack slapping her ass every time he thrust deep inside of her.

"Oh...Oh...Fuck...Ooh Fuck yeah! Fuck me baby! Fuck me babyyyyy!" Vieira can feel her orgasm building as he fucks her. She was so excited.

In and out. Fast and hard. He's rim riding that pussy! The perspiration covering their bodies is not light. It's a heavy sweat pouring off of them. They have only been at it for minutes but the level of intensity is that strong.

He's pounding inside of her so violently that her body is knocking into the wall sounds like someone pounding the wall with their fist.

With his left hand he smacks her on the bottom of her ass. At the same time his mouth covers her tit and he bites down on her hard nipple. Electricity shoots thru her.

"Oh, my fucking Gaaawwwd!" she shouted as a very violent orgasm erupted through her body.

The shock of the orgasm rocked her body back and forth against the wall like she is having a seizure. He drove his cock balls deep inside of her He held there inside of her sucking on her tit the entire time her body is spasming.

When the orgasm subsided, he tossed her unto the bed as if she was weightless. As she bounced on the bed her eyes were glue to his rock hard dick that was covered in her juices.

"Ooh!" Escapes her lips as he scratches her to the edge of the bed.

With both her legs over his shoulders and that ass tilted up he pushed all the way into her. When he reached her furthest depth, he tried to drive his dick even further.

"Aaarrgh!" She screamed out. It felt like she's about to split right down the middle.

He didn't hold nothing back as he fucked her vigorously! Sweat pouring off of him as his balls smacked her ass.

"Aah! Aah! Oooh Yes! Just like that. Right there Baby! Right there!"

Voorheeze dug his feet into the carpet so he could fuck her pretty, little pink pussy harder.

"Uugh. Give me this fucking pussy, bitch!" He grunted. As a response she started lifting her ass off the bed thrusting up to meet that long dick as it invaded her pussy.

"Take it, Daddy! Take this pussy!

He loved that dirty talk. That shit drove him crazy! He turned it up a notch. He reached down with his left hand and smacked her big ass breast that were bouncing all over the place. Then he started choking her as he long dicked her like he was punishing her.

"Ooo! -Oooo. Oo. Fuck me!" Vieira could barely breathe.

The feeling was wonderfully sweet. Neva had she felt this way before. She came twice and was working on the third one as he taunted her.

"Come on, bitch! Take dis mothafucking big, black dick, you white bitch!" He grunted as his face was inches away. From hers. Sweat was pouring off of it into her open mouth. She really felt like she was a wild animal getting dominated by her mate.

"Turn your ass around." He ordered her.

"Why? You wanna see this big fat ass." She teased him.

"*Slap!*"

The slap stunned the shit out of her but she liked it!

Instantly she got on all fours spreading that big white ass in front of him. He knew he wasn't going to last long. Still he dove into her heavenly furnace. Loving the flames of temptation!

"You think slapping me is going to discourage me! Give me that fucking dick, nigga! Give me that fucking dick!" She yelled as she backed that ass up like she was trynna win a Juvenile "Back That Ass Up" Contest.

Voorheeze couldn't do nothing but watch that big ass move as she backed it against him so hard. It was like she was fucking the dick and not the other way around.

"Get it, bitch! You nasty, little, white bitch, get it!" He knew he couldn't hold back too much longer. He could feel his stomach knotting and balls swelling.

He grabbed a hand full of her hair, yanked her head back hard and started smacking that ass like he was a horse jockey.

"Oohh. Oooh, shit! Spank that ass, Daddy. Spank oooo oooh!" When she came it shot out of her like a water hose. The sight of her gushing did him in!

"Turn around, bitch! Hurry up!" she was just in time to open her mouth when that nigga blew a load so fucking strong it was like a fire man's hose.

She barely closed her eyes as he literally painted her entire face. It was so powerful his knees buckled, toes curled and some more shit.

With her eyes closed she reached out for his dick and once she found it, she guided her mouth on it thinking that he was done. She was wrong, but she managed to swallow the rest, sucking on his dick while she did so. Cum dripping off of her chin unto her breast.

"Hold up, let me get you a towel." He told her as he noticed that she couldn't open her eyes.

He got her a hot face towel from the bathroom. After she cleaned her face up she joined him in the shower. They fucked again in the shower before cleaning up.

Later, they were laying on the bed. He was laying on his back with one arm behind his head, while she was laying with her head on his chest, listening to his heartbeat.

"Whew! A girl needed that."

"Shyyyyt! I didn't know you had that in you." He told her, honestly surprised.

She kissed and sucked on his nipple for a second before responding.

"Baby, you bring a lot of stuff out of me, I'll do anything for you, anything with you, and anything behind you, without question, with no hesitation." Vieira didn't care about the consequences of their love affair. She had done the right thing all her life played by the book. And what had it gotten her? Bullshit and heartbreak.

With La'Mont she was truly happy and truly in love. She wanted that every day, all day, for as long as it lasted. Heaven on earth was worth the hell she would pay to attain it.

"Anything and everything?" he asked her.

"You know that's a tall order, lil doll."

"I can feel it, Daddy." She assured him as she climbed on top of him.

Slowly she slid all the way down his hardened pole until she had it all inside of her.

"We'll see." Was all he said as he grabbed her hips and enjoyed the ride.

She rode him slowly and steadily for about five minutes. Then, he lost his cool. He had to beat that pussy up!

De'Kari

CHAPTER XIII

Voorheeze woke up bright and early the next morning. The pussy was good, but he had business to take care of. He was on his way to a meeting. At the light before the freeway, he pulled a bag of coke out of the center console and played with his nose, then he hit the highway.

The weather outside was at the halfway point between chilly and nice. He could see spring trying to take over from winter. The coke had him feeling right so he turned on the radio. First he was going to slap a in CD but decided to fuck with his boy Steve Harvey and see what was good on the show this morning so he turned to 102.9 KBLX.

It sounded like they were talking about violence in the hood.

"Aaaw, fuck that." He said out loud. The last thing he wanted to hear was a bunch of black mothafuckas who ain't neva once visited the hood talk about the hood. Mothafucka's were good for that. How they gone critique the ills of urban life, when the closest they've gotten to Urban Life was a rap song or a statistical analysis sheet?

Just as he changed the station, he thought he was hearing shit. He quickly turned it back to see if he was tripping:

"It's funny Steve ,because it's as if they want me to walk some invisible tight rope or something.." His ears were not playing with him. That was Dok's voice he had heard. He turned the volume up on the stereo and listened. Damn he missed his nigga!

"The part they don't seem to understand, Steve, is before the education and philosophical ideology, I was a street nigga. It's that simple. I didn't step up for notoriety or my fifteen minutes of fame. My aim is to help my people and the only way for me to do that is by truth. Good o'le fashion ugly truth." Steve Harvey had reached out to him, not the other way around. So, he wasn't pulling no punches.

"Okay. Mr. Hayes. You know we all about that good o'le, ugly truth here at the Steve Harvey Show." Steve asked him.

"I mean, hell, Steve, let's start with the most obvious and pertinent truth. Before I state it I must lead with, although I don't necessarily agree with the methods that are being used to do so. Something had to be done to get people's attention about what's been happening to our people here in this country. The rate at which unarmed African Americans are being killed by those sworn to protect and serve is downright devastating. And I stress the "Unarmed" factor. So I can understand why these two men have chosen to take such drastic measures in order to grab the public's attention."

"Steve, marches and prayers weren't doing anything. Rallies and vigils weren't doing nothing. No-one was caring. Well they care now. They're listening now!" Dok's voice rose a little as he spoke.

"Whoa! Whoa! Okay my brotha, good o'le ugly truth it is. But tell me, is it actually possible for something positive to come from so much violence? And why does it have to be violence in the first place?" Steve Harvey asked. Liking the head on this young brothas shoulders.

"Steve, violence begets violence. Ignorance only acknowledges a greater ignorance. When it was just unarmed black civilians being killed, no one cared. But, now that WHITE COPS are being killed, everyone is screaming tragedy. But where was tragedy for fourteen year old Tamir Rice in Cleveland Ohio? He was just a baby, playing with a toy. Or even thirteen year old Andy Lopez here in Cali who was shot and killed for the same reason. These were babies, but no one is screaming tragedy or bloody murda for them! The feds ain't making any "National Alerts" for them!"

"You gotta dig this, Steve. Right now everyone is focused on the death of the cops., which is expected. Yet it is inevitable they will have to deal with the issues that caused the deaths of so many police officers! These situations are both tragic as well as iconic.

"Well, do you think that this situation will wake up the black community and finally get us back working with one another, like in the days of the Black Panthers? Or do you think this will just blow in the wind?" It was Raynell who asked the questions.

"Aaw shit! Now it's gone get deep." Dok told her.

"Hold up! Hold up ma'am I'm the only one that can curse on this show, partner." Steve joked to lighten the mood. "But, getting deep is what we do on the Steve Harvey Show. So, let's have it."

"It's the exact same scenario, reversed."

"Oh yeah, this is bout to get deep." Steve clapped his hands and rubbed them together, with a smile on his face in anticipation of where the young man would take this.

"Jamall Harris, Neal Young, Kenny Hammel, Michael John Chester Mitchell, Sean Carter, Eddie Miles, Man Man, Tyrone Douglas, Anthony Boldin, Tiffany Jackson, La'Quesha Adams. I can keep going for an hour straight, but I'm sure you get the picture. These were all young brothas and sistahs murdered too, but at the hands of our own people. Every years Black Lives are lost in the hoods across America by our owns hands. Either drug related, gang violence or some other idiotic, senseless act of violence. No-one has raised so much as a finger or a voice to bring our own self-inflicted genocide to an end. We've just watched and some say, Oh what a shame. Now that a bunch of WHITE Cops are killing us, we wanna sing Kumbiyah and cry Black Lives Matter! Let me ask you, did they matter when we were the ones doing the killing? Or better yet, if Black Lives Matter, who do they matter to?"

"Whoo now!" Raynell fanned herself. This young brotha was deep.

"Okay. Okay I see you really took it there with that one. But let me ask you something. Are you telling me that you don't support the Black Lives Matter Movement?" Steve just wanted to see where the youngsta would go with this.

"First of all, Steve my answer is not towards you but actually for my people. I urge them to hear my words. I'm a Black Man First and Foremost and I'll neva forget that! With that being said I'm down for and support any and all movements that are for the betterment of my people. If it protects, supports, teaches or advances blacks, then I'm all for it! On the flip side of that coin if it harms, destroys, exploit or hinders hem then I am against it. Even if the threat that's against our people are our people. Then I will rage on them as well." Dok explained.

"Well Mr. Hayes what do you mean by that?" Raynell asked quite intrigued.

"You have something that is called a Philistine. A Philistine is an Agent of Provocateur. A snake, a weasel, spy or a double agent. Someone who infiltrates something and destroys it from within. Unfortunately, that has become our own people through self-hate, undercover homosexuality spreading disease, drive by shootings, and snitching. All of these things have combined to become the single greatest threat to our people. It's our own people that are killing us. And at a higher rate than these police ever could! So I say, if Black Lives Matter… Who do they matter too? Cause it sure hasn't been us."

Voorheeze wanted to continue listening to the broadcast but he had made it to his destination. Reluctantly he turned the radio off and got of the car. He knew that he'd been under surveillance. From the moment he pulled up. Even still the feeling of being watched was just as strong as if he didn't know.

He made his way across the parking lot and entered the office building. Walking up to the receptionist who asked him if she could help him. He told her.

"Yes, beautiful. I was supposed to be at 276 J. Street for the Bill Green Financial Co-Op. I believe I made a wrong turn somewhere." He gave her the code he'd memorized years ago.

The pretty, chocolate thing looked at him for a minute before pressing a button on her desk that locked the front door. When she stood up she had that Janet Jackson "Poetic Justice" body.

"Follow me, sir." She turned and headed towards the hallway.

She stood about 5'6" Her hair was in sistah Locs past her shoulders and she had an ass that swayed like the open seas. He was so engrossed in watching her ass shake he didn't see her when she looked over her shoulder and saw him.

"Trust me, it's too much for you." She smiled and told him as they reached the door at the end of the hall.

"My Junior High teacher told me the same thing, but I aced her class." He shot back

"And just how did you do that?" the look in her eyes spoke all of her intentions.

"Turns out, I was too much for her." He licked his lips so she'd know what his was talking about.

Just then a buzzer sounded and the door was opened. "Saved By The Bell." She told him as she opened the door and turned to leave. She brushed her ass against his dick flirtatiously as she turned.

He just watched her walk back down the hall with a smile on his face. She didn't know that she was playing with fire. He'd have her little ass speaking in tongues. What he didn't know was she knew exactly who he was and she was hoping he'd want to find out who she was.

Through the door, down another short hall and through another door and he walked out into a large warehouse. There was so much activity going on it looked like he was in a chop shop. It was actually munitions depot. And then some.

"Jay!" D-High called out. He was standing by an open office door off to the left of where he was standing.

Voorheeze made his way over to where D-High was. The two embraced then made their way into the office. The warehouse looks like some sort of airplane hangar. The inside office looked like a luxury living room. From the two 65" televisions, the three-piece Italian leather sofas, the plush thick carpet and pictures of black victorious and Revolutionary leaders.

The executive Presidential desk seemed out of place at the far end of the hallway.

"You looking good, little brah." D-High told him as he took his seat behind the desk.

"The busy Bee has no time for sorrow, big brah. You know that because you taught me." Voorheeze sat across from him.

"Yes. But, no bird soars high if he soars with his own wings." This is how it was with them. They could sit and talk through proverbs all day long.

They met in DVI a prison in Tracy California back when Voorheeze was just eighteen years old. D-High took the rowdy, hard headed youngsta under his wings and laced his boots good.

"Lil brah, I got what you asked for right here." He indicated a small black leather carrying case. "I know exactly what you're doing and why first I'm gonna tell you I'll always be there if you need me. But as your big brother, I must remind you that. "A dead body revenges no injuries." D-High looked at him with eyes that could pierce the devils soul.

Voorheeze sat for a moment thinking over what he'd just said. "The cut worm forgives the plough." I don't! I make it regret that it cut the worm."

D-High knew his little brotha. So, he knew he was wasting his time trying to reason with him. Still, it was his little brotha, so he had to try.

With a heavy weight on his shoulders, D-High grabbed the case and placed it on his desk. True, he had no idea exactly what Voorheeze was planning, yet he knew it was big considering what he was giving him.

For the next fifteen minutes D-High showed him how to use the devices. Three times they went over everything. D-High wanted to go over it a fourth time, but Voorheeze assured him that it wasn't necessary.

He walked back down both hallways and back into the receptionist's area here he got the little cutie pie's number then left to go handle his business.

****** N. D. ******
Downtown Oakland

The room was filled with some very important people in the Bureau, including both the Assistant Director Octavian Vaughn and the Director of the FBI himself, Demitri Diaz. Also included were Regional Director Elizabeth Karr and Special Agent in Charge Andreatta.

The meeting itself was called because of e-mail she sent to the Assistant Director three days ago. The meeting took so long to take place because the Director was busy dealing with the recent rise of Guerilla Activity on the East Coast.

"Special Agent Andreatta from your first day in the Bureau you've been a rising star. I myself was the one to recommend your portion because of your analytical mind, your work ethic and most importantly your intuition. But, I have to tell you this one here seems a bit out of there. Now I know we want these guys, but that has got to be grasping for straws." It was Director Diaz talking to her.

She began to speak but Assistant Director Vaughn came to her defense.

"Sir, I know what has been said is hard to believe and a tad bit far-fetched. But, given Special agent Andreatta history, I strongly believe we should put some reverence into what she has said. Keep in mind, it was this same intuition of hers that lead to the arrest and conviction of The Get Money Clique and their entire operation," A.D. Vaughn knew that the Director was pondering that.

"Sir, as I stated in my full report, we aren't dealing with two low level, ghetto thugs, pedaling drugs as we suspected in the beginning. These are well organized, highly sophisticated, goal oriented and achieving, terrorists. Not criminals but terrorists. With terrorist thinking as well as terrorist capabilities.

The video that they just sent shows that they want the attention of a larger demographic. Keep in mind we are talking about the same people who blew up a police station, killing almost its entire force. What could be better for two people who are trying to get America's attention, than by killing a government official?" What she said was clear as day. S.A.C. Andreatta couldn't understand how he didn't see it.

"Miss Andreatta, if I up the security level and tell everyone that we suspect that two black guys from the ghetto were going to assassinate someone in the government, this agency will be laughing stock of the world." After Director Diaz spoke he looked over at A.D. Vaughn, a black man, and regretted that statement.

The entire time Agents Garcia and Daly were viewing what was going on with extreme interest. Agents didn't normally attend meets with the two top Directors.

It wasn't A.D. Vaughn who responded to the senseless racial comment. It was S.A.C. Andreatta herself.

"Well, excuse me for saying, sir but if you refuse to acknowledge my recommendation on this matter, then you and you alone will be the laughing stock of this nation because you ignored the warnings of your Agents. Agents, whom this Agency rely on to prevent just these same matters."

"Excuse me?" The director was shocked beyond belief.

"In the past year or so almost 300 Law Enforcement personnel have been brutally murdered." She stood up from her chair and fixed the sling her arm was in.

"I don't have time to worry about how I talk to you. Or if you'll get offended by something I say. I'm trying to protect my country and everyone in it!" She turned around and stormed out of the conference room. She needed to catch two serial killers, who she knew were just getting started.

S.A.C Andreatta was furious when she stormed out. Her mood wasn't shit compared to the Director's. He started to say something but Special Agent Finnegan, who'd been silent this whole time, beat him to the punch.

"Sir, you'll have to excuse her. The medication from the gun shot's been messing with her head lately." He told the Director as he too started standing up. Once he spoke, he rushed out the door too, followed by Garcia and Daly.

They may have been FBI Agents, but they were a team, a family of their own. They were loyal to the head of that family, Special Agent in Charge Andreatta.

"Hey! Hey! Chief!" Finnegan called out as he came rushing down the hallway, followed by his team.

They caught up to her at the main elevators.

"Are you alright, chief?" It was Agent Daly.

She took a deep breath before answering. She was still visibly upset.

"Yeah, I'm fine." The elevator door opened and they stepped inside. Then she continued, "It just pisses me off that cops are dying. We're all putting our lives on the line to catch these assholes. Instead of helping us, this jerk is busy worrying about politics! This would be the perfect opportunity to catch the assholes." She hated bureaucracy. To her bureaucracy got people killed.

That's what the meeting was about. Since Special Agent Andreatta felt it was clearly evident that they were attempting to take Jim Smith's life, he wanted to set a trap to spring up and intercept them before they carried out their plans. At first A.D. Vaughn was skeptical. After she explained everything in detail, he was on board. Now this piss-ant Director had just put up a road block. She knew, based on the Directors response, that he was more worried about politics than he was listening to her theories and assessments.

Noticing the elevator was passing their floor Special Agent Finnegan asked S.A.C Andreatta. "Where are we headed, chief?"

"Dales. I need a drink while I sort somethings out." She responded without looking up from her phone.

"You mean, "We got some things to sort out." S.A. Finnegan told her.

The others chimed in and they made their way to Dales, a small bar over in Emeryville.

Back in the conference room

Director Diaz was still taken back by the behavior and words of Special Agent In Charge Andreatta. Though he respected the woman's tenacity, he was still her boss.

"I know she should have handled that a lot better, sir. I'll deal with her on that. However, I think you should really reconsider this, sir and really look at what she was saying." A.D Vaughn told the Director, trying to soften the blow.

"Ah. Leave her alone about the attitude. We're all a little wound up. But, tell me, Tom, you don't really think these guys are going to target Jim Smith do you?" Director Diaz just couldn't picture it.

"I'll admit sir…"

Director Diaz cut him off. "Enough with all the sir shit, Octavian, it's only us in here."

"Alright, Demitri. Honestly, I first thought it was the craziest thing that I had ever heard, until she printed some things out to me and explained some other things. Well……Honestly I think she may be on to something."

"Some things like what?" The director was at least now paying some attention.

"Well. Both of these psycho's belong to and are high ranking officials in a Domestic Terrorist Group. And the recent level of activity of the group has been increasing, especially over on the East Coast. Both Chicago and Michigan, as you know, are dealing with this same organization, as is Detroit. With a play like this, these guys would be delivering a serious message. If you ask me, we have to not only consider the threat possible. But, we must deem it plausible."

The ramifications of what his assistant just told him were so ginormous that Director Diaz leaned over and poured a glass of water from the pitcher on the long table. He hadn't considered all of this before. Even though these guys appeared to be operating alone, they would still be very dangerous, just because of the level of training they would have received from the organization,

Then he thought back to the Oklahoma City bombing. The Agency had known all along that the Guerilla Organization had been responsible. They couldn't let the world know the truth , that a Black Militant Organization had delivered such a might blow to America. It was easier to frame the radical Timothy McVey.

The same was done for 911. No Arabs had done that. Again, the Bureau had covered that up. If the blacks knew that their people were able to cripple the American System known as Democracy, the effects would be catastrophic.

Considering all of this, the Director looked at the Assistant Director and asked him. 'What were you all thinking?

CHAPTER XIV
Club Carsjanae's

Linell and Neal were in the office going over a few things. Carsjanae's was a success from the moment he opened the club. Neal, his longtime friend had been his head of security since day one and the only person that he trusted enough for what he wanted to do.

Carsjanae's was so successful that Linell was working out the details to open up a second club. This one he would call "Aniyah's", pronounced A-nie-ah's. The idea that he had for Aniyah's was going to change the game as far as clubs go.

Linell told Neal that he wanted him to take over running Carsjanae's while he focused on getting Aniyah's up and running. They'd been working on this for months. Everything was finally in order. The Grand Opening was scheduled for next month.

"Damn nigga I can't believe yo scary ass actually trusting a mothafucka to watch over and control your baby." Neal joked with him as he passed him the blunt.

"Trust you? Nigga, I done put hidden cameras all over this bitch so I can be spying on you, nigga. When you bring a bitch in here, let her get on top of yo ass. Nigga, I'm trynna see a show. I don't wanna see yo ashy ass!"

They both started cracking up. Then Neal started looking around the office. Knowing, Linell that nigga probably really did have cameras in that mothafucka. Neal knew his partner wasn't really a trusting kind of nigga.

Checking the monitors was second nature to Neal, so as he was scanning the office for hidden cameras, he glanced over to the monitors.

"Kill the cameras, my nigga." Neal told him as he stood up pulling out his Glock 23 with that hockey stick on it.

Linell looked over towards the monitors to see what his nigga was seeing. When he spotted them, his only words were,

"These nigga's done lost their fucking mind!" As he hit the switch to kill the cameras and pulled out his brand new 950 Berretta Jetfire.

Years ago, Clark had introduced him to a kid named Jimmy. Jimmy was a young, black, computer geek that went to Polly high. He designed a system for Linell that would make it appear as if his camera and computers system had a glitch anytime he pressed a certain button to turn the cameras off. This was so it would appear that the system malfunctioned and not the cameras were turned off. So, if it got ugly in the club there wouldn't be any evidence.

Neal was already out the door as Linell came around the corner of the desk. He was right behind Neal out the door, ready to get it popping in this mothafucka.

The Ebony room was called that because all the Italian, butter soft, leather furniture was ebony brown and the tables were all mahogany wood. The room's only contrast was the six inch thick, vanilla cream Persian carpet. The room had three 65" flat screen Sony T.V's and one 85" curve T.V that sat dead center in the room. Right across from the main custom sofa that could seat ten people.

"Look Tip, all I'm saying is it ain't no sense crying over spilled milk. Clark, was my cousin and I loved him, but its rules to this shit and he knew that shit." Cantelope was trying her hardest to cheer French Tip up.

French Tip had finally confided in her cousin and told her what had happened to her brother Clarkola. The whole story of how she'd told Voorheeze that Clark had threatened her when she confronted him about trying to kill Nastasia. Voorheeze had told her then that he would kill his older brother for the threat.

Even though he loved his brother there were rules to this shit, and he lived by them. Their Friday luncheon turned into dinner. It was their first time getting together since Voorheeze and gotten shot up by Sutton. After dinner they went out to the Berkeley Marina to kick it some more. It was here that Voorheeze killed his older brother. He wouldn't allow no-one to threaten anybody he loved. Period point Blank!

Although French Tip knew that Voorheeze was only following the rules of the Family, it didn't make things any easier to accept.

"Girl, I know you're right but knowing that shit don't make it any better. Shit, that was still my oldest brother." French Tip couldn't see that it was guilt that was making her feel all remorseful.

This was the first time a kill had gotten to her. She was unable to process it correctly. Even though she hadn't been the one to pull the trigger, she felt that she was to blame because she was the one to tell Voorheeze about the threat. Had she neva said nothing, both of her brothers would still be alive.

She knew how Clark was. She knew he wouldn't really harm her. He was just pissed off that night. As soon as those thoughts invaded her mind. She forced them out. Fuck was she thinking? Clark knew the rules. He knew what fucking time it was.

"Look alive bitch, we got company." Cantelope's words brought her out of her head.

French Tip's eyes looked towards the VIP entrance because that's the direction Cantelope was looking.

Dok Holiday had just entered the VIP Lounge with Scooter and Rell, his two sons who were also his security team. The entire atmosphere in the room changed as the rest of the She-Wolves who were present picked up on the intrusion.

Once they located who they came to see, the three of them walked over to the main sofa. When they got a few feet away from the sofa, Dok raised both of his hands up in the "I come in peace gesture." Cantelope wasn't going for none of that shit! Her 5-shot 500 magnum was in her hands. All them mothafuckas that think a bitch couldn't bust big shit had Cantelope fucked up! She'd make that big mothafucka sing with precision, Fast!

"Peace, be still ,young sister's. Cantelope we've neva had beef before and I wouldn't bring beef to you." Dok explained once he was in ear shot.

"What's up, then?" Cantelope spoke. Sensing the young killaz uneasiness, Dok figured he would get directly to the point.

"I need to talk to you, French Tip. It's very important, my sistah. Since you've known me, you know that my word is law. I give you my word that I mean neither of you any harm." He spoke in his most sincere voice.

"Oh, I know you don't mean me no harm." Cantelope didn't give a fuck that he was once the General that controlled the reigns for the family.

Shit went down and there was a split. As far as she was concerned, it was Neva Die Dragon Gang or nothing and he wasn't Dragon Gang no more. So, fuck him!

French Tip, on the other hand, knew that he was speaking truth. Dok would neva harm her or brig harm her way, just based on the strength of her brother, Voorheeze.

"You can sit ,Dok, but your boys gotta wait over there somewhere." She told him pointing towards a table by the VIP entrance.

"It'll make my sisters more comfortable." Dok hadn't noticed the other four deadly women that had surrounded them.

Dok nodded his head and Scooter and Rell headed for the table. Their father being the man that he is, he knew exactly how this would work out and had run it down for them before they came into the club.

As they were walking to the table Neal and Linell came busting inside the lounge with a few other security behind them.

"What the fuck you niggaz doing up in my shit?" Linell shouted as he was staring at Scooter down the barrel of the 950.

The hateful look in Linell's eyes would make a Catholic Priest want to give his confessions.

Scooter didn't give a fuck about the nigga gripping the banger. His dad gave specific orders that there would be zero violence. He would follow that order. If the order were receded though, he knew he could get the draw on the big nigga.

"Easy, Big Man. We ain't here on no bullshit! We're here simply to talk to our folks" Dok shouted loud enough to be heard.

The tension was so thick in the room you couldn't fart in that bitch! The gas couldn't go nowhere.

"Don' tell me to be easy, mothafucka! You up in my shit!" Linell looked at Dok as he yelled this shit out.

That split second was all they needed. Scooter and Rell both materialized Glock40's out of thin air. Rell's was pointing at Neal while Scooters was pointed at Linell.

"Peace, be still!" Dok shouted to his sons telling them not to shoot. He knew how they felt about him so they were ready to play Rodeo Cowboys in that bitch!

French Tip knew she had to do something before Carsjanae's made the evening news and they all started their journey to Eternity. She called out Linell.

"L." When he didn't answer she stood up. "Linell! It's all good, big brah. Thank you, but we good." She told him when he finally looked over.

Linell was raging because French Tip had only told Cantelope about what happened to Clark. The streets always talk and right now they were saying that Dok and Gunz had something to do with Clark's disappearance because of the war between Clark and Gunz. Because of this, anybody who fucked with Clark was feeling some kind of way.

Linell wanted to get it popping harder than a mothafucka, but he respected Voorheeze and Clarks little sister like she was his own little sister. Reluctantly, he fell back, but not before shooting one last look Dok's way. Neal followed him out of the VIP

After they left, Scooter and Rell took a seat at the table and Dok sat on the sofa with French Tip and Cantelope.

"So, what's up, Darrell?" She wanted to know right away, addressing him by his real name.

"I see we straight to the point.." When he noticed that she wasn't going to comment, he got straight to the point. "Okay then. I need you to get ahold of my brother. Now, before you say anything, my sistah you, should know two things. One, he told me a long time ago, if I was to ever need him, you could find him, because he loved you so much he would always make sure you could reach him.

"Secondly, all families have disputes, that doesn't stop you from being family. Sometimes, one or the other just needs some space. J is my brotha and I will neva bring him no harm or let harm come his way! I'm trynna help my brotha." His words sounded sincere and his body language easy genuine.

French Tip weighed the two options in her head. If Dok was on some shady shit, then she would be bringing danger to her brother. In case he was being sincere, she wanted her brother to have all the help he could get. She knew her brother was a gangsta, but at the end of the day they were just hood niggaz. The shit that him and Batman were on was some way other. Those niggaz must've watched attack on Precinct 81 too many times.

"Dok, you ain't neva been nothing but right to us. Please don't go wrong. Because behind my brother my girls will go as far as I go!" She leaned closer making sure he saw the death that hidden in her eyes.

"And I'll go to hell and back for my brother,"

"You wouldn't have to, sis. That's my job." He meant exactly what he said too.

"Leave me a number." Considering how much her brother loved and respected Dok, she knew that she was making the right choice,

Dok reached inside his pocket and pulled out a card case. He retrieved a card and handed it to her.

The card was all black and made from thick, expensive, paper. The only thing that was written on the card was the words...

"Neva Die 276!"

She looked from the card up to Dok. Looking at him like.

"Nigga is you crazy." He smiled she looked back at the card. It took her a minute, then she smiled.

"I'll always be Neva Die Dragon Gangs Commander and Chief!" He told her before he leaned in and gave her a kiss on the cheek. Then he left.

She couldn't help looking at the card smiling and shaking her head. Cantelope asked her what was up so she handed her the card, she saw the same thing that French Tip saw at first. Nothing!

When French Tip saw with her eyes and not her mind, she was able to see it. (When the average person sees something, their mind tells their eyes what they are seeing, But if you turn you mind off, your eyes won't see what your mind says is there. Your eyes will see what is actually there. The card actually said:

NEV ADI E276 which is (638) 234-3276 Dok's phone number, but the average mind will only see NEVA DIE 276. That was some Gangta shit. After explaining it to Cantelope, French Tip pulled out her phone to call her brother.

De'Kari

CHAPTER XV

Sniff! Snifff.

After his meeting with D-High, Voorheeze had gotten into a heated argument with Keak. The plan was simple, at least he thought it was. He and Kwashay would ride the two Road Kings which were kitted with all the necessary shit needed to make them look like police motorcycles.

Voorheeze would have the main bomb and Kwashay would hold the secondary. To him the plan was so simple, that's why it would work. He wasn't counting on Kwashay crashing one of the big motorcycles during training. When he fell, Kwashay sprang his arm severely enough that he wouldn't be able to control the big Road King.

The plan called for two riders. Voorheeze didn't want either of his sons getting involved that deeply. Like Keak told him, "something of this magnitude, the only way to be involved was deep." Shit involved was involved!

SNIFF!

SNIIFF!

He knew his son was right but that didn't make shit any better. Just like he knew he shouldn't be snorting coke while they were planning this shit, knowing better and doing better, were two totally different fucking things.

He was starting to see things he'd neva seen and he wasn't liking the shit he saw. He was all the way gangster 100% but he was a fucked up father. What kind of father would have his sons out with him doing some shit like this?

Getting money was one thing. He didn't feel bad about providing a way for them to feed themselves and secure their futures. But they were about to kill Jim Smith. There was no coming back from this shit. These mothafucking white folk would hunt them down forever! How could he put that on his boyz?

Before he could answer that, his I-Phone began ringing.

"What's up beautiful?" He asked his baby sister when he picked up.

As he listened to her talk, he held his head back to get a drain. While Lil Boosie rapped in the background about mothafuckas handling the truth.

"Yeah, it's cool. Hold up let me get a pen." He was about to get up until she told him that he didn't need a pen.

On the other line French Tip could tell something was wrong. He brother didn't sound right. It wasn't just the stress that she could hear in his voice. He sounded like he was high. Whatever it was that he was thinking about doing, she knew it was major cause she knew her brother. She also knew he would need a clear and level head.

"Are you serious?" He asked her once she told him what Dok's phone number was.

He hung up the phone and cracked a brief smile. Only Dok would think of some shit like that. The smile quickly evaporated as he remembered his earlier thoughts about being a father.

His father was neva there for him as he was growing up. It fucked him up and scarred him mentally and emotionally. After he was grown, they had a bullshit broken relationship, but the nigga still had neva been there for him.

How could he follow in that niggaz footsteps he wondered? He may have been there financially and physically, but right now he wasn't being there emotionally.

"*Knock*! *Knock*!

"What's up?" He called out to whoever was knocking on the door.

"Brah, I need to holla at you." It was Batman.

"So, come holla, nigga."

Batman opened the door and walked into the room. Only a night light was on so it was dark in the room. The ECO speaker was playing low and Voorheeze was laid up on the bed with a plate of powder in his hands. He could tell by the thin layer of sweat on his forehead that Voorheeze was high.

Batman walked over to the desk in the corner and grabbed a chair then sat facing Voorheeze.

"Before you cut me off, brah. I need you to really listen to what I got to say." When Voorheeze nodded, he kept going "I ain't gone

164

lie, brah, I don't know how you feel. I can only imagine though and honestly you got a reason not to want your boys riding in the thick with you. But what else can we do? We don't have another uniform and we damn sure can't take that mothafucka nowhere and get the size taken in. More importantly he does have a point. If this shit go bad, them crackers on all of us tough. You can bet they gone investigate us tough. When that happens, it ain't gone matter what role you played. If we get caught, dey gone kill us. Period. In for a penny in for a dollar, dawg." The truth of Batman's words stung even more.

"That's why I'mma tell 'em both to cut. If we can't do this shit on our own, then fuck it, it ain't getting done!" He wasn't about to say fuck his kids like his father said fuck him.

"V. It's too late for that." When Voorheeze looked confused Batman broke it down.

"Like I said, these crackers gone dig all the way to the core. They gone find out about us practicing all our movements on the bikes . They can even track us to Windsor. I'm sorry, Robin, but the moment you called them you put them in it."

Once Voorheeze realized Batman was absolutely right, he silent tears fell from his eyes and slid down his cheeks. The anguish that he felt was unbearable. In a sense he had inadvertently become the same son of a bitch that his father had been.

"Vell, what the fuck did I do?" It was rare for him to call Batman by his real name, that's how fucked up he felt.

"Look, man ,'I'mma keep it real. Them lil niggaz ain't kids no more. You guided them and taught them well enough and long enough for 'em to make sound, conscious, decisions. Dey doing what dey wanna do, because dey wanna do it. Period, point blank! Dis shit ain't you fault. It just happens to be our life." Once he saw that he had his brotha's attention. He had to wake his game up.

"Now what you need to do is get off yo ass and get on yo feet! Dey might've chosen to rock with their cock out, but it's you job to keep them safe. You ain't bout to do that like that." He pointed to the plate then he stood up to leave.

Batman stopped at the door when he reached it and turned around. "And Robin. You're a better father then that man ever could've been. Now put my fucking chair back, nigga! Batman laughed his way out of the room.

When Batman closed the door Voorheeze couldn't do anything but laugh to himself. His brotha was crazier than a mothafucka, but he was right. Fuck some *"Poor Me"* shit! Now was the time to get active.

He made a nice line about a gram and some change and snorted it. The one thing the nigga was wrong about was Vanna White, when that bitch whispered in his ear he was on point! Fuck he mean put the shit down?

**** N. D. ****

"Come on Starr, we out." French Tip said to Cantelope before standing. Dok left about twenty minutes ago. Her conscious was fucking with her.

When they got up to leave their sisters followed them out of the club.

"What's up?" Cantelope asked her as French Tip reached inside of her pink and black Challenger for her other phone and took a seat.

"Starr I know I should be happy and focused on Satin Doll and Mom Snacks. But I can't be happy knowing that my brother needs me and instead of being there for him. I'm off doing me." She told Cantelope while she powered on the phone.

"So, what's up? We rock'n?" Cantelope already knew how French Tip felt about her brother. She been expecting this play ever since Voorheeze went incognito.

"Squad up." Was all she said replied.

Cantelope turned around with a Kool-Aid smile on her face as she shouted out.

"Let's go bitches, squad up!"

Lady J, Chocolate and Tasha were all smiles as they headed to their vehicles, ready to kill some shit. It had been a while since the

She-Wolves had seen any real action, and they were past ready to do the damn thing.

Once the phone was on, she clicked on the find my iPhone feature. After tapping in the login and password she looked for her brother's phone. Once the tracker was activated, she took off into the night with her sisters following her.

All the women had their own homes, but they shared a mini mansion which they often used before and after, a big job. With the death of Anne and the Twins retiring, they didn't use the house as frequently. They stopped by to grab their gear and to switch cars. Cantelope decided that their customized cars would draw too much attention considering how flashy they were.

Two hours later they were almost to Angel's Camp. French Tip picked up her phone and called her brother.

"What's up, beautiful?" He asked when he picked up the phone.

"Dok came out to see me today. He said he needed to talk to you. He left you a number, saying it was urgent." She relayed the message knowing what his response would be.

"Yeah, it's cool. Hold up let me get a pen."

"V. You don't need a pen!" She called into the phone before her brother got off the phone. "It's Neva Die 276."

After talking to him, French Tip was now convinced more than ever that her brother needed her. She could hear in his voice that he was higher than a mothafucka! A nigga couldn't think straight like that. Now as she reflected on it, this was the first time that she'd had to reflect on his mental state since he'd gotten out of the hospital.

She remembered walking into his house after they thought Clark was dead. Seeing all the empty picture frames, the shrine and the picture of Lisa that said Danika on it. Hell, yeah her brother needed her! Shit, he might need more mothafucking help then she could give him.

They pulled into the time share about ten minutes after she got off the phone with her brother. Lady Luck must've been on their side because the time share was relatively empty. That meant two things, they. couldn't draw too much attention and they also had ample parking spaces.

Still the Wolves were on point as they got out of their vehicles. French Tip Cantelope and Lady J all walked up to the door, the other ladies stayed posted up on security. The night was pitch black and they blended into the shadows.

Keak was the one to open the door. He had a banger in his hand and a mug on his face, until he saw who it was.

"Oh shit! What's up, auntie!" He stepped outside and bear hugged French Tip, lifting her completely off of her feet.

French Tip was by far Keak's favorite aunt. The only time anyone saw him acting over joyous was when he was around her.

"What's up, nephew?" She greeted him once he finally put her down. He stepped aside and let the three of them in. Keak greeted Cantelope and Lady J as they walked past him.

Inside the living room, D.J. and Kwashay were playing Madden. DJ always kept a PS4 in his trunk so he could take it wherever he went.

"What's up, y'all?" Was all he said when he looked up and saw them walk in.

DJ wasn't being rude. Niggaz just took that John Madden that seriously.

French Tip was shocked to see Kwashay there sitting on the couch engrossed in the game. Seeing him only confirmed her suspicions. Her brother was up to something big.

"D. ,what's up, nephew? What's up, Shay? Since y'all can't pause that silly ass game for one second, where yo Pops at?" French Tip wasn't tripping she knew how niggaz were about their John Madden. She didn't understand all the hoo-raw though. She just chalked it up as boys will be boys.

"Down the hall, last door on the left." This time he didn't even look up from the game.

She turned towards the hallway and headed into the living room.

"I got next. If you betting, I'll match whatever the bet is and I'm not trynna have problems up in dis bitch!" She heard Lady J tell them as she made her way down the hall.

Silently she said a prayer hoping they didn't make Lady J show her ass up in this suite.

"Come in." She heard her brother call out from behind the door when she knocked.

When French Tip stepped into the room she was shocked as hell. The room looked like a Military Command Post, A black tarp was dropped over the two windows. There were maps and blue prints that were all marked up, hanging on all of the walls inside the room. In the middle of the room was an eight-Foot long collapsible table. It was covered with enlarged maps and blue prints.

French Tip just stood there in awe trying to take it all in and figure out, just what the hell was going on. Voorheeze was bent over the table studying one of the maps. A desk lamp was on the table hanging just above his head, illuminating the map so he could see easier. He neva once looked up to see who came into the room.

After a moment or two more he spoke.

"What are you doing here? His eyes still neva left the map.

French almost asked him how he knew it was her, but then she reconsidered. Voorheeze stayed on his security. She wouldn't be surprised if the nigga had hidden cameras throughout this bitch.

"I could feel it in my heart that you needed me, so I came."

"You mean y'all came." That confirmed the camera hunch.

"When do you track me with your phone?" This time he took his eyes off of what he was doing, lifted up and focused on his little sister.

He stepped toward her outstretching his arms for a hug.

"Hey, Booger," he whispered into her ear as he hugged her like he was scared to let her go.

They hadn't seen each other since the night he'd killed their older brother. Unlike French Tip, Voorheeze didn't feel guilty about killing Clark. He did what had to be done. That nigga knew the rules to this shit. Although he didn't feel guilty it still fucked him up. After all, that was his big brother and he'd loved him dearly.

Even without the rules to the game, French Tip was his baby sister. It was his job to protect her. He would've killed Clark anyway, just based on that.

"He threatened someone I love, Booger." She knew exactly what he was talking about. His comment told her that it was bothering him too."

"I know, brother. I know." She whispered back to him, fighting the tears from falling.

French Tip felt like if she grieved Clark, she was slapping Voorheeze in the face for loving and protecting her. However, if she accepted what Voorheeze did without feeling remorse for Clark, she was shitting on his grave.

Finally, he pulled back breaking the embrace. He studied her for a moment, then turned his attention back to the maps on the table.

"You should not have come." He simply told her,

"Why what's all of this? What are you up to?" She asked him. She too walking over to the table and looking down at the maps. That she could now see, were maps of Sacramento, and Old Sacramento.

When he answered her, he still didn't break his concentration on the maps

"I'm gonna kill Jim Smith." He stated plainly.

She had heard some farfetched shit in her time, but she knew she had to be hearing wrong. She knew this mothafucka didn't just say he was going to kill Jim Smith, the leader of the white supremacist group! Shit she didn't like the racist mothafucka either but killing him...

Just then she thought maybe she should've stayed away. The thought faded just as quickly as it came. If her brother was about to become a terrorist, then she was about to become a motherfucking terrorist too! Cause she wasn't about to leave him or her nephews! Period!

CHAPTER XVI

"I know some of you are tired of meetings. I personally can understand that. We've been having so many meeting lately my head is spinning." S.A.C. Andreatta tried a rare moment of humor to lighten the mood. She knew the agents in the room were tired.

" For those of us in this room, I can assure you that with the exception of in the field briefings, we will not be having another meeting until this assignment is over and done with." That got their attention,. The agents begin to look alive. "First to quell any rumors and all guessing. We are still in pursuit of two of America's Most Wanted, Levell Jenkins and La'Mont Simpson."

"Based on the studied analysis, we have it on good authority that all of the prior acts of violence committed by this duo have been leading up to a climatic finish."

There were laptops in front of everyone. All of which were connected via Bluetooth to the laptop she was now pushing buttons on. Instantly, all the screens came to life. A PowerPoint was being played. It summed up all of the destruction the Bureau felt these two were responsible for. The presentation concluded with pictures of Jim Smith giving his speech in San Diego last month.

This puzzled everyone in the room except her team. While they were at the bar in Emeryville the A.D. called her giving her the green light. She'd told her team immediately.

"Uh excuse me ma'am, but why are we staring at a photo of Jim Smith?" It was special Agent Roberts who spoke up and asked the question.

She made sure to look him straight in the eyes when she responded. "We believe Jim Smith is, in fact, the next target."

The room as already silent to begin with, after she said that, a cemetery like silence overtook the room.

It was a four year agent by the name of Holly who broke the eerie silence.

"Special Agent, are you telling us that these two intend to try and kill Jim Smith?"

"That's exactly what I'm telling you! Our two teams have been selected to form a special task force to intercept them before they can carry out the heinous plot that they have concocted to further destroy the moral of our country. We have no idea as of yet which venue they will attempt to strike at whether San Francisco next week or Sacramento at the end of the month. So, we have to be ready for both because they plan to strike at one.

"We do not have a full detail. It will only be our two teams. Yet, the A.D. has assured me that any and every last resource that the Bureau has is at our disposal Fellas, we have one of the most important assignments that the Bureau has ever had with a very short, personal unit. It will be the seven of us in this room now, we will be joined late by Agent Allman." She pause to think if she had forgotten anything.

"Special Agent Andreatta, if this assignment is so important, which it sounds like it is. Why are we only using two smaller teams instead of two full security details? Hell, maybe even three?' Special Agent Roberts was a young, very intelligent Black man. He had one of the sharpest minds in the Bureau. There was even talk of him possibly becoming the director one day. But, even if his mind wasn't sharp, something about this still wouldn't feel right.

Only for a brief second she teetered on whether she should answer his question or not. Everyone waited to see if she would answer his question or not and if she did, what she would say.

It wasn't a hard decision. She personally felt that, if people were going to voluntarily risk their lives they at least should know why and what they were rushing in for.

"Because the analysis of the data collected and presented before us was done by me. I presented my findings to the A.D. who concurred with my findings and set up a meeting with the Director. The Director doesn't necessarily concur with the findings. He thinks they may be a little far-fetched. However, he sees enough truth and reasoning within the data to take necessary precautions. With it being election season and all, I don't blame him for being cautious." Andreatta was neva one to bite her tongue, she damn sure wasn't going to start now.

Everyone in the room got the innuendo. The Director believed the assignment was bullshit, he was only covering his ass because it was election year!

"Hell of a gamble. I'd hate to be him if your assessment is right and things go south." S.A. Roberts was throwing S.A.C. Andreatta a bone. She knew exactly what he was doing and made a mental note to thank him later.

"Well, for all of our sake, let's hope it doesn't go south." With those words, the meeting was over. It was time to work. They had a lot of work to do.

**** N. D. ****
Long Beach

"Bitch! Do I look like some Rooty Poot ass, Poot butt to you?" The question was followed by a back hand to the mouth.

The woman stumbled backwards from the blow. Blood ran down her chin from her busted lips.

"Fuck you! You o'le bitch ass, nigga. You think you hard cause you hit a woman, cuz? You ain't hard nigga, fuck you!"

The woman yelled as she attacked her attacker. She didn't have as much power behind her punches as a man, but she threw them mothafuckas with the speed of Mohammed Ali.

She connected a four piece with a biscuit to his chin and jaw. Her long red hair flared about like the Phoenix as she threw her punches. Punches that would've been much faster were it not for the big jacket she was wearing. The jacket looked out of place with the Crip blue booty shorts that she was wearing. More of her big, yellow, ass cheeks were hanging out of the shorts then was covered by them.

That didn't stop her from following up her punches with a quick three piece. Her ass cheeks bounced with every step and punch, drawing a crowd of spectators. The crowd of people had gathered to watch was going crazy!

"Aaw, bitch, you done lost yo fucking mind!" Baby Blue yelled out after Blue Tasha connected the last punches to his jaw.

173

This time he punched her in the jaw like she was a nigga. The punch knocked her on her ass. Cars were honking.

"You a fucking, pussy ass, nigga! Won't you fight a grown man instead of hitting on some little helpless girl! You o'le faggot ass, nigga! Some lady yelled out the window of her car as she drove by. When Baby Blue heard the bitch call him a faggot, he wanted to turn around and air that bitch out. It took all of his self-control to stick to the script.

"Aw, nigga come on, cuz!! Blow fo blow, nigga. Now I'm bout to knock you ass out!" Blue Tasha staggered back to her feet.

Everyone could hear police sirens ,but they didn't give a fuck! Everybody knew who Blue Tasha was. She was known in the hood for knocking niggaz out. Niggaz wanted to see this.

She quickly stepped in. Just like she figured, Baby Blue swung with a haymaker. She dipped low and to the left. When she came up his entire right side was exposed. She gave him a one-two to the body. The left stung his ribs while her right caught him in the solar plexus. He bent just slightly to his right side, stunned that he'd let her out maneuver him.

She stood up and gave him a two piece to the head that dazed him. She caught him just behind the ear with the left and followed with a stunning uppercut afterwards.

He wasn't faking, Baby Blue was actually dazed, Her adrenaline was driving her now so Blue Tasha moved in for the kill like a red nose pit-bull.

At that moment two police cars came screeching to a halt beside the gas station. They were responding to the call of a domestic disturbance that went out over the radio.

"Hey, Freeze!" One cop yelled.

"That's enough, Buddy!" Another one shouted.

This being Long Beach, the police knew not to draw their weapons. Too many times, the gangbangers high on PCP neva heard the words freeze. All they saw were monsters with guns, so they themselves drew down and opened fire.

It was now department policy not to draw their weapons unless the situation called for force.

Blue Tasha was still advancing.

"I said freeze, God Dammit!" The first cop yelled.

She looked at Baby Blue, who was smiling at her. She licked her lips and then blew a kiss at him. They both began unzipping their jackets.

It was the training Sargent who hadn't gotten out of the squad car, who peeped the move. He started to open the door so he could warn the two officers but it was too late!

Baby Blue stepped to his right making sure Blue Tasha was out of his way. The officer's eyes got as big as saucers at the sight of the Chinese AK 47 in his hands that was concealed under the heavy jacket he had on.

Blaaaada! Blaaada! Blaaaada! Blaada! When he squeezed the trigger. The cop who was yelling freeze got hit with a barrage of bullets that chopped his chest up and tore off the entire side of his face.

Blue Tasha spun around with a viscous looking Mac 12 in her hands. *Taaat! Taaat! Taaat! Taaat! Taat* 380 bullets ripped through the other cop. Knocking him on his ass!

They both walked steadily toward their prey. The Sergeant was on his knees praying when they walked up on him. They looked at each other then back at the Sergeant. "Black lives matter, Cuz! They opened fire simultaneously, knocking his face off and various other parts off of him.

After walking to the two cops that were down, they filled their bodies with the remainder of the bullets.

The deadly duo reloaded their weapons and headed for their 64' Impala. Most of the spectators kept it moving when the shooting started, all except Lil Half Bread and his team. Their job was to make sure that the two Big Homies got away.

When they drove off, Tiny Locs looked at the gas station owners dead body bent over the counter. If he would've showed them where the CD player was for the cameras, he would be alive. Now ,he could go talk to the same God that the sergeant was praying to. Only, he could not go to talk to him face to face.

Up ahead they could see Blue Tasha kissing on Baby Blue. It was a deep, wet, lust filled kiss.

"Gawd Damn!" She yelled when she finally broke the kiss. She took a few deep breaths before she tried to speak.

"Daddy, you had a me so turned out I didn't know what to do!"

"You almost made me knock yo crazy ass out! Fuck you trynna do, punk me in front of the little homies." Baby Blue was dead serious.

"Aaw, come on, Daddy." She purred as she snuggled up close to him.

"If you promise to be gangsta, I'll let you knock this pussy out."

"All I know is Gangsta, Cuz. I'mma Long Beach Rollin 20 Crip, cuz! That's all I know. Now hit the Big Homie and let 'em know C's up." Baby Blue grabbed a half a blunt out the ashtray.

Blue Tasha picked up the phone to carry out the order.

CHAPTER XVII
San Francisco, a week later

It was very bright and beautiful, sunny, Saturday afternoon. There was a slight gentle breeze coming off of the San Francisco Bay.

Two young college kids held banners in their hands that read "MAGA:. One was white. He stood 6'3. his buddy was a Hispanic kid who stood almost 5'8." The street they stood on was Hayes Street.

Around the corner on McAllister Street, a white couple walked hand and hand, slowly making their way through the crowds of people that had gathered for today's speech. He was shorter than her. She was slim whereas he was husky, but they looked good together.

A young black couple was on the outskirts of the crowd gathered on Van Ness Street. Both of them had on matching "MAGA" T-Shirts and campaign hats. The t-shirts had the slogan 'Make America Great Again" underneath the acronym "MAGA." His t-shirt barely fit his muscular torso and his hat was pulled down low on his eyebrows. She on the other hand, looked like she should be a runway model with her petite, curvy body that complimented a face that was made for the big screen.

They were downtown San Francisco gathered at City Hall listening to Jim Smith give his speech. They've been in place for two hours now, scanning the crowd and studying faces. They were looking for the slightest tell-tell signs of their two suspected Terrorists or any of their affiliates. They were all Federal Agents, undercover assigned to the special strike team formed to prevent the assassination of Jim Smith.

S.A.C. Andreatta was positioned in the heart of it all. She was a mere two feet away from the steps leading up of the podium. Not only was she a marksman with any pistol she was also top ten of the entire bureau in hand to hand combat. If anyone tried to breach the barriers at the front of the crowd, she would put them down without question.

"Special Agent Roberts, anything?" She discreetly spoke in other comms, 160 yards behind her, the young black man in the

"MAGA" clothes and hat discreetly spoke into his on microphone. "So, far we're not picking up on anything. There were a couple maybes but none panned out." He was referring to the portable, digital, hand held Ultrasonic ex-ray device that his partner Agent Allman was secretly scanning the crowd with.

The miniature machine was the equivalent to having an x-ray machine in your hands. The Feds have had this device for a few years. It neva got the popularity that inventors had hoped because the Feds found it much more beneficial secretly using it on the Urban communities, without them knowing.

"Copy that. Night Hawk, how are we looking?" She spoke again. This time hidden within a man-made shaft connected inside of the silver and gold dome of City Hall, Agent Holly answered.

"Chief, I don't see any threats or possible threats. But, I'm ready should the need arise."

Agent Holly was a highly decorated Delta Force Sargent before joining the bureau. Though he didn't brag about it, he had seventy-seven confirmed sniper kills in battle and a few unverified. In other words, he knew what he was doing with a sniper rifle.

The dome of City Hall had the secret ducts built into them for these type of scenarios.

**** N. D. ****

In the courtyard was Agent Galarza aka The Walking Death. He'd received this nick name because to date he had twenty-three kills while on the force. He was Internal Affairs private pain in the ass. They had gone after him a dozen times. Yet, all of his kills had been ruled justifiable. Although he has neva been in any form of military service, he carries himself like a real mercenary.

He smoked a Marlboro Red as he eyed a black man who looked like he is just idly walking around.

"Come on, you son of a bitch, just give me a fucking reason." He mumbled to himself as his heart rate climbed.

The adrenaline that surged through Agent Galarza every time he engaged someone was euphoric. It's a high all of its own. He lived for it.

"Agent Galarza, anything?" Just the sound of her fucking voice made his skin crawl.

"Fuckin' bitch, should be a school teacher." He say to himself.

"Agent Galarza, do you have anything to report?" The frustration is clear in her voice as she asked again.

"If anything moved on this end I would've dropped it where it stood, Special Agent in Charge." He refused to say her name.

Her and all the other females who ran around acting like men, he figured they should all go fuck themselves, then kill themselves. Galarza's definition of a woman was Suzie Home Maker.

S.A.C Andreatta couldn't stand the smug son of a bitch. When the A.D told her he would pair her team with Roberts's team, she dreaded it because of Galarza. Everyone hated him. He was an excellent agent and that fact only made him more of an asshole.

Now wasn't the time or the place, but she promised herself that after this, she would formally let him know exactly who he was fucking with.

"Everyone keeps your eyes open and stay alert. I'm sure he'll be wrapping up shortly." She instructed.

**** N. D. ****
Meanwhile

Voorheeze slid his wet tongue down the center of her back. He paused to plant soft kisses on both sides of her lower back. They were e already covered with sweat because they had been at it for over an hour.

Her pussy lips were swollen and sore from the beating he had put down. She'd stopped counting her orgasms after five. The first three were served right in his mouth and Voorheeze greedily drank them down.

What followed that was a pounding of a lifetime. It was a shock the neighbors didn't call the police, as loud as she was screaming and hollering for Jesus. He had her exhausted, feeling like she was nineteen all over again.

Over an hour later and Voorheeze still hadn't climaxed He figured now that he had her attention, he would wake her game up!

His soft kisses had him back up her back. When he got to her neck he gently nipped her neck. A moan escaped her partially parted lips. She could feel the imprint of her Steele hard dick pressing up against her ass cheek. When he bit her irresistible body. The wet sweat that covered her body made it resemble melted milk chocolate. His dick jumped and smacked her ass at the sight of her body.

"Roll over." He whispered softly into her ear. But, to her it sounded thunderous like a might roar from Heaven.

She bit her bottom lip and slightly opened her legs while her eyes were closed, in anticipation of his rod once again being buried deep inside of her.

Sweat dropped off of his face unto her huge beast as he hovered over them, licking his lips. His neck and hips were in sync. Voorheeze lowered, his head ready to swallow her thick nipple with his mouth at the same time that his manhood penetrated her heavenly gates.

"Ssss" inhaled through her teeth as Voorheeze penetrated her while taking as much of her breast into his hot mouth as he could.

She arched her back from the pleasure. This allowed every inch of him a free passage so he hit rock bottom and buried himself balls deep inside of her. He just stayed there while he feasted of that one tit.

"Oooh…Yes….Ssss. Oooh" the way she was moving and grinding under him he didn't have to move.

"Mmmm this feels sooo good! Mmmm"

She kept on grinding. Not only was his dick touching every hidden corner from the way she was rotating, the top of his shaft was rubbing up against her clitoris along with his pubic hair.

The combination was building another orgasm. Her head felt like it would incinerate, she was on fire.

Fuck that! This was his show! He couldn't let her take over. He had to show her after all these years.

He began sliding in and out of her slowly. He was moving like she as a delicate virgin. IN and out slowly, he snaked his way through that pussy.

"Aaaaaw…Shyyyyyyt Daddy! Ssss, Mmmm."

Now she controlled her slithering to match his slow, powerful, deep thrust. If someone would've video tapped it, this is what Love Making 101 looked like.

His left hand squeezed and massaged her other tit. Fuck raining, that pussy was flooding his dick. The knocking above his head was a different thump from the head board.

He looked up and noticed the head board was banging so hard into the wall, that the sign that hung above the bed was smacking the wall too. He smiled when he read the sign Mr. & Mrs. Simpson."

She grabbed both sides of his ass and tried to force him deeper. As he stroked in and out of her, he felt his balls swell in preparation to cum.

First he licked then he bit down on her right tit where his name was tattooed.

Bang! Bang!

Knock…. knock.

Bang!

Bang!

He began speeding up!

"Talk to me, daddy! Fuck me, daddy! Daddy, fuck me! She shouted over and over

Bang!

Bang!

"Fuck!" Voorheeze yelled as he woke up. The shit felt so real.

He grabbed his rock-hard dick that was standing at attention.

"What's up?" He called out to whoever was knocking at the door.

"Brother, you need to check it out." French Tip called sheepishly through the door.

"Aaight, here I come" He smiled as he responded knowing that they knew he would've flashed on anyone else for waking him up.

He laid back for a brief moment and thought about the dream. Mr. and Mrs. Simpson the sign read.

"Damn, Lisa I'm sorry." He whispered once he realized that it could neva be reality. His guilt had him questioning his own methods and actions. Here he was madly in love with Lisa, but fucking the dog shit out of Vieira. The fact that he was only doing it for the cause, didn't make him feel any better.

He threw some sweats on and went to see what's up.

In the living room everyone was gathered watching KPIX/CBS5 news on the flat screen. He didn't say a word. He stood and listened while Dana King reported from the anchor desk about the rise in attacks towards the police in California. Although they refused to play the video of Batman calling on the gangstas in the United States to take a stand for themselves. There was a clip of the beginning of the video shown next to her while she talked.

"One officer was killed in an area of Los Angeles known for being a Bounty Hunters neighborhood just this morning. The day before yesterday, while making a traffic stop in Watts, a veteran officer was gunned down by a passing motorist. All of this seems to have followed a triple Homicide of three police officers down in Long Beach."

The footage of the killings at the gas station was very poor. It seemed that a good Samaritan took the video from an old cell phone from across the street. It showed a couple engaged in a domestic dispute which concluded with the couple turning on the officers that responded, killing them in cold blood.

She went on to talk about Jim Smith's rallies on making America better. The reporter also speculated on whether or not Jim Smith would continue his tour in the wake of the string of violence.

Batman was smiling ear to ear when he looked over at Voorheeze and asked him. "Do I see the Bat sign in the sky?"

"That bitch is gleaming, nigga." He responded with a corny ass smile on his own face.

It's was hard to believe that two stone-cold killers could be so fucking goofy. They took that Batman and Robin shit to heart.

"Okay why the fuck you two so happy? This right here gone put some shit in the game." Cantelope already didn't want to be here. She thought killing Jim Smith for the fuck of it was the dumbest shit she had ever heard of.

Now if some paper was on the line, she could feel that. Getting it how you lived was the American way. She stayed and went along with this fuckery solely on the strength of French Tip. Now after all their time training and shit, it looked like it wasn't even going to pop off now.

"Naw, cousin, dis ain't gone put no shit in the game." He rubbed his hands together, licking his lips and looking like a mad scientist."

"This actually helps us more." Seeing that they were lost he broke it down. "Aaight peep, game check play. See, Jim Smith is so fucking arrogant and cocky, that he won't even consider someone trynna get at him, let alone some niggaz. So he's coming hands down! If he doesn't, his racist ass gone feel like he's a coward to some ignorant niggaz. Now security agents, on the other hand, along with the rest of them pigs, they gone be so mothafuck'n spooked that they gone bump security up like it's Dooms Day in dis bitch! It's gonna be so many cops that nobody will pay attention to us. It will just be two more cops in uniform riding motorcycles." Voorheeze was smiling like a high school freshman who fucked the captain of the varsity cheerleading squad.

"Nigga, is you crazy?" Cantelope was looking at him like he'd lost his mind.

He hadn't told them the part about them dressing as police officers yet. He was holding that for the punch line.

"Bat shit crazy!" There was no smile on his face. "But, I guarantee this shit gone work, cousin."

Right on cue, Kwashay walked into the living room like a kid who saw the teacher's panties. He was carrying a metal box in one hand and a weird gadget in his other hand. If that wasn't weird enough, he had on a police motorcycle helmet with the visor flipped up.

"Alright now, dis shit is going too far! What the fuck is all of this? French Tip called out at the sight of Kwashay. then she erupted in laughter.

He looked so damn goofy standing there that everyone couldn't help but to laugh at his big ass.

"Laugh all you want, sis. I bet you mothafuckas stop laughing after this." He puts the oversized lunch box on the counter. Then he pulled something out of his pocket that looked like a dart and tossed it in the air a few times and caught it.

"This right here, it'll take too long to try and explain. Just know…" He threw it hard up against the wall. Nothing happened. "Know that it is unbreakable and completely safe. He walked over and picked it up. For the first time they realized he was holding a type of gun.

"This button right here" he pointed to a red button at the top of the gun. "This activates the bullet. Trust me we don't want do that now." He smiled before pointing to a button on the side of the gun where the safety should be "hitting this button is like putting one in the chamber. There's 3-D retina display inside the visor of the helmet for the lazar painting of your target. The lazar itself is invisible to the eye. It can only be seen on the lens inside of the visor. Once it's pained it doesn't matter where it's pointed after you've painted your target. The bullet will finds its destination. Big Brah put the box by the door. Everybody else stand over here in the kitchen unless you wanna get shot." Once that was done, Kwashay painted the box with the Laser then walked to the back room.

"Aaight! Watch out now!" He called out from the back.

They waited, anticipating some type of bang from the gun itself. What they heard, instead, was a sound similar to disk soaring through the air.

"*Ssssmack*!

They all looked on shocked as the oversized lunch pail rocked back and forth. The dart was protruding from it.

Kwashay came out of the back happier than a parent watching their kid graduate. "Now that's that H-Town, shit!"

"That's what's up, Lil Brah!" Voorheeze knew his lil brah would come through. This was why he sent for him. This was way more then he'd expected though.

Kwashay had felt like shit when the bike went down and he'd fucked himself up. He'd felt he needed to make it up to them so he put his all into his project.

"Okay, hold up. Now understand this, cause it's really some life and death shit." He pressed the red button at the top of the gun. The dart like bullet began to illuminate. The greenish liquid inside glowed.

Everyone stood there wondering what kind of James Bond shit they were seeing.

"Once the red button is pushed and the bullet is activated, shit ain't a game. This little mothafucka will bring two Sky Scrapers down." He hit the red button again. Instantly it stopped glowing. "Harmless as a butterfly. Once it's activated, it will blow in ten seconds. I can adjust the time if you want. I've also got a remote-control detonator that can both activate it and detonate it." He held up something that looked like a zippo lighter.

"Nigga, you in here throwing bombs around this bitch like dirt rocks! Have you lost your mothafuck'n mind?" To say that Lady "J" lost her composure would be an understatement.

"The chemical components which make up the liquid explosive are completely harmless unless activated by these." He held his hands up showing the devices. "Without it, a feather could do you more harm.

No-one else said a word. They all looked at Kwashay like he was the mad scientist, until Voorheeze finally spoke.

"Let me see that." He said reaching for the gun.

Kwashay grabbed his gun, like Voorheeze he got familiar with it.

The buzz of the excitement was over so everybody went back to chilling except for Keak.

They'd all been training and planning so hard these past couple of weeks that they took the day off just to lounge.

Keak was stoked. He hated the fuck out of rednecks. Ever since he first learned about slavery in school, he'd hated everything about them, from their wet dog smell to their pink fucking skin. Being able to kill the racist ass, lying ass Jim Smith would be the best shit he could ever imagine. With that in mind, he made sure he was just as familiar with the shit as Kwashay.

CHAPTER XVIII
Milpitas

What's good wit it, sis?" J. Styles answered the call after seeing French Tip's number on the screen.

"What's up, brah? I'm just checking in with you to see how school's going and to make sure you're straight." She told him.

"I'm good, sis, you know me. Got this one new teacher, she be giving niggaz hella fucking work to do. But, me and a couple classmates we studied together and knock that shit out."

"You need me to call your teacher and get her to lighten the work load?" She asked. Seeing if he would tell her the work load is too much.

"Wow!.... I'm surprised you would even come at me like that." He told her feeling offended. "You know I'm the smartest cat in the class! Cut the homework? You might wanna tell 'em to throw in a couple test or pop quizzes or something!" He joked into the phone.

She knew he was only covering his feelings. She had to make a mental note to apologize to him later in person.

"Alright then. Grandma has been feeling a little sick so we gone stay here a bit longer. Will you be good on your own a while longer?"

"Sis, I'm straight, don't worry about me. You just make sure NaNa's alright."

"I'll call you later and check on you."

"Aight, sis." J. Styles hung up the phone and took a hit of the blunt he was smoking before the call come through.

He savored the taste of the purple in his mouth as if filled his lungs. Sure, there was all that new shit out right now, but Styles was old school when it came to his weed. So, he only smoked 'Grand Daddy Purple. Every now and then he'd fuck with the Platinum Cookies, but that was it.

"What's up wit sis and them?" C-Murda asked from the passenger seat.

Styles blew out a thick cloud of smoke before responding.

"Shit. You know sis, she just staying on point. Making sure niggaz on they square."

"I feel it." C-Murda left it at that. If Styles wanted to tell him more, he would've done so. Murda leaned back against the Italian Ostrich seat and hit the blunt as his mind drifted to the little chick he'd met the other night.

J. Styles, on the other hand, was thinking about the four kilos of heroin that was in the back. They had taken a hard hit when Clark defected. Then, after Dok and Gunz split it was almost a crippling blow. A blow that could've easily been the final blow that did the Mobb in for good. Because of all of this, J. Styles stayed on his grind.

Somebody had to step up and with C-Murda by his side, Styles did just that. He always believed that he didn't need to be the head of the table to be a boss. J. Styles had been making power moves for years now. He had $120,000 worth of heroin right now in the back of the track for a connect that he'd found. This particular buyer was good for four keys a week. If $480,000 a month on one client wasn't boss shit he didn't know what was!

A while back Voorheeze had taught them all how to spit talk, the best form of code talking there was. One conversation could mean a number of things. It all depended on the initial topic. The conversation with French Tip could've meant new heat from the police was causing problems. Or even new competition taking away some clientele. In this case though, he was letting her know that the new shipment arrived and it was extra chunky

They were on their way to East Side San Jose to drop these off. Afterwards they had something small to straighten out before making five more drops today. Niggaz in the Bay Area were getting money. But, how many mothafuckas could say they touched damn near a mill (million) in one fucking day?

Now that...Was that Neva Die Shit!

**** N. D. ****
An empty warehouse somewhere in the Bay Area

Everybody was tired after a day of being out in the sun on their feet. The day was incident free. There wasn't so much as a J-walking citation issued.

S.A.C. Andreatta was in a good mood, still. Even though the threat assessment of Jim Smith being attacked was her win. She would rather the attack didn't take place than for her to be right. Not everyone agreed with that philosophy.

Agent Galarza felt this whole assignment was bullshit! He knew damn well two mothafuckas from the streets wouldn't try and attempt some shit as crazy as killing Jim Smith. He knew that the moment they were given this assignment. To make matters even worse, they were following the orders of some incompetent she bitch!

His frustration showed clearly on his face as he entered the warehouse. This warehouse was their base of operations. And old factory warehouse the government seized years ago from a drug dealer who used the warehouse as a drug depot.

S.A.C. Andreatta was the first to enter the old warehouse followed by Agents Garcia, Daly and Holy. Special Agents Finnegan and Roberts were directly behind Agent Galarza. They could both tell Galarza's attitude from all of his huffing and puffing and mumbling under his breath the entire way back.

"Okay, listen up guys!" Andreatta called to get everyone's attention. "I know everybody's tired. It's been a long week, so, I'll be brief. Take tomorrow off to rest. Be here at 2:30 a.m. the day after tomorrow. Don't think that because today was peaceful that this threat isn't real because I assure you it is. I could feel it out there today." S.A. Roberts nodded his head in agreement because he felt the exact same tingle and pull at his instincts today out there. "With all of my years of experience I believe Sacramento is it. We got to be ready. Galarza?" She called while stretching. She wanted to loosen up her muscles especially where her wound was.

"What?" his complete lack of respect was forcing her hand.

"If I give you an order in the field, if I ask you a question. I don't care about your little boy in the sand box attitude, you will answer the question and carry out that command without question or hesitation! You got that?" Even with her being roughly ten feet away from him, the fire that burned in her eyes that was proof of her controlled anger. It could be seen clearly.

Like a stubborn child being scolded, he just stood there in defiance!

The only person in the room not holding their breath was S.A. Finnegan. He had a huge smile on his face. He was the only one in the building who had ever seen her prove a point.

"I see" she said after realizing he wasn't going to respond.

"I can be disrespectful too", turning towards the table, she turned and took her service weapon out of her holster and placed it on the table while she was doing she told him." In case you're not intelligent enough to realize it, Agent, we are still in the field." She cracked her neck and her knuckles and then she walked up and got directly in his face.

S.A Roberts looked over to Finnegan, knowing that he had been around her the longest and gave him a head nod like 'what's up." The smile on Finnegan's face became a grin as he shrugged his shoulders saying "I don't know"

"And I just gave you a directive stating that while we are in the field and you are under my command you "will" answer all of my questions. Now you could be a good field Agent and answer the question. Or you can be a spoiled little boy and not say a word." She got even closer to where he could smell the sweet fruity smell from the energy drink she drank earlier.

"But I promise you, if you keep testing me, I will kick your motherfucking ass all over this warehouse like you were my bitch and make you answer my question!"

This white girl is crazy. Agent Allman thought walking up. She waited outside making sure no-one followed them here. She was just entering into the warehouse and wondered just what she'd walked into.

Garcia and Daly were stunned. Sure, Finnegan told them stories about their fearless leader. But they thought he was only trying to scare them.

Agent Galarza was about to be his normal self and say something else rude to the little, manly, whore. Something in her eyes stopped him. The anger and fire was gone. He knew he had to be crazy cause he could swear that her eyes were smiling! She wanted him to say something slick.

They were taunting him. Screaming "Motherfucka I wish you would." He looked around at everybody staring at him. He was more embarrassed than if he had shit smeared all on his face.

He couldn't let her get away with this! But what could he do? He knew about her MMA background and her reputation. Sure, he was being an asshole but he didn't think she would go this far.

"Are you going to follow command or do I have to teach you your place?" She really did want to fuck the guy up but fuck it!

"Wait! Wait!" He yelled just as she was swinging to knock his fucking head off.

"Y-Yeah. Yeah. I got you! I don't have a problem following orders or answering questions." He may be embarrassed but he realized he would really be embarrassed if everybody saw her kick his ass.

"Good! Everybody out of here and get some rest....She paused with a smirk on her face.

"That's an order!" She couldn't help it, she had to have some fun.

She didn't have to tell them twice. Everyone left immediately, each in their own world. Most were thinking about what just took place with shock and amusement.

Agent Galarza was still utterly embarrassed about having his card pulled. His mind was set on paying the little, dyke acting, bitch back for what she'd just did! His ego was so bruised, right now he was thinking thoughts that could get him life in prison.

Agent Allman picked up her cell phone as she got into her vehicle. She was thanking God for the time off as she punched in some numbers.

"We need to talk." Four simple words were all she spoke and then she hung up the phone.

**** N. D. ****
Later that night

Dok sat in his lazy boy recliner inside his den with a glass of Cognac in his hand, a cigar in his mouth and the world on his shoulders. Jeanette was sound asleep in the master bedroom, oblivious to the perils that haunted her husband. She'd gone to bed over an hour ago, when he received his visitor.

Dok couldn't believe the shit that he heard.

They say that being the best and most efficient leader is knowing when and how to lead. A leader often finds himself having to make the tough decisions. The calls that no-one else could make. That's the penalty of leadership.

This was far beyond a tough decisions. This was the type of shit that could either destroy someone's entire existence or make a mothafucka legendary. Some Matrix "Red or Blue pill" type of shit.

Dok twirled the cigar in his mouth as he inhaled the smoke. The sweet smoke rolled across his tongue like his thoughts rolled across his mind.

It wasn't a matter of making the right decision, he only had one decision he felt he could make. Anything else would not be an option! He could only hope that its execution was flawless. Anything less than perfection would cost them everything!

In his heart he knew forty-five minutes ago what he was going to do. He just needed time to digest and except it.

He sat the glass of Cognac down, grabbed the phone and dialed a number.

Mtambo picked up on the first ring.

CHAPTER XIX
Sacramento, 2 ½ weeks later

Governor Costa was testing the limits of his patience and tolerance level by hosting a dinner for Jim Smith, a politician that most government officials knew was a racist. He was wealthy, donated lots of money to charity and always talked about building a better America for all people. But those that knew him well, knew that he hated anyone that wasn't white and his better America was whites only. To say that he hated the fucking guy would be on understatement. In fact, it would be the understatement of a lifetime.

The entire night it took everything that he had in his reserved strength to keep his composure. As a political diplomat he always had to live his life as if someone was watching. So, the Governor had long since mastered the art of deception and hidden faces, Everything he'd ever learned was being tested tonight.

The Governor sat in his lounge with a room full of politicians and two wealthy contributors, listening to the asshole sound more and more moronic with every word that he spoke.

"…..You see although everyone knows how I feel you will neva catch me making phrases like them people or their kind." He pointed towards the senator of Oregon as he spoke. "Scott, you know as well as anyone that a duck can't change his feather's twice. Although I haven't had a need to change my feathers I've utilized its meaning when I needed to do what needed to be done. See I tell you guys that's why my work is so important. Them darkies are getting out of hand and they need to be contained." Jim Smith was smiling like what he said was the equivalent to the Gettysburg Address.

Massachusetts Senator Elizabeth Warren looked beyond confused at hearing his words. "So, what do the African American people have to do with your work?"

As always the question lingers in the air while Jim Smith looks at his watch. When he's finished he looks up at the senator and smiles.

"Mrs. Warren, come on now." He makes a gesture with his right arm palm facing up like. "You know" as he continues speaking. "We all know that where there is crime they are there. Wherever there's illegality, they have part in it. See, my foreign policy will let the world know that we have a zero tolerance to bullshit." He told her.

"The only bullshit that's anywhere, is coming from you. It's always came from you, from your corrupt campaign to the way you've managed to bully the investigation. You, sir, are the disgrace to American People." Howard Schultz doesn't have political ties. He's a Billionaire CEO of Starbucks, who happens to be throwing his hat in the ring for 2020 race for the Presidency. It was him who spoke.

The look on Jim Smith's face was priceless. Pure rage neva looked so evil. It only lasted a very brief moment. Most didn't catch it. Michael Bloomberg, the other billionaire in the room was one of the people who did. As a former Republican turned Democrat, he loved to see Smith sweat.

"You gotta admit, Jim. You've managed to dodge some pretty hefty bullets so far. One could only wonder just how many more you can dodge. And at the rate that they've been coming you're due for one right now." Michael Bloomberg told Jim Smith as he savored the taste of his hand rolled, special blend cigar.

At eight hundred dollars apiece, his cigar was worth more than all of theirs combined.

Jim Smith was not too smart of an individual. Yet, he was far from a dummy.

"See, Michael, what you and Howard fail to realize is that I am Jim Smith. I don't spend my time worrying over mediocre things like you do. If I want something done ,it's done." Although this was said with poise, one could tell Smith was irate by the position his toupee slipped to.

It was Senate Majority Leader Mitchell Connell of Kentucky, sensing the coming fireworks, who changed the subject. "Mr. Smith, have you heard the rumors about the supposed plot against you?"

"You know, Mitch. I've heard the rumors but I gotta be honest with you. He took a pull on his cigar rolled the smoke around his tongue and blew the smoke and before finishing he leaned back in his chair and said. "I believe that has got to be by far the most outrageous crock of bologna I have ever heard."

All conversation ceased when a knock came on the door.

"You may enter," the Governor called out.

His wife Khaury came in and walked over to him. She hated the smell of cigar smoke. If this wasn't important she would've neva come to this room.

When she bent over to whisper in her husband's ear one of the men almost had a heart attack! He'd neva in all his years seen an ass that big especially one being less than two feet away from his face.

No-one in the room could blame him for the way that he was staring at Khaury's ass because they were all staring the exact same way. All except Senator Warren. The way she was staring at the big o'le ass would make any director of a porn movie cast her as the star character, confirming the many rumors that the Senator is in fact a lesbian.

Governor Costa was well aware of the fact that all eyes was on his wife's juicy ass as she left the room. That is why he'd staged the make shift emergency. He knew his wife's ass was to die for and he got a kick out of knowing others fantasized about it but he was the one indeed fucking it. The distraction was a good way for him to control the conversation.

"Now where were we?" He asked with a huge smile on his face as he turned back to the room.

****** N. D. ******
Meanwhile at Angels Camp

"I love you like oxygen, Booger. I can't breathe without you." Voorheeze was squeezing French Tip so tightly in a hug that she could barely breathe.

"Aaaw, brother I love you too!" The tear that slid down her cheek is not one of sorrow.

The tear is from the love that she felt knowing that her brother's affection is genuine and pure, she'd always known how much her brother loved her. Still, she feels it now more than ever.

"Don't cry, Booger." He told her as he broke the embrace and wiped her tears away. "Remember no weakness, always show strength."

"Happiness is strength, brother. I'm crying because I'm happy." The big smile on her face proved it.

Voorheeze took a step back and turned to address his family. He took a deep breath to gather his thoughts then he spoke.

"Look we all know what time it is. We all know what's what. So, I'm not about to make no long drawn out speech. I love each and every one of you more than I could ever say. What we are about to do, ain't no telling where that's gone lead us. We all know that everybody ain't bout to make it. It is what it is. I'd rather die for what I believe in then to live in shame any day. This started as some personal shit to make then pay for what they did to T'Rida. Now it's grown into something bigger than any of us. Let's make them mothafuckas respect our gangsta!" He looked at every face in front of him and for the first time he didn't see his folks. He saw his people….Black People "One Aim One Struggle One Goal!"

They all called out "Neva Die!"

"That's what's up!" Voorheeze called out afterwards.

They were at the farm where Batman had killed San Joaquin Deputy Purtle on live video feed. Voorheeze decided they should move there the day after Kwashay completed the explosives. He figured they would draw too much attention moving around at Angel's Camp and there were too many of them to have been caged up in the suite. When Batman told him about the farm it was a no brainer.

The She-Wolves were the first to leave, everybody knew what they needed to do. Tomorrow would be the moment of truth. They were either gone shit or get off the pot.

"What you thinking bout, Robin?" Batman came walking up to Voorheeze.

"Brah, shit.." He took a big deep breath and blew the air out. "Brah, I'm trynna figure out if I made the right choice letting them get involved.

Batman knew his brother conscience was bothering him because of how big his heart was. "Truthfully, I don't think you could've stopped 'em. Especially yo boyz, them niggaz love you to death. Shit, nigga, you wasn't stopping them.'

"There you go with that ,shit. Them lil niggaz think they gangsters. Nigga, I ain't that old yet. They'll still do what I tell 'em."

"I can't stop them." Voorheeze mumbled to himself shaking his head.

"Oh yeah, here we go. O'le big, bad ass, Jason Voorheeze!" Batman was walking around with his arms out wide at his sides imitating a giant.

"What you doing? Showing brah, what his future wife look like?" Everybody busted out laughing at Kwashay' s comment as him and the boys walked up.

DJ had a bottle of Remy in his hands. Keak had a blunt already rolled. Then figured since this might be their last night together that they might as well have one for the road.

**** N. D. ****
Meanwhile

An armed escort was in the lead vehicle as well as the end vehicle. Both vehicles were bullet proof as was the limousine they were escorting. Two guards were in the front SUV and two armed guards were escorting. Two guards were in the front SUV and two armed guards were in the back.

"Uh, guys, looks like we got a broken-down school bus up ahead" The passenger of the first SUV called into the mic.

"Can you get around it, Steve or is it a total blockage?" Patrick Mahoney, Lead Agent for the convoy, asked.

"That's a negative, the position of the bus has the entire road blocked off."

"Any signs of foul play?"

"Uh, no, sir. Looks like some old guy struggling to change a flat air. Request permission to take a closer look, sir." Agent Steven Laney radioed back.

It was a nice quiet morning. Light traffic so far on the roads, clear skies with a promise of sunshine. All in all, it was the making of a beautiful day Agent Laney was thinking to himself with a smile on his face.

"Keep your eyes and ears open, Steve. See what's going on with this guy. We may need to back it up and take another route." L.A. Mahoney instructed.

"Roger that, sir." Agent. Laney responded as he climbed out the Triple Black Chevy Tahoe.

His head stayed on constant swivel and his eyes alert, taking in everything about the surroundings. Part of his mind was at ease knowing that his partner Ramirez had his back.

In was one of the old 1990's school busses and from the looks of it the thing it should've been out of commission a long time ago.

"Say uh, how's it going today, sir?" Agent. Laney asked the older gentleman whose back was to him. he was busy messing with the tire.

Agent Laney figured surely the old guy must be hard of hearing because he kept right on fussing over the tire. Neva one acknowledging his presence.

He took a step closer and bent down. He placed his left hand on the old guy's right shoulder and said. "Excuse me there sir, do you by any chance need a hand here?"

The old man slowly turned his upper body around in response to the question and the arm that was resting on his shoulder.

The smile on Agent Laney's face instantly disappeared while his eyes became as big as saucers. He stumbled backwards and opened his mouth. Nothing ever came out.

**** N. D. ****

Agent Tang looked in the rearview mirror at the two approaching vehicles. One was a navy blue Chevy Trail Blazer. Behind it was a black Jeep Grand Cherokee.

From the passenger seat he looked at his boss. "Hope we can get her moved. Looks like back tracking is no longer an option."

Lead Agent. Mahoney turned around to see what Tang was talking about. Something was all wrong about the Trail Blazer. He couldn't quite put his finger on it, but something was off.

"Holy Shit!" At the alarm in Tang's voice Mahoney spun back around in his seat.

He was just in time to see Agent Laney's dead body falling backwards. He wasn't in time to see the old man blow the back of Laney's head off like Tang did.

"Son of a bitch! Radio it in, we need back up!" His voice trailed off as he watched the passenger and driver's door open up and two men climb out with assault rifles in their hands.

He wasn't worried about the bullets of the assault rifles penetrating the bullet proof armor. However, seeing the type of artillery they were carrying told him that these weren't amateurs.

"Uh sir! Sir! We got movement at the back of the bus sir." Agent. Fitzgerald's was so scared that his voice squeaked. "Heavy arms, sir! What do I do? What do I do, sir?" The sound that pierced the morning air in response was not the answer he was looking for.

**** N. D. ****

BOCCA! BOCCA!

The sound of gun fire drew her attention away from the work that she was going over. She looked up with a horrific look on her face.

"What's going on, Samuel?" She asked the Agent who sat across form her. The panic was clearly audible in her voice.

"Nothing to be alarmed about maam. There's a minor situation that is being tended to." He tried to reassure her, but failed terribly.

199

Senator Harrison worked very hard her entire life fighting through setbacks and adversity to get to where she was today. The first African American Female Senator of the State of California. One thing that didn't help her achieve her position was ignorance or stupidity. Two gunshots and the constant radio static she could hear coming from his ear piece didn't sound like a minor situation to her.

Her heart began beating faster as she wondered what was really going on outside. The drawn partition and the tinted windows prevented her from seeing what was going on.

"Samuel, that sounds like gun shots. That's not a minor situation Samuel. Not to me. Now I asked you what is going on and I expect you to be honest with me." Though she tried to sound stern, the quaking of her voice confirmed her fear.

The thunderous sounds that erupted through the air proved there wasn't anything minor about what was going on.

The huge barrel was the first thing to stick up thru the open window. The second thing that followed was the thick lion like mane of dreadlocks. They hung over a pair of eyes that looked like they belonged to the devil.

The big, black, mothafucka who was behind the gun looked himself like he had escaped the brimstone gates of hell. His butter yellow teeth seemed like they were glaring in contrast to his midnight, black skin. The smile was indeed satanic.

****

"*KUNK*! *KUNK*!*KUNK*!

The mightiest sound to ever be heard by human ears was the firing of the 50 Cal Gatlin Gun. Its massive missile-like bullets chopped through the armored plating with ease. The monster behind the big gun laughed maniacally as Agent Fitzgerald body was thrown violently all over the drivers and passenger seat of the Tahoe.

In less than five seconds the SUV resembled an abandoned personnel vehicle in Desert Storm. The windshield was blown backwards into the lifeless body.

The two men carrying the AK-47's walked up toward the sides of the second escort vehicle and took huge steps back. A third figure in all black came strutting up to the vehicle.

The white men inside stared at the sexy figure with awe. The skin tight, tights that wrapped around and covered a set of long, thick, luscious legs that belonged on a panty hose commercial instead of or an assassin.

When she got close to the driver's door she smiled and lifted her hands. Those hands held five pineapple grenades. The men inside didn't know if they should take their chances with the pineapples or with the assault rifles and exit the vehicle.

The shooters already knew the answer to the question regarding the armor holding up. They were there in case the Agents tested their luck outside. The AK47's would quickly put an end to that. She tossed the grenades under the truck and everyone backed up even further. They waited in anticipation of the blast.

"Oh my God! Samuel what in God's name is going on?" Senator Harrison screamed loudly after hearing the 50 Cal as it made mincemeat out of the first Tahoe.

"Calm down, Senator. Everything will be fine." He didn't believe himself. Being ex-military, he knew the sound of a Gatlin Gun.

"That doesn't sound like everything is fucking fine, Samuel!

KAMOOM! BOOM! BOOM!

The force of the multiple explosions sent the Tahoe three feet into the air.

BOOM! BOOM!

The last two grenades exploded seconds later!

Looking at her face he could tell that the Senator was screaming. He couldn't hear a sound though because the blast temporarily took away his hearing. The limousine shook violently from the shock waves. He could only imagine how frightened she was because he was scared shitless himself!

TATA! TAT! TAT! TATA! TAT!

The distinctive sound of two AK 47's erupted loudly vibrating through the Limo next. Senator Harrison was in complete shambles. She had no idea what was going on. It sounded like they had driven right into the middle of a war zone.

Tears of fright flowed from the Senators eyes, as she was on the verge of hysteria. The gun fire ceased. The loud pounding that Senator still heard was the sound of her own heartbeat. She looked to Agent Samuel Peterson for some type of assurance but the gun in his shaky hands and the look of uncertainty on his face told her that she was looking in the wrong place.

"Senator Harrison, my name is La'Trisha Combs.. "The voice was sultry and smooth yet very powerful. "Senator, I have direct orders to retrieve you and lead you to a safe secret location. Senator, time is of the essence here."

Agent Samuel whispered." Don't listen to her Senator. It's all lies.

"I assure you that you will be leaving here with us. The question is under what circumstance and condition. You can open up the door and step out like a lady and I assure you no harm will come to you. Or I can throw five live grenades under the limo. I promise you if necessary we will drag your body out of there. I'll give you five seconds maam to make up your mind. Please don't make me blow you up." Trisha learned a long time ago that fear was the best motivator there was so she knew that the Senator would come out. She also knew that the Agent would play hero.

Senator Harrison was scared shitless, but she was no dummy. With all of the wreckage and carnage caused today. there was no doubt in her mind that the woman would do exactly what she said.

Agent Samuel was warning against it, but she wasn't trying to hear shit he was saying. The Senator told the driver to unlock the doors. He was only too happy to oblige, shit, he was just a driver he wasn't trying to get involved in shit.

She opened the door, took a deep breath and slowly climbed out of the limo. The morning sun greeted her, causing her to squint from its brightness. It took a moment for her eyes to adjust to the light. While she stood motionless, her heart raced a thousand miles an hour.

Finally, when she could see, the Senator's eyes took in the features of one of the most beautiful woman she had ever laid eyes on. Her smooth brown skin resembled cocoa butter. She stood 5'4 with jet black hair that made her jet-black eyes that much more deadly.

"Thank you, Senator. I assure you, we mean you no harm maam. But, we must go now, please follow me." Trisha told her.

The two men holding the Ak-47 lead the way. The Senator and Trisha followed, leaving the limo sitting vulnerably in the midst of the wreckage.

Senator Harrison couldn't believe her eyes as she looked around at the destruction and carnage. It actually looked like a war zone. Smoke was in the air, still arising from the blown-up car. The smell of gun powder was very thick.

They were heading to the two SUV's in the back. The look on the Senator's face was horrific disbelief.

"Believe me, there was no other way. They would have neva given up. And trust me, the people need you." Trisha was saying this they reached the Grand Cherokee.

"*POW!*

As if to prove the point of what she'd just said, a single shot rang out. Trisha placed a comforting hand on the Senator's back, gently urging her to climb inside the truck. There was no need to look back for confirmation. She already knew Agent Samuel couldn't live with the fact that he had just sat there while the Senator was abducted.

He had tried to make a last-minute heroic stand thinking that they were dumb enough to leave him unattended. Unfortunately, the sniper that Trisha had ready for that play sent a 7.62 x 5lmm missile that plowed into his skull through the center of his forehead. The mightily force of the impact snapped his neck and knocked his body up against that limo.

In less than twenty seconds the entire cadre had disappeared.

After riding in a fear-driven silence for ten minutes, Senator Harrison found the courage to muster up a question for her captor.

"Young lady, you stated that you were taking me to a safe and secure location. Dare I ask what the meaning of all of this is? Who or what are you protecting me from? And why do you care?" Behind the fear, strong and intense piercing eyes looked at Trisha.

After what she'd just gone through Trisha figured the Senator could use a little information to help calm her nerves. She figured it couldn't hurt anything.

Trisha smiled at the Senator and told her, "Maam, I'm here to save your life. Trisha explained there was a hit out on her. The only way to protect her was by kidnapping her. They were informed that Jim Smith's group was behind the planned hit. Smith felt she was getting too big and too much exposure helping people of color. She shared about the organization and explained everything they were trying to build. She also left the Senator enough money to continue her good work in building up urban communities. The Senator was very much aware of the corruption in the government but she had a strong belief in peaceful protests and non-violence. So, she didn't agree with their methods.."

**** N. D. ****
Later that night at the Governor's Mansion

The 100 plus years old Victorian-style Mansion was built in 1877 originally for Albert and Clemenza Gallatin, neither of whom held any political position. Albert was just a mothafucka with money who built his wife a house.

He scaled the concrete wall that ran along the Historic Alley. His all black fatigues and stealthy movements made him nearly invisible to the naked eye. The night was pitch black and still. One of those moonless nights that made people uneasy. The air was bone chilling with zero wind factor.

It didn't take any time at all for him to scale up to the second story balcony. Once he safely made it, he took a moment to quiet his breathing. When you are 262 pounds, scaling anything was work, no matter how fit you are.

Once inside the very old house, he made his way silently to his destination. With so many rooms inside of the mansion one could easily get lost and spend over and hour looking for the right room. Good thing that Mtambo knew exactly where he was going.

The room he just came out of housed a beautiful hand-crafted marble fireplace. It had crafted hinges with doorknobs on them. This let him know that he was close to his target. He'd studied the layout of the floor so much that he knew exactly where everything was.

He stalked down the hallway, all his senses on high alert. The Persian rugs that his feet stepped on aided in his stealth, drowning out all sounds of footsteps.

He reached his destination and stood immobile for a full minute. The light snoring of his intended victim was barely audible through the thick door.

With the silent speed of a trained predator, he opened the door and entered the bedroom. There was no need to close the door behind him because he wouldn't be in there long. In his hand was an all-black SIG Sauer P226 with a silencer on it.

PSST! PSSST! PSSST!

The sound was barely audible. Three quick taps of the trigger seat, three slugs into the victim's head. The small twitch of the body and the breath that escaped its lips, were signs of a direct hit and clean kill

Mtambo spun around on his heels and exited the mansion the same way that he came. Not a soul would know of tonight's activities until tomorrow afternoon.

De'Kari

CHAPTER XX
5:09 A.M.

The bathroom was full of steam from the hot shower. Voorheeze reached for the baby oil and squirted a generous amount over his muscular, scar covered body. The water began beading up quickly all over his body because of the baby oil. Next, he stepped out of the shower and walked toward the sink. As he walked, the beads of water escaped from his body like a refugee. He'd been air drying like this all of his adult life.

After turning the cold water on, he cupped his hands under the nozzle filling them up with the ice cold water and splashing it in his face six or seven times. The contrast from the piping hot shower to the ice-cold water on his face was exhilarating. The feeling was indescribable.

He took one hand full of water and wiped the mirror clear. Then he splashed more water on his face. When he stood tall and looked in the mirror he doesn't see his face. His mind sends him years back in time"

His homeboy Kevin was a young hot Poet taking the Poetry Circuit by storm. To show his folks some love and support he and T'Rida went to Tommy T's with some of the family to check him out. His first poem titled "What If" silenced the room and had everybody up in that joint on some reflection shit. Including Voorheeze and T'Rida.

"What if God froze time
And gave you a split second to make a better decision?
What would you do?
Would you even care, or would you just push through?
"What if you died today?
Do you think people would care?
How well do you know yourself?
Anyone can be a dad. I just want to be a father.
Every minute of every hour
I just want to lead the way
Show them a righteous path. But....

What would happen if I died today?

His eyes blinked and he shook his head trying to clear the cob webs. He didn't know why that memory came to him right then.

He remembered that he and T'Rida shared a look that spoke volumes at the end of the poem. For a young white boy, Kev was deep. Voorheeze remembered thinking that if niggaz recited this poem before every major decision that they made, then mothafuckas would do a whole lot less of the dumb ass shit that niggaz did.

He didn't know why he flashed back to then or why he thought of that poem, but a chill ran down his spine leaving goose bumps in its wake.

He threw more cold water on his face and shook his head some more. Now was not the time to be getting all philosophical and shit. Motherfuckers had shit to do, with that he left out the bathroom to get dressed.

**** N. D. ****
6:22 a.m.

"Alright now. I want everyone to keep their eyes and ears open. With all that we've seen we still don't know what these guys are fully capable of. Nor do we know when they plan to attack. So, from the moment we touch ground everything's live!" S.A.C. Andreatta addressed both teams before they headed out.

Her wounded shoulder tingled and her gut rumbled with intuition. She knew that she was correct. Today would be the day and God dammit she was ready.

"Any questions?" Looking around she waited a second to see if anyone would say anything. "Finnegan, give me a moment. Everybody else, let's load up."

The two crews gathered their gear and loaded their perspective vehicles. Andreatta waited patiently until everyone was out of ear shot.

"So, chief, what's up?" S.A.C. Finneagan asked. Although he had a feeling it had something to do with Galarza.

She didn't waste any time beating around the bush.

"I don't like the way Galarza has been acting. I don't trust him. I didn't even before what transpired a few weeks ago. I want you to keep an eye on him."

Finnegan had to admit to himself that Agent Galarza had been acting funny. He didn't think that he would jeopardize an operation.

Even so, he knew his place was to follow orders, not to give his opinion. "I got you, Chief. Whatever you say." He told her.

"Be safe out there. Now, let's go catch these bastards." She grabbed her duffle bag and headed to her vehicle where Agent Garcia was already waiting for her.

Meanwhile Agent Galarza was already behind the wheel of his black Chevy Tahoe. He glared at S.A.C. Andreatta while she walked to the passenger seat of the Charger. The amount of heat coming from him was unbelievable.

Agent Finnegan observed it all.

**** N. D. ****
2:17 p.m.

Lil Trill was walking down 10th St. He had to maneuver and barge his way through the heavy crowd that lined the street. Concert stage speakers and amplifiers carried Jim Smith's voice for a mile in every direction from the steps of the Capital Building.

Smith began his speech at 2:00 p.m. precisely. Lil Trill wasn't late. He was on time, if not early. He wasn't here to hear the Smith's speech. He was here to get a glimpse of Jim Smith himself. Just like so many of the rest of the patriotic Americans that lined and crowded all of the sidewalks surrounding the State's Capital.

His black True Religions, eggshell Louis Vuitton button down shirt, bald head Caesar fade and Louis Vuitton spectacles on his face, gave Lil Trill the look of a student at SAC state instead of one of the member of a notorious gang. The Louis bag hanging off of his shoulder matched the look perfectly. It resembled a nice book bag.

He finally made it to L St. and turned left. His destination was somewhere in between 11th St. and Lincoln Highway. He reached his destination, adjusted his bag and waited patiently for Jim Smith to drive by.

****

Meanwhile

Lil Yankee-AR was on the opposite side of the street dressed similar to Lil Trill in a pair of Black Cavalli Jeans, white button down and Gucci frames. A Gucci knap sack was over his shoulder as he waited.

Lil Yankee A.R. was more of a people person then Lil Trill. It was only natural that he would engage the people around him in conversation especially the white women. His jet-black skin and well-toned body gave him the appearance of the singer Akon. Only that face was on a body that resembled Wesley Snipes back in the Passenger 57 days.

One white lady in particular couldn't help herself. While all of them in the area talked an joked, she couldn't keep her eyes and hands off of him. Twice, when her eyes lingered on him, he looked at her only to have her lick her lips seductively at him and bite down on her bottom lip. She was a natural blonde with tanned skin, big o'le Dolly Parton titties and a nice ass, all on a 5'8 170 lb. frame. She was wearing white Daisy Dukes with a tank top that lost the battle holding her big ass chest in place.

Lil Yankee A.R. was a young, spunky nigga. So, under normal conditions he'd blow her back out. But, that wasn't what he was there to do. At one point she pressed her monstrous breast up against him and whispered in his ear, "My pussy is so wet, she's drowning." Just when he was about to let his fingers play 'Slip and slide' in all that wet-wet, he looked down and read the words. 'Make America Great Again." On her tank top and it snapped him back to reality,

"Just wait, I'mma really make it wet." He whispered back in her ears.

Her response was to turn around and plant her plump ass up against his dick. He didn't have a problem with that at all. When she started rubbing that mothafucka back and forth, his lil man woke up fast.

He looked around him and realized that they were standing shoulder to shoulder. No-one could see what was going on. So, he said fuck it and wrapped both arms around her.

He let his left-hand slide in her pants and wreak havoc on her pussy that was every bit as wet as she climbed. When she reached around and pulled his dick out and jacked him off. All he could think was. "White Bitches, go Yankee!

****

S.A.C. Andreatta checked her watch for the thousandth time. It was 2:27 p.m. It had only been ten minutes since she last checked her watch, but it felt like hours.

Her makeup was very clammy from the sweat. The temperature was a good 89 degrees on this sunny day. Looking at her one would think the sweat was from the sun that was beaming down. In actuality it was caused by her nerves. She was so far on edge she couldn't move.

"Eagle one, status?" She spoke into her comm.

"Uh, nothing's changed, chief. Everything's still calm." Agent Holly's voice came back in her ear. He was positioned on top of the Capital building scanning the crowd through the 5K scope attached to his British Sniper Rifle with a range of 1400 meters.

Andreatta didn't understand it. She felt it in her guy that this was going to be it. Hell, she could still feel it now!

Again, she checked her watch. The two teams were spread all throughout the crowd surrounding the State Capitol. There was a set of eyes covering every entry point of area they deemed likely for some sort of sabotage.

Jim Smith was nearing the end of his speech. Though it was unlikely, she was actually beginning to question herself. Could it be that she was wrong? Did she allow the trauma from being shot to cloud her thinking? If so she didn't care about the embarrassment.

She could live with that. What she couldn't do is live with herself if her instincts were correct yet she didn't act on them.

****

16 minutes later

Lil Trill had just finished taking off his button down and putting it inside of the Louie bag. No-one was paying him any attention. Everyone in the crowd was busy looking towards the street. They were anticipating the security team with the fancy line of cars, trucks, motorcycles and security that Smith was known for when he traveled (he thought he was on the Presidents level since he came from generations of influential people and long money). . They were scheduled to come up this street any minute now.

No sooner did he stand up, now wearing the white T-Shirt that was under his button down. He looked down the street and all the vehicles were just turning on to L St. from 15th St.

****

Lil Yankee-A.R turned his head in the direction of the vehicles. Something in the distance caught his attention. He turned his head back in that direction. He was staring at the North East Side of the Capital Building.

Everyone around him was looking to the left but he was looking right.

He couldn't see it anymore. "Where did it go?" He wondered. Right when he was getting ready to turn his head back towards the vehicles he saw it again. It was right there clear as day.

Light was reflecting off of something. No doubt there was a sniper on the roof. "Fuck 'Em!" He told himself, it'll be what it be because that thing in his hands was about to wake this bitch up!

There were eight motorcycle cops at the front of the vehicles in two columns. Four bikes road in each column. Two bullet proof black Suburban's followed that. Followed by Smith's limo which was followed by two black Tahoe's and eight more bikes.

The vehicles crossed 13ᵗʰ St. this caused Lil Yankee-A.R. to turn his attention back towards that direction. The motorcycles were just passing where he was.

When Jim Smith's vehicle was passing by him a mighty roar went up through the air and vibrated the ground. Two all-black Ducati 1299 Superleggera's came speeding up the street.

****

The 1,285cc engine 215 horse powered bike vibrated powerfully underneath him as DJ pushed the twin-cylinders to the limit. As bad as he wanted to look over at Batman and Lady J, he knew that he was traveling too fast to risk taking his eyes off the road.

The carbon fiber wheels were spinning so fast that they appeared to be motionless. They zoomed by so fast that no-one had time to react.

"Brace yourself, cousin" he spoke into the mic built into the helmet. Cantelope's response was to wrap her arms tighter around his waist.

He squeezed the clutch, threw the bike in neutral and murdered the brake.

The Agent was frantic. All sorts of codes and commands were being screamed inside of the vehicles. People outside couldn't see through the tints. If they could they would see bodies and heads turning in every direction.

The motorcycle cops didn't know what to make of the two super bikes. The first thing that came to mind was pranksters and thrill seekers, like those guys that streak across the field butt ass naked at baseball games and football games.

Aaaaarrrrrghhhhhh!

Clouds of smoke filled the air along with the smell of burnt rubber, as the tires skidded to a loud, screeching stop. The smoke completely concealed both bikes and their riders.

Nobody saw Cantelope as she swung her thick leather clad leg around fractions of a second faster than Lady J. Both women had Military Galil's strapped to their bodies.

Blaaada, blaaada, blaada, blaada, blaada, blaaada
The reflection of the flame from the tip of the barrels could be seen in the visions of their helmets.

Pandemonium was not a strong enough word to use to describe the hellacious tumult that followed. The hollow point 5.56 mm's tore through the bullet proof vests of the cops with ease.

As the bullets caused the cops to jerk, the big Harley Road Kings they were riding became too much for the cops to control.

Blaaada! Blaaada! Blaaada!

The ladies didn't let up as the cops went down. They continued to empty the full 100-round C-Mag drums.

People were literally fighting each other while screaming, trying their best to get to safety. In the chaos no-one took the time to realize that the police were the target. When people heard gun shots, they got the fuck out the way. Or at least they tried to.

BOC!

The sound of a single rifle shot echoed through the air. The shot forced people to pause momentarily in fear of where the bullet would land.

****

The crack of the high-powered rifle snapped Lil Trill out of his daze. When the Ducati's first came to a halt, he looked that way like everybody else. The random gunfire that came after had him stunned.

Until now.

With the heart of a lion, Lil Trill barged through people. He was throwing 'bows like he was in one of the clubs of Atlanta. The young killer took aim at the motorcycle cop that was closest to the streets. Them niggaz in L.A. have been giving the police the blues ever since them Neva Die niggaz made that video. It was time to let mothafuckas know what that Underworld Zilla was about.

"Black Lives Matter! Uzzzz. Underworld Zilla, nigga!" He yelled out at the top of his lungs.

Taata! Taata! Taata! Taata! *Taata!*

214

****

The vehicles came to a complete stop when the gunfire from the front started. The motorcycle cops all froze temporarily, not knowing what to do. This made things easier for Voorheeze ,who was at the back of the motor cade passing as a motorcycle cop.

Voorheeze broke formation and rolled up the outer flank of the column. All gangster shit aside, he was nervous as hell. He was sweating like a run-a-way slave under his helmet. While his heart thumped away in his chest.

In his right hand was the dart gun that Kwashay made. It was already locked and loaded. Ready for him to squeeze the trigger and shoot. Seconds later he felt he was close enough to take the shot.

Irregular movement to his right caught his attention he couldn't allow himself to be distracted. From the hip he aimed and took the shot. The titanium tip dart penetrated the armor of the vehicle beneath the metal fender. Once secure, its claws came out of the dart clasping it tight.

The erratic movement caught his attention again. This time he turned his head in that direction. It was a good thing that he did.

"Black Lives Matter! Uzzzz! Underworld Zilla Nigga!" Black Live Matter was on the little niggaz white T in big, bold, blood red letters. Neither the shot nor him yelling is what got Voorheeze attention. The Baby AR-15 that he had pointed directly at Voorheeze demanded his full attention.

Taata! Taata! Taaata! Taaata! Taata!

The shooter opened fire.

****

FBI! MOVE! Move out of the way! All teams this is team leader! Move! converge on L St. I'm heading south towards 11th. Smith's Convey is under attack. I repeat the Smith is under attack! Everyone converge on the convey!" S.A.C. Andreatta yelled as she pushed and elbowed people out of the way.

"Hold up, lady!" Some random jack ass said as he tried to grab her.

She didn't have time for bullshit. Her right arm came up with the speed of lightening. When it came down she made sure it was with force.

Crack!

The sound of his nose breaking, was the result of the service weapon that was in her hand colliding into his face. Blood sprayed everywhere! She turned her head so it wouldn't spray her face.

The blistering sun was causing her to sweat profusely. This almost caused the 9mm to slip out her hands.

Taaata! Taata! Taata! Taata! Taata!

S.A.C. Andreatta almost jumped out of her skin. The devil had to be a lie, because there was no way what she was seeing was real. Not even ten feet in front of her off to the left., a young black man had opened fire on the police.

"FBI! Drop your weapon!" The gunman just continued to fire.

"FREEZE!"

POP! POP!

He staggered forward but didn't go down.

"Come on buddy, don't do this to me. Go down buddy." She mumbled under her breath. She was poised, ready to do what it looked like he didn't want to do, put him on his ass

BOCACAA! A loud bang was followed by a long echo.

The young man holding the assault rifle was lifted off of his feet from the force of a sniper's bullet violently crashing into his chest. The .50 caliber bullet destroyed his heart when it tunneled straight through it. Lil Trill's lifeless body was thrown ferociously up against a white man who was looking down at his brand new white MAGA T-Shirt. The stunned look on his face had to do with the rapidly spreading red stain messing up his shirt. If he could scream he would but the bullet that exited Lil Trill pierced his lung making it difficult to get air.

"Thanks, Eagle one." She spoke into her commas.

"Chief, I didn't take the shot." Holly responded.

"Everyone, we got bogies in the field. Heads up." All the Agents "Roger that" for acknowledgement..

S.A.C. Andreatta made her way to the suspect to confirm her guess. He was dead. People were looking at her like she was a science experiment until she picked up the Baby AR he had dropped.

She made her way through the people that was still stampeding.

Scuurrrrr! Kunk! Kunk! Kunk! Pop! Pop! Pop!
BOCA! KUNK! BOC! KUNK! KUNK! KUNK!

It sounded like a war was going at the front of the convoy. People went from frantic to berserk. Agents had decided enough was enough, they were getting Jim Smith out of there. The loud horn of the Suburban drew attention as the drivers swung the trucks toward the sidewalk.

Pedestrian life was meaningless as those who didn't get out of the way were mowed down. S.A.C. Andreatta had neva seen anything like this in her life. They were actually running Americans over with no regard to human life.

She made her way over to of the motorcycle cop who was down. He was the first one to go down when Lil Trill opened fire.

Andreatta knew it would be best to announce her presence. "FBI, are you okay ...."

****

The force of the high-powered slug to knocked Cantelope back down in the seat. DJ heard her scream seconds before she crashed into his back.

"We got a sniper on the roof! Cantelope's been hit, we got to get outta here!" He called out through his comms that were connected to the blue tooth inside of his helmet. "Hang on cousin, I got you!" After telling Cantelope this. DJ threw the Ducati in gear and gunned it.

Batman watched in horror from the other bike as Cantelope flew backward off the back of the bike. Instantly, he and Lady J bounced off of their bikes and returned fire at the motorcycle cops who hadn't been gunned down and the agents that climbed out of the first Suburban.

Both Lady J and Batman knew, with the sniper being out there, they could die any minute. That understanding only gave them more adrenaline. Hell, for then it was NEVA DIE TILL THE CASKET DROPPED!

Taaata! Taata! Taata! In unison they let the Galil's in their hands spit round after round.

Lady J only had enough ammo for one burst before she clicked on empty. She used two clips in the first hail of shots. Just when she looked over Batman to call out of him.

Scuuuuuuurrrrrrrrr!

Two customized triple black Lincoln MKT's appeared from nowhere. They skidded to a halt in front of Batman and Lady J as well as DJ and Cantelope

DJ hopped off the bike and rushed to Cantelope's side. As soon as he looked up at the truck, its customized door slid open.

"Throw the women in the truck! Y'all do it moving on the bikes!" Some big nigga with Rasta dreadlocks shouted out.

DJ brought his Galil around and pointed at him. "Who do fuck is you, nigga?"

"Dragon Gang! Now let's go!"

While they were talking, the side, door slid horizontally on the second truck. Rell was a sight for sore eyes!

Kunk! Kunk! Kunk! Kunk!

"Dragon Gang! Bitch!" He shouted before opening fire.

He held his finger clamped on the trigger and swung that .50 Cal Gatlin Gun like Sampson. The downed Harley's bucked and flipped as the bullets slammed into them. It looked like a Hollywood action movie.

The Agents scrambled to get back into their Suburban's. The armored plates in their trucks meant little to the big gun. Lil Rell didn't let up. He chopped the shit out of everything.

On the other side of the Lincoln, DJ wasn't about to be swindled by a nigga he didn't know. He had a decision to make, fast. Trust the nigga or kill him.

"Damu, Askari! Mimi Venus WeWe Gaidi Jamaa." Hearing his Swahilli name called was enough to catch Batman's attention, because it was a name he neva used. But the declaration that the nigga was part of the guerilla family gave him answers.

"Lady J., help get Cantelope in the truck. Y'all ride…" His words was interrupted when a bullet from Agent Holly's rifle knocked him off his feet.

****

"Got it!" Cuana was finally able to locate the FBI sniper when he fired that shot.

She adjusted the optics on her Scope, held her breath with her tongue out and took the shot. One minute she was seeing his head, the next a cloud of red filled the lens. She turned her attention back to Voorheeze. After killing Lil Trill, Cuana saw the Fed bitch approaching him. She didn't want to take her eyes off him but that sniper was fucking shit up. So, as much as she wanted to aide her comrade, she knew she had to take care of the sniper. He was the imminent threat! She had to kill him first.

De'Kari

CHAPTER XXI

FBI. Are you okay, buddy?" Voorheeze was turning around as the words left her lips.

He stepped fully into the swing and connected with his right fist. She flew backward like the nigga in Friday, when D-Bo knocked him out. The baby A-R fell out of her hands. He didn't even wait for her body to land before he took off heading toward the Hyatt Regency.

"In foot pursuit of suspect Simpson! Suspect was last seen running in the direction of Hyatt Regency Hotel. Suspect is disguised as a motorcycle officer. I repeat. Simpson is wearing police uniform. Full motorcycle gear." God damn S.A.C. Andreatta's head and jaw hurt like hell.

She's neva been hit so hard in all her life. Little did she know the only reason she wasn't knocked out was because Voorheeze is left handed. He'd punched her with his right.

She shook her head and retrieved the assault rifle. What was left of the Smith's security team continued running over Pedestrians. Andreatta ran in the opposite direction after the motherfucker she'd been chasing for months!

****

He looked over his shoulder as he knocked people out of the way. He didn't see her anywhere but Voorheeze could feel the bitch on his heels.

"Hey, watch it guy! Oh, sorry officer." The white man didn't see the uniform when he felt Voorheeze bump into him. He neva felt the left hook that knocked him out and broke his jaw either.

Voorheeze kept pushing. Finally, he broke away from the thick crowd and was able to run. Some people looked at the big black cop sprinting full speed away from the problem instead of towards it. The majority of people were too preoccupied with staying alive.

Voorheeze was an old school gangsta. Wasn't no skinny jeans ever going on him. As he struggled to run in the tight ass motorcycle pants, he couldn't help wondering how a grown man could wear those pants so tight.

As he made his way to the front of the lobby he slowed down his pace. A bunch of rich onlookers were crowding the mezzanine, trying to get a look. He took one last look back, then entered the door to the lobby.

****

Meanwhile

Now was not the time to see where they were hit or how bad it was. Lady J and DJ got Cantelope and Batman inside the Lincoln.

Batman told them that it was good. That the niggaz were on their side. Now they had to pray his judgment was good.

While the two of them got on the bikes Mtambo called out. "We good back here."

Suja spoke into his mouthpiece. "Ndugu let's go."

With precision both trucks backed up and made reverse U-turns in sync. Suja looked to his right just as the shot-up Suburban was turning the corner on 10th Street. He locked eyes with the driver and smiled.

****

The minute Voorheeze went down Keak grabbed the Glock .40 that he was carrying, His heart told him to knock the little niggaz dick in the dirt. His mind told him stick to the script. His had won out.

That was a good thing because he was on his bike, ready for whatever when the agents started to drive off. Before pulling off Keak saw his Pops knock the white bitch smooth off her feet.

Jim Smith's convoy or at least what was left of it, was now miles away from the disaster area. One agents Suburban, one Tahoe and five motorcycle cops were all that was left of the protection team. The lead Suburban broke down two blocks away from the fire zone. The two agents that were inside jumped into the other truck and they continued on.

Keak positioned his bike sideways at the beginning of the on ramp. It looked as if he was sealing off the ramp so no one else could get on. He climbed off of his bike.

Sirens could be heard off in the distance. No doubt heading to L Street. Inside of his hand was a small device he'd retrieved from his pocket.

"Black Lives Really Matter, my nigga." He said to himself before he pressed his thumb on the button.

K-A-B-O-OM!

Even at over a mile down the freeway, the blast concussion was formidable where Keak was. He had to use all of his strength to keep the big Road King upright. He didn't have to wonder about the results. A blast that big no doubt, killed.

A huge black smoke cloud mushroomed in the sky over the Freeway. Horns could be heard now blending in with the rest of the noise. The sound track of destruction!

Jim Smith was dead!

****

Meanwhile

Lil Yankee A.R. got his name cause he was known to get on shit with an AR-15 or the Baby A.R. Much like the one he held in his hands.

He started to seize the moment when the shooting started but the mayhem that followed shocked him to the point of mobile paralysis. Neva in all his nineteen years had he witnessed anything remarkably close to this shit.

When he finally broke out of the paralysis, the only emotion that drove his young heart was fear. Fear saturated every ounce of his body.

He dropped the AR right where he stood. Since he was kicked out of his parents' home at sixteen, he'd been trying desperately to make a name for himself. He'd succeeded in making that name.

Unfortunately, all of his bodies were either unarmed or unsuspecting niggaz. Seeing an actual battle unfold before his eyes was traumatizing.

He was knocked back and forth as he did his best to push through the rambunctious crowd. They thunderous roar of the 50 cal. sounded to him like the voice of God!

His heart thumped like tribal drums.

Tink!

A bullet ricochet off of a pole less than a foot from his head. This caused Lil Yankee A.R. to dive toward the ground. A fat white bitch had the same thought. When they collided, she screamed at the top of her lungs. The woman thought Yankee A.R, was attacking her. This drew attention of some who were running by as well as a few police officers who had responded to everything.

Lil Yankee A.R. climbed to his feet nervously. He tried to help the woman up. She only made a bigger scene. He was about to take off when…

"He's one of them!" Like everybody else he looked to see where the conviction came from "Right There! Somebody! That guy right there! He's one of them!"

The white bitch from earlier that was having her very own sexfest with him was bouncing up and down in the middle of the streets pointing at him screaming her head off. Her antics and words caused people to stare including the cops.

"I saw him with a gun." As her words registered so did the BLACK LIVES MATTER! Spelled across his chest in blood red letters.

"Freeze!" They drew their guns in unison.

After instructing him to lie down with his hands clasp behind his head. an officer cuffed Lil Yankee A.R.

He hadn't busted a grape in a food fight with boots on ,still he was getting locked up.

****

Meanwhile

He was only passing the fourth floor and already Voorheeze legs was burning like he'd been running bleachers for an hour back in high school. He wasn't about to make it too much further.

After running inside the hotel, he raced to the stairs. He didn't have a destination. He was moving all on impulse. At the landing for the fifth floor he decided to catch his breath until he heard someone running up the stairs below. Before he stopped he didn't hear her over his own heavy breathing.

Instincts told him to dip out the stairwell and he listened to his instincts. The hallway seemed like it ran on for miles. He knew that was his mind fucking with his out of shape ass.

Voorheeze believed he had passed nine or ten doors before he saw a room ahead of him with a nigga who was just putting his key card in the door. He had gotten off of the elevator and was walking towards his room when Voorheeze opened the door at the end of the hall. He hadn't seen Voorheeze cause he was busy sending a text a message on his phone.

Voorheeze barged into him like a middle linebacker forcing the nigga into the room and causing him to drop his shit. Voorheeze quickly closed the door.

"What the fuck?" The nigga called out.

As he was going head first into the wall, he was pulling his .40 Cal off his hip. He spun around with it pointed at Voorheeze. Seeing the police uniform he immediately lowered it and began stuttering.

"I-I got I got a permit for this."

Voorheeze ushered the nigga to the front room to get him away from the door.

"Daddy, what the fuck is going on?"

"Bitch, what I tell you 'bout questioning me, hoe?" The nigga called out.

"S-Sorry D-Daddy I was j-just making sure you were okay."

Voorheeze had seen it all but if this shit didn't take the cake nothing would. Standing asshole, butt naked, dripping with water and soap suds was a little white midget. She couldn't have been no bigger than 3 ½ feet, 4 tops. Her titties were so big, they each was bigger than her head. A head that was covered by blonde and pink dreadlocks that hung down her back to her ass.

Voorheeze was neva a disrespectful nigga but he couldn't help staring. He ain't neva seen an ass that big on a regular size bitch. Cherokee D'Ass and The Body XXX was getting shitted on by this midget.

When Voorheeze focused back on the nigga the nervousness was replaced with a smirk.

"My nigga, I ain't the police ,rogue. I'mma gangsta." He didn't know why he kept it clean with this nigga. Something about this nigga said "Realism"

"Nigga, I know who you is, you dig? Yo face been all over the television. You more famous than Obama, you dig." The nigga that stood before him was about 5'8 he looked to be some type of Middle Eastern mothafucka but he sounded black than a mothafucka.

"Man you got something to do with all that shit that's been going on today? No scratch that, just tell a Playa what you need, ya dig, it's all good Gangsta." He told Voorheeze.

"Brah, a nigga just need something to drink and a minute to think." Voorheeze honestly told him.

"Sit down, Gangsta. Bitch fix this nigga something to drink." He told the midget before sitting down himself.

"Okay, daddy. Let me put some clothes on." She said and turned to leave.

A bitch with a big ass was like heaven to Voorheeze cause he was an ass man. He almost had a heart attack when she turned to leave. Her ass had to be sixty inches.

The nigga bounced off the couch quicker than flash.

"Hoe, did you just talk back to me?" He asked her.

"No, daddy, I just wanted to cover up yo money maker." She cowed down.

"You should've thought of that before you brought yo funky ass out here to begin with, ya dig? Now walk that big ass in the kitchen and fix him something to drink." His gold teeth sparkling as he told her.

As he sat back down he told Voorheeze, "Check it, you dig, my name's 'Moe Dollars.' I been check'n trap since the cat in the hat, ya dig. That lil Buffalo butt white girl earns me two stacks every night. She a good hoe. I mean that. But I stay on her ass still until that trick check a mill, ya dig. Now dig dis, I'mma stomp Down P but I'm always "G" tell me what you need? Ya dig?" The way that shit rolled off his tongue was magic.

To a bitch, this niggaz words probably were Holy Grail Sacred. To Voorheeze he sounded like any and every slick talking Pimp. The difference was Voorheeze could sense the gangsta in him.

****

"Chief, I'm coming through the lobby doors right now. Which way you want me to proceed?" S.A.C. Andreatta was just getting ready to open the door to the stairwell when she heard Agent Allman in her ear.

"South East stairway, trailing suspect. Follow and proceed with extreme caution." She opened the door and stepped in, gun ready.

- She could hear him racing up the stairs so she followed behind him. Before she made it to the second flight of stairs things went silent.

"What we got, Chief?" Agent Allman whispered as she came up to S.A.C. Andreatta.

"He got out of the stairwell on one of the floors." She was still trying to listen while she talked. "I'mma take three and four you take five and six." Agent Allman nodded her head in agreement.

S.A.C. Andreatta closed the door gently behind her. As quickly and silently as possible she made her way down the hallway. She paused briefly at every door to see if she could hear any type of commotion. She made her way back to the stairwell and shot up the fourth floor.

Halfway down the hall a couple came walking out of the door leading to the back stairway in her direction. S.A.C. Andreatta didn't give a damn about what they were arguing about. She wished they would shut the fuck up so she could hear.

"Are you looking for your partner?" The woman asked S.A.C. Andreatta.

"Shut the fuck up and mind your business." The middle Eastern man pulled her down the hall.

She broke her arm loose.

"Then she turned towards S..AC. Andreatta.

"Actually, I'm FBI. Now yes it's your business and your duty to serve your country by helping your government anyway you can. Now what partner are you talking about miss?" She couldn't conceal her excitement. It spilled out in her voice.

"The black cop that was running after somebody," she looked at S.A.C. Andreatta with a look that said. "Woman are you a retard?"

S.A.C. Andreatta was hoping she was talking about Simpson when the girl said, "Your partner." She was sure now that the girl was.

"Which way did he go?" She asked the girl.

"The girl looked to her boyfriend for approval." She's the FBI, daddy!" She pleaded.

His response was to turn around and walk off. S.A.C. Andreatta sat waiting. Her heart almost pounded out her little chest. The girl watched him walk away then turned toward Andreatta. Her voice was quieter than a mouse but Andreatta heard her loud and clear.

"He ran up the stairs. He was on the phone telling someone to meet him on the roof." Afterwards she turned and scurried away. Hoping that she would be able to catch up to her boyfriend.

S.A.C. Andreatta rushed to the exit door they had just come from.

She didn't hear any noise when she entered the other staircase. She took the stairs two at a time, figuring he was already on the roof. In her mind that's why she couldn't hear him.

Three flights later she slowed down. Her spider senses were going crazy. How convenient she thought that the Good Samaritan just happened to show up. Then again considering all that happened a Good Samaritan wouldn't be far-fetched.

She radioed that she was heading down to the garage. Her instincts told her that the good Samaritan was a staged decoy. That meant S.A.C. Andreatta should go in the opposite direction as she was told Simpson went in.

****

"FBI. FREEZE!" Like fuck he would!

Voorheeze knew that stank, white bitch wouldn't fall for the misdirection.

Now he wished more than ever that he had his banger. It had fallen when he fell off the motorcycle. He couldn't allow himself to surrender. There was no doubt he would get the chair.

Fuck that! He bolted

BOC! BOC!

He crashed thru the door to the garage he crashed into the last person he ever thought he would see.

"Whoa, Bredren!" Dok called out as Voorheeze landed in his arms.

His nickel plated 45 magnum was in his hands. Dok had pulled it out when he heard the shots.

Just as he felt the blood on Voorheeze lower back the door came crashing open.

"FBI!"

With no warning Dok dropped Voorheeze like a sack of potatoes. Dok's 45 was pointing at her seconds before Voorheeze hit the ground.

"Devil, I don't care what Agency you're from. You got two options you can leave or you can die." If he could've seen himself, he looked more like the devil then she did as he said this.

"Listen. Buddy you don't know what you're doing. That is a very, very dangerous man. Sir, put your weapon down and put your hands in the air!" S.A.C. Andreatta was nervous as hell, but she'd be dammed if she coward.

"Bitch, do I…"

"Shut your fucking mouth and drop your gun, nigger!" Agent Galarza demanded not even giving Dok the opportunity to speak.

"Fuck!" Dok mumbled under his breath. He would risk shooting it out with the white bitch. She looked like she snorted crystal meth anyway.

He couldn't see exactly where the dude was behind him. How could he risk it against both of the pigs? Reluctantly he lowered the canon. After just doing twenty years in prison, he wasn't looking forward to going back. But, he would live to fight another day. Dead Niggaz couldn't fight.

When he stood up he saw the white bitch had a "Gotcha" smirk on her face. Her confidence was back. She was swagged up.

BOC! BOC! BOC!

Dok jumped! The smirk on her face was erased. At first Dok thought he was tripping until three tiny red dots appeared on the front of her blouse and began to spread.

BOC! BOC! BOC!

This time Dok turned in the direction of the gunfire Voorheeze couldn't get up to see past Dok's car. It didn't matter because Agent Galarza was walking towards S.A..C Andreatta who had fallen to the ground.

The six shots to her torso put her down easily. He still stood over her and fired two shots to her head. Emulating the way the gangstas did it.

"You guys just don't stop. Mighty bold shit y'all been pulling off." He was looking at Dok and Voorheeze now with his Glock .20 pointed at them. "Hell, I mean why you would bat your nigger eye at killing a FBI Agent. You just murdered a government official for crying out loud." Neither one of them could respond.

Dok was kicking himself in the ass for not picking the Desert Eagle back up while the commotion was going on.

"Your deaths are gonna make me a hero. A Patriot! Let's Make America Great Again!"

BOC! BOC! BOC! BOC! BOC!

The first two bullets hit the side of his head knocking off majority of the other side. The third on hit him in the shoulder, spinning him around which let the last two hit his chest.

Agent Galarza's eyes were as big as saucers with a surprised look on his face. Although they were open they couldn't see Agent Allman because he was dead.

It was Voorheeze turn to be shocked. He just saw one FBI Agent shoot another. Only to then be shot by another.

The acrid smell of gun powder lingered heavily in the air of the parking garage ,causing him to cough,

"Come on help me get him in the car." Dok told her as he opened the door of Lil Rell's Challenger SRT and rushed to pick Voorheeze up.

Minutes later they were pulling out of the underground parking garage on 12th Street heading for the Lincoln Hwy. Taking I-5 was out of the question due to the bombing.

"What you trynna do, set a record for the most times getting shot?" Dok finally broke the silence.

"Naw, I gotta have buzzard's luck or some shit." Voorheeze hadn't known he was shot until Dok let him go and his legs gave out on him. "Shit don't feel bad though. But, fuck that! What just happen back there?"

"I can't tell you what that was with o'le boi and the white chick. Brah, that shit had me just as fucked up as you. But, the sistah is a Mwezi. Her grandfather was the legendary Matasia. She's from Los Angeles. Part of a Secret Intelligence Cadre that moves throughout different Law Enforcement and Government Agencies gathering Intel for the collective while feeding the enemy information that our Military Counter Intelligence Cadres manufacture to throw them off our scent.

"She was forced to surface. Once the Feds began investigating Batman. She reached out and made contact with Zair months ago. It was her that let us know 'bout this crazy ass idea you and him concocted." If Voorheeze didn't know Dok so well he would've thought he was bullshitting.

"That explains a lot." He noticed that his leg was going numb but there wasn't shit that they could do about it, so he just ignored it. "How'd you know where I was?"

"Check your phone."

Voorheeze reached in his pocket for his iPhone. He didn't know what to expect since the volume was turned off. That was why he hadn't heard it beeping. The screen was flashing off and on. "Find My iPhone" was written on the phone. He couldn't do anything but smile.

"French is a very intelligent sistah. And she loves you to death."

"Thanks, big brah. After the way I got down I don't know why you helped me, but thank you." Shame was all in his voice.

"Blood, the fuck you mean? You one of mines! One of my most-if not THE most loyal of the few good men I salute as a thorough 1000% 7-star General of this Neva Die La Familia! Nigga, we been back 2 back against the world from day one!"

"Nigga, I'll neva leave you or go against you! You were going thru some shit, so I just let you go thru it. But, nigga dis Neva Die For Life and we Neva-Eva-Die!" The fire in which Dok breathed those words silenced Voorheeze.

In his heart he knew he was wrong. Hell, he'd been wrong about a lot of shit. Most of all killing Clark! How in the fuck could he kill his big brother? His idol. The one nigga he'd look up to his whole life.

They rode on in silence from there. Both men were lost in their own thoughts. Dok was thinking it was officially time to take back over Neva Die. He was liking the feeling of building and doing positive shit instead of destroying and killing. It was time to take the family to new heights. He couldn't lie though, he was liking the sound of Dragon Gang at the end of Neva Die. They were fa'sho keeping that.

Voorheeze was thinking he at least owed it to Mama B to let her know what had happened to his brother. He couldn't be a coward now. He also thought about Lisa wondering where she was. His love for her had him wishing shit was different. Thinking about his brother and Lisa caused a reaction he'd neva experienced. For the first time in his life tears of regret slid down his face!

De'Kari

CHAPTER XXII
A few months later

To say he was paranoid would be a severe understatement. The government cracked down on any and every known individual remotely connected to Voorheeze, Batman and The Neva Die Organization.

They were relentless in their approach. The first to feel the government's wrath was Mama B. She was kidnapped the day after the assassination. She was grabbed in the middle of the night by a team of government TSU agents and held at a non-disclosed federal detention center.

One by one, family and friends of the Organization were getting arrested by FBI agents. They were all held and interrogated for hours.

All the arrests were sanctioned under the 2002 Patriot Act. All members and family of Neva Die were deemed domestic terrorist.

As much as Voorheeze wanted to do something about what was happening, he had to stick to the plan. That was the penalty of leadership. His resilience paid off.

Two weeks after the assassination, with the help of a couple of Russian connects of Kwashay's, Voorheeze was able to hack into the States Capitol computer system. He had complete control of Sacramento's traffic, surveillance and retail cameras.

He demanded the immediate release and immunity of everyone detained in the federal detention center. Along with the introduction of a Senate Bill that would force law enforcement to release documents and footage of officers involved in shootings to the public.

The thought behind the Bill was officers would think twice about their actions if they knew they would be monitored and held accountable.

As expected, government officials were in an uproar. Homeland Security and the FBI tried everything they could to catch those responsible, while the National Security Agency did everything in its power to break into the worm that hackers created that poisoned Sacramento's technology.

Unfortunately, none of the agencies were successful. Forcing the government to meet the demands. Reluctantly they did.

Voorheeze wiped the sweat off his brow. They'd finally did the unthinkable. Voter's voted the Bill into law proving to all that black lives did matter.

As he picked up one of the burner phones, he sent Vieira a message. He couldn't help but reminiscence. Something he found himself doing quite a bit.

The victory was sweet, but it came at a price and it was costly. Many sacrifices were made, but it was all for the people. That was the price of being a Vanguard for the people.

He typed a simple and clear message to Vieira.

"Meet me at the airport at 2:40pm."

The Feds had a net circled around them and it was closing fast. If they didn't make their escape now, they would not be able to make it.

After sending her the message, he called out to Batman.

"What's up, Robin?" Batman asked, coming out the restroom.

"It's time to go." He looked at his big brother. Neither had to say a word. They both knew the odds were against them.

"Say less!" Was all Batman said.

Voorheeze had wanted to see the press conference but they couldn't jeopardize it. They grabbed their things in a matter of seconds and were walking out of the motel room that was rented under an alias with their hands on their guns and their eyes on the swivel.

**** N. D. ****

She pulled into the parking space reserved for "CEO" The sign sat on a post planted in front of the parking space. She was listening to Tupac's "Dear Mama." She always played this song when she thought of her big brother.

"I shed tears with my baby sistah/ova the years we was poorer than the other lil kids/ and even though we had different daddy's. The same drama/when things went wrong we blamed mama."

She rapped right along with Tupac as she remembered how her brother used to tell her 2-Pac somehow was rapping their life in the song. She still remembered when he requested the song on the old school Juke Box Video Station, brought Mama B into the living room and rapped the song to her like he was Tupac himself.

She opened the door to the triple black Mercedes Maybach and climbed out. The Starburst pink on the butter soft Italian leather really looked like the actual candy. The interior combination was Bonkers.

She looked up at the sign in front of the building with admiration. No matter how many times she saw it, she always felt the same butterflies and sense of pride.

"Satin Doll Fashionista LLC." This wasn't some little store space at some strip mall. The entire building belonged to French Tip. It was a 15,000 sq. ft. warehouse she had bought and remodeled.

She finally sat behind her desk after greeting a few people and directing a few others and taking care of a couple minor issues..

The office was very elegant and spacious. The equivalent of three normal offices. The walls were a warm summer paint. Plush thick Persian carpet covered the floor. A Liz Claiborne design theme is how it was put together. Tip had all of the furniture, including the leather, sectional imported from Italy.

Hanging on the wall to the left of the desk was a blown-up photo of the top echelon of the Neva Die Dragon Gang. The picture was taken on the main stage at Carsjanae's the night that T'Rida proposed to Monique during his birthday celebration.

She grabbed her cell phone out of her Chanel clutch bag. Finding Na'Shay's, name she sent her a text message:

"Hey niece. Just making sure everything is okay. Thank you again for calling me. Remember you are family and I love you. I'll always be just a phone call away and it's Neva a bother."

The initial plan was for French Tip to ride on the back of the Ducati instead of Lady J. at the last minute she received a call from T'Rida's daughter Na'Shay telling her that Titas had been dealing with somethings that had gotten out of hand and blood was spilled.

Titas was starting to deal with it on his own to show that he was a man but Na'Shay was scared for him so she called French Tip.

It took a minute but it was handled. Now French Tip made sure that she checked in with them at least once a week. Her phone vibrated letting her know that she had received a message.

"Hey Auntie, all is well and we're doing fine. Thank you again for coming and helping us. I know we're family, auntie. That's why I love you. Mamma said thank you, too, She's still sober.

Smiling to herself. She looked for Dok's contact info to send him a message. She was thinking that Shay Shay indeed was a sweetheart but she was no doubt a heart breaker.

She found Dok's name and brought the message screen up. Once she was there she began typing the message.

****
Meanwhile

"Sup, big brah. Crazy two years, but I wouldn't take any of it back if it meant we wouldn't be where we are now. I'm proud of you. And when I said "I'm" I am sure you know that it isn't just me, it's him too! Anyway, go on out there and do you. This moment is what it was all for. Remember ain't no turning back after this. The whole world is watching.

One Aim One Struggle One Goal

NEVA DIE!

Dok smiled to himself as he read the message from French Tip. He placed the phone in his pocket, took a deep breath and stood up. Today indeed was an important day for all of them, but mainly for him. After today there could be no illegal activity around him because people would be watching.

He grabbed his suit jacket and walked to the door. It opened immediately after he knocked on it. When he stepped through and began walking down the hallway. Rell and Scooter fell in step with him walking on his flank. As they got closer to their destination a woman's voice could be heard speaking.

"So as your newly elected President, it brings me a great pleasure to bring to you a brother who has truly became a Patriot. a fighter for the people and an advocate of truth. Ladies and Gentlemen, Mr. Darrell Hayes." President Kam Harrison smiled and clapped as she turned to face Dok.

He took another deep breath then walked out the open doors and onto the patio overlooking the West Lawn of the White House.

The President shook his hand and left the floor to him. Dok took a moment to look out over the sea of rich blackness. The applause was loud and genuine. His speeches have become a world-wide phenomenon. He'd single handedly brought a degree of understanding to the Black Lives Matter Movement that didn't exist before.

He took off his suit jacket and laid it down. When the crowd saw the "Black Lives Matter" logo on his T-Shirt they cheered and applauded again. Once they settled down enough he began to speak.

****** N. D. ******
United States District Courtroom

The courtroom was packed beyond the max. This was the biggest trial of the century and it was finally over. Spectators in the room where divided in their beliefs regarding the case. There was no-way to tell concretely which way the verdict would come back. But, it was in now.

"Well the defendant rise" Judge Garrett spoke. At fifty-nine years old, the white woman looked beyond tired and ready to get past the case.

Once the defendant and his court appointed Federal Public Defender stood up, Judge Garrett read off the verdict.

"Theodore Carnicious Johnson on the Charge of Conspiracy to willfully commit violence and murder of Jim Smith, you have been found... Guilty. On the charge of Conspiracy to discharge an illegal assault rifle in public with the intention of committing mass mayhem. You've been found...Guilty..."

Theodore Johnson passed out. The news he was receiving was too much on his young soul. Hearing what was happening to her son Mrs. Rebecca Johnson fainted as well. Theodore woke up before his mother. When he did, he learned that he was convicted on every one of the seventy-nine conspiracy charges as well as the two felony federal charges. One was possession of a loaded military type assault rifle. The other being first degree sexual assault on the white woman who testified against him. She was the prosecutor's main witness.

When he came to he learned that he would spend the rest of his natural life in the Federal Prison System and he began to cry. He was sentenced to eleven life sentences. When they were finally able to awaken his mother, she had a heart attack upon hearing the news. His father neva said one word.

Although he'd told people he had been kicked out of his home, he had actually runaway from a nice middle-class family. His love for rap music and reality T.V. gave birth to his love for street life. When he ran away he wanted so much to be accepted, he did the craziest things. When he had first been given the name Lil Yankee A.R., he did everything he could to live up to it. Tikashi 69 was his idol. He wanted to be just like him.

The shooting at the rally was his initiation to Underworld Zilla. Being a part of them was his street dream. Instead of being embraced by the gang he was now being embraced into Federal Prison.

**** N. D. ****
San Jose International Airport

Voorheeze checked his Audemar for the thousandth time.
"Come on, rogue, where the hell is she at?" He asked himself.
Finally, he saw her truck driving toward the hanger. Even though everything was rented in a legit alias, a nigga always had to be on point. Him and Batman were the new Bin Laden and Sadam Huerrae. Voorheeze was damned if he went out the way either of those two did.

When she finally stop the car and got out. She rushed over into his arms. The two of them kissed deeply and passionately. Tears were sliding down Vieira's face. The kiss seemed to last forever. They finally separated, both of them were nearly out of breath.

"Were you getting second thoughts?" He asked her once he regained some oxygen.

"Baby, why would you asked me something like that?" Vieira was genuinely hurt. "I would neva do that to you. I'll always be in love with you."

"Then what took so long? You're almost forty-five minutes late."

"Okay I don't know if you realize it but these bags are heavy and lugging them and this big, fat ass was hard work." She smacked her gigantic ass when she said it for emphasis.

On cue, he turned to the baggage handlers that he'd rented and instructed them to remove the bags from her Toyota Sequoia and carry them onto the plane. Then he turned back to her.

The combination of her tears and the sunlight dancing off of them made her eyes sparkle in a way that touched his heart.

"Will I ever see you again?" She asked. Her heart ready to explode under her hefty breast.

"You neva know. Anything's possible." He knew he was full of shit but he couldn't bring himself to hurt her anymore.

This white girl turned out to be a real" Ride or Die Chick!

"How many more y'all got?" He asked the last two dudes who were passing him.

"These are the last two, sir." The first guy told him.

"Put those two back." He instructed.

Goodbyes are always hard so there was no reason for him to prolong it. After tipping the luggage handlers nicely, he said goodbye to her.

Then he said a prayer because he knew he was truly a blessed man. For him to be on a G-7 headed to paradise instead of being dead or in jail was truly God's doing.

Once he boarded the jet he looked at Batman who was holding a glass of Cristal for him.

"Damn, I thought you was having second thoughts." Batman told him.

"You know me, I hate hurting people, brah." Voorheeze walked over to the bar.

"You can keep that B.S." He pointed at the bottle of Cristal. I'mma hood nigga, I'll always drink hood shit." He lifted a big bottle of Remy Martin XO for emphasis.

"What's in all them bags, nigga", Batman was curious.

While he was sitting down Voorheeze replied, "Nigga, open one and see."

Batman did and got the shock of his life.

"Nigga how much is this?"

"That's a ticket, brah." Voorheeze told him.

"You mean to tell me it's a ticket in each and every one of them bags, nigga?" Batman couldn't believe that shit.

There were fifteen bags total with him giving Vieira two that left thirteen million.

"Nigga I counted thirteen bags. Aaww, nigga you balling, shit."

"Shit, that ain't my shit." It was a bitch holding the smirk in.

"Brah, that's yo shit." Batman looked like he was having a heart attack.

My nigga you been loyal from day one. Truly my big brother. Nigga, you neva faked, neva faltered and that shit , mean something to a real nigga. Besides, I got you in all this shit. The least I can do is make it worth it. Make sure you got a way or a means out of it." Batman looked over to his wife who was seated next to him.

She didn't say a word. Rachel was ready to mess Voorheeze up for getting her husband in this mess to begin with. She just thanked God nothing had happen to her man.

"Damn, nigga, that's some gangsta shit." Batman had neva seen a nigga do a more gangsta move.

Niggaz always talk that' you my brotha shit" but they didn't hold it down.

"Real niggaz ,do real shit." Was all Voorheeze said.

"What about you."

"She gonna hold me down." He leaned back into Lisa's lap. "Lil Thickems you gonna hold me down?"

"You know it, Big Daddy." She leaned down and kissed him on the forehead.

When he looked at her crazy she said. "Nigga please, you was just kissing that white girl." Everyone laughed but him.

"I'mma hold you down though, Boo Boo."

He had to respect it. He told Batman technically the money was Gunz. Since he and Nastasia were both gone Voorheeze wasn't gone let the money go to waste. There was no need for him to keep it because Lisa had his money. Everything was Gucci.

As they flew over the waters Voorheeze turned on that Meek Mills "I'mma Boss" He looked over at the woman of his dreams and thanked God that she was finally his after all these years of waiting patiently for the right time to approach her. Little did he know, if he would've stepped to her, she would've been his years ago.

As Nipsey Hussle's "Victory Lap" came on he knew in his heart that they'd finally made it!

He was going to miss his family but he knew with Dok at the head of the family, Neva Die Dragon Gang would be straight. With the new direction Dok was taking them in, success was guaranteed.

BLACK LIVES REALLY MATTER!

One Aim. One Struggle. One Goal!
Neva Die
276
Long Live the Will to Win!

NEVA DIE!

Stay tuned for Blood of My Father! The Jason Voorheeze Story"!

"R.I.P. NIPSEY HUSTLE"

Submission Guideline

Submit the first three chapters of your completed manuscript to ldpsubmissions@gmail.com, subject line: Your book's title. The manuscript must be in a .doc file and sent as an attachment. Document should be in Times New Roman, double spaced and in size 12 font. Also, provide your synopsis and full contact information. If sending multiple submissions, they must each be in a separate email.

Have a story but no way to send it electronically? You can still submit to LDP/Ca$h Presents. Send in the first three chapters, written or typed, of your completed manuscript to:

LDP: Submissions Dept
Po Box 870494
Mesquite, Tx 75187

DO NOT send original manuscript. Must be a duplicate.

Provide your synopsis and a cover letter containing your full contact information.

Thanks for considering LDP and Ca$h Presents.

Coming Soon from Lock Down Publications/Ca$h Presents

BOW DOWN TO MY GANGSTA

By **Ca$h**

TORN BETWEEN TWO

By **Coffee**

BLOOD STAINS OF A SHOTTA **III**

By **Jamaica**

STEADY MOBBIN **III**

By **Marcellus Allen**

BLOOD OF A BOSS **VI**

SHADOWS OF THE GAME II

By **Askari**

LOYAL TO THE GAME **IV**

By **T.J. & Jelissa**

A DOPEBOY'S PRAYER **II**

By **Eddie "Wolf" Lee**

IF LOVING YOU IS WRONG… **III**

By **Jelissa**

TRUE SAVAGE **VII**

MIDNIGHT CARTEL

DOPE BOY MAGIC

By **Chris Green**

BLAST FOR ME **III**

DUFFLE BAG CARTEL **IV**

HEARTLESS GOON **III**

By **Ghost**

A HUSTLER'S DECEIT III

KILL ZONE **II**

BAE BELONGS TO ME III
SOUL OF A MONSTER III
By **Aryanna**
THE COST OF LOYALTY **III**
By **Kweli**
THE SAVAGE LIFE II
By **J-Blunt**
KING OF NEW YORK V
COKE KINGS IV
BORN HEARTLESS II
By **T.J. Edwards**
GORILLAZ IN THE BAY V
De'Kari
THE STREETS ARE CALLING II
Duquie Wilson
KINGPIN KILLAZ IV
STREET KINGS III
PAID IN BLOOD III
CARTEL KILLAZ III
Hood Rich
SINS OF A HUSTLA II
ASAD
TRIGGADALE III
Elijah R. Freeman
KINGZ OF THE GAME V
Playa Ray
SLAUGHTER GANG IV
RUTHLESS HEART II
By Willie Slaughter

THE HEART OF A SAVAGE II

By Jibril Williams

FUK SHYT II

By Blakk Diamond

THE DOPEMAN'S BODYGAURD II

By Tranay Adams

TRAP GOD II

By Troublesome

YAYO II

A SHOOTER'S AMBITION II

By S. Allen

GHOST MOB

Stilloan Robinson

KINGPIN DREAMS

By Paper Boi Rari

CREAM

By Yolanda Moore

SON OF A DOPE FIEND II

By Renta

FOREVER GANGSTA

By Adrian Dulan

LOYALTY AIN'T PROMISED

By Keith Williams

THE PRICE YOU PAY FOR LOVE

By Destiny Skai

THE LIFE OF A HOOD STAR

By Rashia Wilson

<u>Available Now</u>

RESTRAINING ORDER **I & II**

By **CA$H & Coffee**

LOVE KNOWS NO BOUNDARIES **I II & III**

By **Coffee**

RAISED AS A GOON I, II, III & IV

BRED BY THE SLUMS I, II, III

BLAST FOR ME I & II

ROTTEN TO THE CORE I II III

A BRONX TALE I, II, III

DUFFEL BAG CARTEL I II III

HEARTLESS GOON

A SAVAGE DOPEBOY

HEARTLESS GOON I II

By **Ghost**

LAY IT DOWN **I & II**

LAST OF A DYING BREED

BLOOD STAINS OF A SHOTTA I & II

By **Jamaica**

LOYAL TO THE GAME

LOYAL TO THE GAME II

LOYAL TO THE GAME III

LIFE OF SIN I, II III

By **TJ & Jelissa**

BLOODY COMMAS I & II

SKI MASK CARTEL I II & III

KING OF NEW YORK I II,III IV

RISE TO POWER I II III

COKE KINGS I II III

BORN HEARTLESS

By **T.J. Edwards**

IF LOVING HIM IS WRONG…I & II

LOVE ME EVEN WHEN IT HURTS I II III

By **Jelissa**

WHEN THE STREETS CLAP BACK I & II III

By **Jibril Williams**

A DISTINGUISHED THUG STOLE MY HEART I II & III

LOVE SHOULDN'T HURT I II III IV

RENEGADE BOYS I II III IV

By **Meesha**

A GANGSTER'S CODE I &, II III

A GANGSTER'S SYN I II III

THE SAVAGE LIFE

By J-Blunt

PUSH IT TO THE LIMIT

By **Bre' Hayes**

BLOOD OF A BOSS **I, II, III, IV, V**

SHADOWS OF THE GAME

By **Askari**

THE STREETS BLEED MURDER **I, II & III**

THE HEART OF A GANGSTA I II& III

By **Jerry Jackson**

CUM FOR ME

CUM FOR ME 2

CUM FOR ME 3

CUM FOR ME 4

CUM FOR ME 5

An **LDP Erotica Collaboration**

BRIDE OF A HUSTLA **I II & II**

THE FETTI GIRLS **I, II& III**

CORRUPTED BY A GANGSTA I, II III, IV

BLINDED BY HIS LOVE

By **Destiny Skai**

WHEN A GOOD GIRL GOES BAD

By **Adrienne**

THE COST OF LOYALTY I II

By Kweli

A GANGSTER'S REVENGE **I II III & IV**

THE BOSS MAN'S DAUGHTERS

THE BOSS MAN'S DAUGHTERS II

THE BOSSMAN'S DAUGHTERS III

THE BOSSMAN'S DAUGHTERS IV

THE BOSS MAN'S DAUGHTERS **V**

A SAVAGE LOVE **I & II**

BAE BELONGS TO ME I II

A HUSTLER'S DECEIT I, II, III

WHAT BAD BITCHES DO I, II, III

SOUL OF A MONSTER I II

KILL ZONE

By **Aryanna**

A KINGPIN'S AMBITON

A KINGPIN'S AMBITION **II**

I MURDER FOR THE DOUGH

By **Ambitious**

TRUE SAVAGE

TRUE SAVAGE II

TRUE SAVAGE **III**

TRUE SAVAGE **IV**

TRUE SAVAGE **V**

TRUE SAVAGE **VI**

By **Chris Green**

A DOPEBOY'S PRAYER

By **Eddie "Wolf" Lee**

THE KING CARTEL **I, II & III**

By **Frank Gresham**

THESE NIGGAS AIN'T LOYAL **I, II & III**

By **Nikki Tee**

GANGSTA SHYT **I II &III**

By **CATO**

THE ULTIMATE BETRAYAL

By **Phoenix**

BOSS'N UP **I , II & III**

By **Royal Nicole**

I LOVE YOU TO DEATH

By Destiny J

I RIDE FOR MY HITTA

I STILL RIDE FOR MY HITTA

By **Misty Holt**

LOVE & CHASIN' PAPER

By **Qay Crockett**

TO DIE IN VAIN

SINS OF A HUSTLA

By **ASAD**

BROOKLYN HUSTLAZ

By **Boogsy Morina**

BROOKLYN ON LOCK I & II

By **Sonovia**
GANGSTA CITY
By **Teddy Duke**
A DRUG KING AND HIS DIAMOND I & II III
A DOPEMAN'S RICHES
HER MAN, MINE'S TOO I, II
CASH MONEY HO'S
By Nicole Goosby
TRAPHOUSE KING **I II & III**
KINGPIN KILLAZ I II III
STREET KINGS I II
PAID IN BLOOD **I II**
CARTEL KILLAZ I II
By **Hood Rich**
LIPSTICK KILLAH **I, II, III**
CRIME OF PASSION I & II
By **Mimi**
STEADY MOBBN' **I, II, III**
By **Marcellus Allen**
WHO SHOT YA **I, II, III**
SON OF A DOPE FIEND
Renta
GORILLAZ IN THE BAY **I II III IV**
DE'KARI
TRIGGADALE I II
Elijah R. Freeman
GOD BLESS THE TRAPPERS I, II, III
THESE SCANDALOUS STREETS I, II, III
FEAR MY GANGSTA I, II, III

<u>BOOKS BY LDP'S CEO, CA$H</u>

<u>TRUST IN NO MAN</u>

<u>TRUST IN NO MAN 2</u>

<u>TRUST IN NO MAN 3</u>

<u>BONDED BY BLOOD</u>

<u>SHORTY GOT A THUG</u>

<u>THUGS CRY</u>

<u>THUGS CRY 2</u>

<u>THUGS CRY 3</u>

<u>TRUST NO BITCH</u>

<u>TRUST NO BITCH 2</u>

<u>TRUST NO BITCH 3</u>

<u>TIL MY CASKET DROPS</u>

<u>RESTRAINING ORDER</u>

<u>RESTRAINING ORDER 2</u>

<u>IN LOVE WITH A CONVICT</u>

<u>Coming Soon</u>

BONDED BY BLOOD 2

BOW DOWN TO MY GANGSTA

De'Kari

www.ingramcontent.com/pod-product-compliance
Lightning Source LLC
Chambersburg PA
CBHW060542260626
47161CB00003B/1018